ELIZA NEVIUS

Professionally Unprofessional

PROFESSIONALLY UNPROFESSIONAL
Eliza Nevius

To the coffee that kept me conscious, the playlists that made me feel powerful, and the people who never said "maybe try a real job." This book is for the dreamers, the overthinkers, and those who build something from scratch—one late night, bad haircut, or purple wall at a time. Lexie's journey from chaos to confidence was inspired by the real hustle of starting something on your own, and the unexpected people who make that journey unforgettable. Especially the annoying, suit-wearing ones.

Contents

Foreword

Writing this book was equal parts therapy, chaos, and caffeine overdose. Lexie and Ben took over my brain and refused to shut up until their story was told—snark and all. If you've ever felt like the underdog in a boardroom, a misfit in a blazer, or the sarcastic one in the group chat, this one's for you.

Bound Books Publishing may not exist in real life (yet), but its spirit was inspired by every creative who decided to bet on themselves. Thanks for letting me share this love story with you—I hope it made you laugh, swoon, and maybe even believe that enemies can be more than just insufferable... sometimes they're the beginning of a plot twist.

A little red number one sits next to my inbox, mocking me with its indifference. I click it, half expecting a new bill or a reminder about a dental procedure I forgot to schedule. It's not. The first word that jumps out at me is "Congratulations." I reread it, thinking maybe the text is blurry, and it's actually some fancy font that spells out "Constipation." Then the whole sentence hits me like a toddler's kick to the shin: "Congratulations! Your novel hit the bestseller list!" I stare at it, eyes bulging like a pufferfish, then spring up from the couch. My half-empty coffee mug goes flying, and I knock a stack of books off the table with a thud. "Holy sh—" The rest is drowned out by me dancing around my apartment in my mismatched socks. I must look like one of those inflatable tube guys that flop around in front of used car dealerships. My long brown hair is swinging wildly, and I'm sure the old man next door is about to bang on the wall. Let him. I'm a bestseller.

I land on the couch, out of breath and grinning like an idiot. "Oh my God!" I yell at the walls, the ceiling, and the upside-down stack of books on the floor. It's not the first time I've done that, but it's definitely the first time I've gotten good news from one of them. The email is still open on my laptop screen, flashing at me like it's trying to signal aliens, and I take a moment to soak it in. "Congratulations, Lexie!" I yell again, letting it bounce off the walls and ring in my ears. Who knew those twelve-point bold letters could sound so good? I try to sit still, feeling the couch sink down like a whoopee cushion beneath me. The words blur as I read them over and over. A crazed laugh escapes me, and my grin just gets bigger.

I snatch my phone from the coffee table, my hands jittery with excitement. Maci has to hear this. She needs to know she's best friends with a best-selling author. I stab at her contact and listen to it ring. "Come on, Maci," I chant. "Don't you dare have a life right now. Pick up, pick up, pick up." My mismatched socks are tapping, and I can't sit still. This must be what those bugs in old cartoons feel like when they get stuck in a lampshade. I pop up again, shaking out my hands to stop the pins-and-needles. Everything looks brighter and messier than ever. A dozen bookshelves line the walls like jumbled-up Tetris pieces, a few colorful pillows make the couch look like a clashing rainbow, and half a dozen coffee cups sit scattered around the apartment. The table is covered in sticky notes and manuscripts. Even the dust on the bookshelf looks better when I'm on a bestseller high.

When I'm one second away from dying of impatience, Maci finally answers with an out-of-breath, "Hey Lex! What's up?"

"Only my novel hitting the freaking bestseller list!" I yell so loudly that she could probably hear me even if the call dropped.

"What?!" Her voice is like I just told her I adopted an elephant. "You're serious?"

"As serious as a reality TV breakup," I say, even though I'm smiling so hard my cheeks hurt. "You're now speaking to a number-one, certified, bestselling genius."

"Oh my God, Lexie! That's amazing!"

"Of course, it is. Did you doubt me?" I pretend to sound offended. "Why do you think I've been ignoring your texts for three years?"

Her laugh is high-pitched and bubbly, like usual. "This is so insane! We have to celebrate. Drinks! Dinner! All the things!"

"Can you make sure to bring an oxygen tank for me?" I ask. "I don't know if my heart can take it."

"We need to frame this email and hang it up like an art exhibit," she says, almost breathless.

"I know," I say, gesturing wildly even though she can't see me. "And we can call it the 'Lexie Is Amazing' collection. Ten dollars per viewing."

"Okay, we need to meet right now."

"Yes! You read my mind. When can you get here?"

"Maybe two hours?"

"Fine. But if I'm dead by then, my ghost will haunt you," I say. "And all I'll say is, 'You took too long.'"

"Deal." I hear her start to say something else, but my over-caffeinated excitement kicks in.

"We can finally afford name-brand cereal!" I blurt.

"Look at us! No more mystery flakes!" Maci giggles, then pauses. "Oh, and also—"

"Also, we should probably expand the business," I say before she can finish. "We'll have bestseller bucks to play with."

"Like a bigger office," she says. "One where the bathroom isn't also the storage closet."

"Yes, exactly! I can't believe we did it, Maci. How do we live with ourselves?"

"Expanding is going to be amazing! Our little publishing empire in the middle of the city." I hear rustling in the background. "Maybe one of those fancy places with windows."

"And doors," I add. "And walls that weren't found in a dumpster."

"And rats that don't pay rent."

"Why are you wasting time?" I ask, already back to tapping my feet and pacing around. "You should be halfway here by now!"

"Okay, I'm going to throw on pants and get there as soon as I can!" Her voice is full of anticipation. "We're going to celebrate so hard, and then I'm going to sleep for a year. See you soon!"

I hang up, staring at the phone like it just made me breakfast in bed. I should probably sit down, breathe a little, and let my pulse stop sounding like a bad dubstep song. But who am I kidding? I'm already making another round through my tiny apartment, singing the "Hallelujah" chorus and planning the rest of my celebration.

I reminisce about my epic odyssey from clueless dropout to slightly less clueless bestseller author. At nineteen, I ditched college faster than a bad blind date to chase my writing dreams. Maci was my best friend and fellow drop out. As my cover artist and editor, she has been my rock through this whole thing. Fast forward four years, and after collecting about a hundred rejection letters—enough to wallpaper my bathroom—Maci and I decided, "To heck with those snooty literary gatekeepers, we'll just DIY this thing." We pulled our measly funds together and incorporated Bounds and Books Publishing.

Now, the manuscript they turned down like a bad prom date is topping the bestseller list, and they can all take a long walk off a short pier.

There's a bottle of cheap champagne hiding in the kitchen cupboard that I bought five years ago as a joke. The label's all in French, which means I have no clue what it says, but it's a screw top. I rip it open and find the least dirty mug in the apartment. "Cheers, future Lexie!" I shout, then down half the glass before it hits my lips. The bubbles tickle my nose, and the sticky-sweet taste is almost enough to kill me. Worth it.

I collapse back on the couch, swinging my legs up and sprawling like a cat in a sunbeam. I reach for my laptop, click on the bestseller list, and there it is: My name. It still looks so crazy that I expect the screen to start laughing at me. It doesn't. It's real. I'm real. And I'm number freaking one. I take a huge gulp of champagne, scroll through the emails I haven't checked yet, and snort champagne out my nose. I swear there are hundreds of messages from readers congratulating me and asking when my next book will be out. I blink at the screen a few times, wondering if it's going to sprout a mouth and start yelling at me too.

"Maci! I'm not sure I'll make it 'til you get here," I text her, then snap a quick selfie with my laptop, my hair all crazy and my smile taking up most of my face. I'm going to remember this moment forever. Or at least until I wake up from this dream.

The tiny apartment feels smaller than ever, even as it bursts with energy. I lean back, legs propped up on the table, take a deep breath, and close my eyes. Then I jump up again, grinning like I've lost my mind. Maybe I have. It feels amazing.

I don't know if the excitement is making me dizzy, but the walls of my apartment are definitely spinning. No, it's me. I'm spinning around like a record in a vintage shop, champagne mug in hand, yelping random syllables of excitement. I don't even care that I look like a crazy woman, dancing around in my living room with a glass of bubbly that costs less than a cup of coffee. This is what being a bestselling author feels like. "Where are you?" I shout at my phone. It's sitting on the couch, not doing its job, and not bringing Maci to me fast enough. "Is it the future yet?" I pick it up and yell into it. "Are you on your way? Do you have anything other than pajamas on?"

I pace the apartment like it's going to speed up time, I pause for half a second to breathe, flop back on the couch, and send my brain a signal to chill. It doesn't work. I'm up again, my long hair flying all over the place, almost knocking more stacks of books over. The place is a mess, even worse now that I've gone on a celebration rampage, but I don't care. I love it. It feels like me.

A minute feels like a year, and when my phone finally rings I answer it so fast I almost drop it. "Maci!" I yell. "Are you on your way yet? Are you dressed? Are you bringing the oxygen tank?"

"I'm literally walking out the door now!" she says, her voice high-pitched and cheerful. "Calm down! Don't pass out before I get there!"

"Too late," I say. "I'm on my second ghost already."

"You better save one for me!" she says, then giggles. "This is crazy, Lexie! I still can't believe it."

"I'm not sure I'm awake," I say, taking another sip of bubbly. "If I'm not, and I wake up, I'm going to be so pissed."

"This is so insane. You deserve it! Are you still going to be able to see me from your penthouse?"

"I'll install a camera to buzz you in," I say. "Your own private security line. You can bring a guest."

"And I'll wear a fancy dress just to visit you."

"Is that why it's taking you so long?" I ask. "Are you buying one now? Getting your hair done?"

"Nope, just getting pants."

I collapse onto the couch again, still too excited to stop bouncing my feet up and down. "Oh my God, Maci! It's really happening!" I shout. "Can you believe we're going to be rich? With a real company? That's almost a real business?"

"No, I can't believe it," she says, her voice rushing with enthusiasm. "But I've always known it!"

"I haven't!" I say. "I'm pretty sure we're committing a crime right now."

"We're doing it, Lex. We're really doing it!"

"Remember our old place?" I say. "Maybe we can finally have a space where the walls aren't made out of cardboard."

"And where the bathroom isn't the size of a toilet!"

"And where there's not a family of rats named the Hendersons living in the closet!"

"This is too exciting," she says. "Is it weird I'm scared?"

"No," I say. "I'm scared out of my mind. And a little tipsy."

I get back up again, more energy zipping through me like I'm a ball in a pinball machine. "We're going to do this!" I yell. "We're going to be the biggest company ever! Bigger than all the other companies combined!"

"This is what we've been dreaming about!" Maci's excitement matches mine, and I can hear that she's started moving faster.

"You better hurry," I say. "Or I'll eat all the fancy dinner by myself. It's already in the microwave."

"Be there soon! If you pass out, save me a ghost!"

I hang up, and even though it's only a few seconds, it feels like forever. Maybe I really should wait and catch my breath before I collapse. I plop down on the couch, watch the room spin around me, then jump up again. No way I'm sitting still.

I dance another lap through the apartment, sending sticky notes and half-empty mugs crashing to the floor. I laugh and don't even care. The whole place feels like it's going to explode. I take a big gulp of my drink and text Maci again, just to tell her I might not survive the next five minutes. "Bring cereal," I add. "I don't trust the microwave."

I slow down for all of ten seconds and imagine what tomorrow will be like. If we actually do this, if we actually make it, what does that mean? What's next? And will we know what to do when we get there? A second later, I shake off my doubts and laugh at myself. Who cares? We'll figure it out. We always do.

When Maci finally gets here, she's going to have to scrape me off the ceiling. I take another sip of champagne, dance around the room one more time, and imagine all the crazy things that will happen when I'm a bestseller for real. Then I imagine myself with the only cereal that doesn't come in a bag.

One

Welcome to the War Zone: Office Edition

∽♥∾

Three Best Sellers and Two Years Later.

It turns out that it takes a while to reach the coveted spot of being wealthy enough to rent your own office space.

Maci and I burst out of the elevator like a couple of confetti cannons, the sleek white walls of the downtown office building a stark contrast to the shoebox we're currently working in. I can't help but wonder if we're even allowed to be here—two publishers in their mid-twenties, giddy with the smell of cheap perfume and ambition. Our real estate agent leads the charge, a crisp folder in hand, while Maci dances across the open floor plan like she's auditioning for a Broadway musical called New Office Space.

"Lex, can you believe this?" Maci squeals, spinning in a circle. "It's perfect!"

I glance around at the modern interior, the kind that screams adulting but in a chic way. "I think I've died and gone to IKEA heaven."

Maci stops long enough to give me a mock glare. "You could show a little more enthusiasm, you know."

"Oh, I am!" I assure her, raising my hands like I'm praising the almighty Office Space Gods. "I just don't want to get too attached before they figure out we're used to paying rent in vape shop gift cards."

The agent smiles politely, like she's not sure if I'm joking. Spoiler: I am not.

Our footsteps echo as we wander further into the space, a satisfying clack against the hardwood floors. Massive windows give us a view of Chicago that our current digs can only dream of, unless strip malls and parking lots are your thing.

"I mean, check out the size of this place," I say, peering around. "We could fit three of our current offices in here and still have room for a life-size cutout of Stephen King."

"Or one of you!" Maci chimes in, grabbing my arm.

"Yes, Lexie the Author," I muse, "available for birthday parties and book signings."

The agent, a no-nonsense woman in a blazer sharp enough to cut glass, consults her notes. "Shall we continue? There's quite a bit more to see."

Maci practically bounces as she trails after the agent. I'm tempted to remind her that we haven't signed anything yet, but it's hard not to get swept up in her enthusiasm.

The open floor plan stretches out in front of us, a blank canvas just waiting for Maci's grand designs. She pauses to point out imaginary walls and invisible desks, her imagination running as wild as her chin-length blonde hair.

"I think we could do our editorial team over here," she announces, gesturing to an empty corner. "And the marketing folks can go right next to them."

"Keep dreaming big, partner," I say, trying to keep up with her. "If we sign this lease, we might even have a real break room instead of a coffee pot balanced on a stack of paperbacks."

We reach the end of the space, and the agent gestures to a hallway leading to another set of offices. "And of course, your neighbors will be a financial advisory group."

I pull up short, the words slamming into me like a bad review. "A financial what now?"

"They're already established here," the agent explains, flipping through her folder, "but with this much room, you shouldn't have any issues coexisting."

"Coexisting," I repeat slowly. "Like two peaceful nations, sharing a border and not launching paperclip missiles at each other."

Maci nudges me, eyes sparkling with excitement. "I'm sure we'll hardly notice them."

"Yeah," I mutter, "but what if they notice us?"

Maci shrugs it off, the picture of optimism. "Lex, it's going to be amazing. We'll have all this space and be right in the heart of the city."

I want to believe her, but all I can picture are men in suits giving us the side-eye because we're a couple of free-spirited publishers cramping their corporate style.

The agent points out the newly renovated kitchen area, and we walk over, the promise of more amenities leading us onward. "This is quite a rare find in the city," she says, the practiced lines rolling off her tongue. "Especially at this price point."

I can feel Maci vibrating with happiness beside me, like an

over-caffeinated jackrabbit. "We could actually afford it?"

I chuckle at her enthusiasm, even as I weigh the pros and cons in my head. "That depends. Do they accept payments in back issues of our failed magazine project?"

"Are you always this skeptical?" the agent asks, one eyebrow arching over her horn-rimmed glasses.

I give her a wink. "Nope, only on Mondays."

"It's Thursday…" She says giving me a look that is both scathing and confused.

"Think of it like this," Maci jumps in, wrapping an arm around my shoulder. "Our little company. Big, beautiful new office. The only thing that could ruin it is your worrying."

I glance around at the high ceilings and natural light streaming through the windows. It's tempting—way too tempting for someone like me, who's spent the last year crammed between a laser printer and the world's most irritating neighbor. Not Maci, the vape shop.

We close the door to our - possible- new place and head towards the boundary where our creative haven meets its financial adversary. I can hear faint sounds from the other side—keyboards clicking, phones ringing. The kind of sounds that probably accompany daily TPS reports and discussions about stocks and bonds.

"Do you hear that?" I whisper dramatically to Maci. "Corporate drones preparing their attack."

She swats at me playfully. "I think it sounds perfect."

For a second, I let myself get swept away in her dream, picturing our desks filling the empty space, creative chaos where there's now only polished perfection. Then the reality of sharing with a group that likely irons their socks brings me back down to earth.

I let out a long breath, taking one last look at the beautiful, expansive space. "We could really make this work, huh?"

"We really could," Maci says, linking her arm through mine. "Come on, let's go sign before the bank changes their minds on our loan."

The city buzzes beneath us, the hum of distant traffic a reminder of everything this place offers that we don't have yet. I still have my doubts, sure, but when the chance comes to grow your dream, you don't let it slip by without a fight.

The closer we get to financial territory, the more I feel like I'm sneaking into a corporate fortress. It's sleek and shiny, all minimalist furniture and muted colors, and Maci and I look like rebels infiltrating an army of suits.

I was hoping to make it to the elevator before we had the chance to run into any of the corporate dudes, but just as we pushed the button their office door opens as a group of men dressed in fancy suits make their way towards our position.

My eyes land on the king of them all: six feet of arrogance in a tailored suit, his glare sharp enough to shave with. I barely have time to register his whole smug vibe before he opens his mouth, condescension dripping from every word. "Are you lost?"

Before I can snark out a reply, the relator steps forward, hand extended, "Hello, I'm Francie Mavis of Mavis Realty; my clients with a publishing company and I were just taking a look at the open office space down the hall."

He looks at Francie's hand as if he were personally offended by her addressing him. "Ben Maddox." He says in a tone that sounds both bored and dismissive. "A publishing company?" he says, drawing out the words like they're foreign to him. "How… quaint."

I can almost feel my spine snapping straight as his dismissive tone slithers into my ears. "Quaint, yes," I reply, fighting to keep my voice even. "But we like to call it charming."

Ben's gray eyes scan me from head to toe, taking in my casual jeans and t-shirt. He might as well be inspecting a piece of gum stuck to his shoe. I flip my long hair over my shoulder, an old habit that kicks in when I'm irritated.

"Do you always greet potential neighbors this way?" I ask, injecting as much sarcasm into the question as I can manage.

"Only the charming ones," he says smoothly, a hint of a smirk playing on his lips.

Maci jumps in, her voice bright and cheerful despite the tension. "I'm Maci, by the way! So nice to meet you all."

Ben barely nods, and I can almost see the thought bubble over his head: Cute. They're letting interns tour the building.

"Alexandria Phillips," I introduce myself, even though he hasn't asked. "Co-owner of the publishing company that may or may not be infiltrating your precious corporate bubble."

Ben's eyebrow twitches at the word "owner," like he's mentally recalibrating his assessment of me.

I can't decide if I'm more annoyed or amused, but I'm leaning toward annoyed.

"Publishing," he repeats, rolling the word around his mouth like it's a foreign concept. "Books and… magazines, I assume?"

"No, porn," I shoot back just to get a reaction. For the record, we do not publish porn. We are classy. Mostly.

His eyes go wide as one of the men behind him snickers.

Maci elbows me sharply in the ribs. "She's kidding," she says quickly, her cheeks flushing pink. "We publish fiction. Contemporary, romance, that sort of thing."

Ben's expression settles back into practiced indifference, but there's a glint in his eyes that wasn't there before. "I see. Well, Ms. Phillips, I hope your— fictional endeavors don't disrupt our very real business."

"Oh, I don't know," I reply, tapping my chin thoughtfully. "Have you seen our latest bestseller? 'How to Remove the Stick from Your—'"

"What my partner means," Maci interrupts, stepping slightly in front of me, "is that we run a very professional operation. You won't even know we're here."

"Somehow I doubt that," Ben says, his gaze still locked on me.

The elevator dings behind us, and I've never been so grateful for the sound. "Well, this has been enlightening," I say, backing toward the open doors. "Can't wait to bring our chaotic creative energy to disrupt your… what is it you do again? Count other people's money?"

"Financial advisory," he corrects, his jaw clenched so tight I'm surprised his perfect teeth don't crack. "We help people build wealth and security."

"How noble," I reply, not at all impressed. "We just help them escape reality for a while."

Maci practically drags me into the elevator, smiling apologetically at Ben and his crew. "It was lovely meeting you all!"

As the doors begin to close, I catch Ben's steely gaze one more time. Something flashes across his face—annoyance, curiosity, or maybe just indigestion from whatever fancy lunch he probably had.

"Lexie!" Maci gasps, but she's fighting a smile. "Did you have to antagonize him?"

"Me?" I press a hand to my chest in mock innocence. "I was being delightful. He's the one who acted like we were selling friendship bracelets instead of running a legitimate business."

As the elevator descends, Maci nudges me with her elbow. "His eyes were kind of dreamy, though. All stormy and intense."

I look at her like she's just suggested we publish a cookbook written by crack heads. "Excuse me? Did we just meet the same person? The human iceberg with a superiority complex?"

"I'm just saying," she shrugs, "hate-flirting is still flirting."

"We were not flirting!" I sputter. "We were establishing boundaries, like two neighboring countries with nuclear capabilities."

Maci rolls her eyes as the elevator reaches the lobby. "Right. Well, if we take this office space, you two can continue your cold war from opposite sides of the hallway."

I follow her out into the marble-floored lobby, my mind still replaying Ben's dismissive tone. Something about him just gets under my skin like a splinter. "Did you catch that look he gave us? Like we were peasants trespassing in the kingdom of his oversized ego!"

"To be fair," Maci says as we push through the revolving doors into the Chicago afternoon, "we did start in your parents' garage."

"That was years ago!" I protest, squinting in the sudden sunlight. "And now we have one part time editor and a four bestsellers."

Maci links her arm with mine as we navigate the crowded sidewalk. "Which is exactly why we need this office space."

The image of Ben's irritating smirk flashes through my mind, followed quickly by the memory of those floor-to-ceiling windows and all that space. Space we desperately need.

"You know what? Yes." I nod decisively. "We're not letting some arrogant finance bro scare us away from our dream office. We're taking it."

"Great," Francie says, already typing on her phone. "I'll send over the contracts this afternoon."

I can't shake the image of Ben's disapproving glare. There was something about him that got under my skin immediately, like a papercut from a particularly pretentious bookmark.

"You know what?" I say to Maci as we head for the train. "Maybe this will be good material. I've been wanting to write a villain with really cold eyes."

Maci laughs, linking her arm through mine. "Just remember, in your books, the cold-eyed villain usually ends up being the love interest."

"Not this time," I assure her, even as a tiny voice in my head whispers, "Yeah, good luck with that."

But I'm a writer. I know how these stories go. And Ben Maddox is definitely not getting a redeeming arc.

Two

Assaulted by Lavender

⁓⟡⟡⁓

Three Weeks Later

Maci fumbles with the lock before the door finally swings open. Our new office space, waiting for life to be breathed into it, smells like dust and possibility. There are boxes stacked taller than I am, furniture cocooned in plastic wrap, and painting supplies scattered everywhere. "Ready to tackle this mess?" I ask, grinning at Maci. She nods enthusiastically, already hauling a box towards the reception area. I dive into my office, wrestling with my desk and bookshelves like they're wild animals. We're still laughing and joking about paint colors and book launches when there's a sharp knock.

A moment later, in struts the embodiment who shall hence forth be known as the Wicked Witch of Wacker. Compared to this snooty nuisance, Ben Maddox might as well be a teddy bear. Her nose crinkles in disgust at our delightful mess. Her hair is yanked back into a ponytail so tight it could launch a rocket, and her lips are pursed like she's just sucked on a particularly sour lemon.

"Can I help you?" I ask, as she remains glued to the doorway, her glare still burning holes into my soul. "I am Angel, executive assistant to Mr. Maddox across the hall. The racket you're making is wreaking havoc on our customers and disrupting our business," she snaps, like it's the most tragic event of the century.

I flash her my sweetest smile. "Are you that bad at your job that people in an office down the hall from you- who can't possibly be making the amount a noise you claim- distract you enough that you can't get your job done?" I ask, earning a muffled snort from Maci.

Angel's face flushes an impressive shade of crimson. "I'll be speaking to Mr. Maddox about this," she huffs, spinning on her designer heel so fast I'm surprised she doesn't drill herself into the floor.

"Looking forward to it!" I call after her retreating back. "Tell him that I've missed his sunny disposition!"

Maci collapses against a half-assembled bookshelf, giggling. "You know," Maci says, composing herself and swiping at her eyes, "if this whole publishing thing doesn't work out, you can always fall back on diplomacy."

I grab another box and head towards my office, trying and failing to hide my grin. "Might as well quit now and join the UN," I say.

I start hauling books towards my office. It's cramped and smells like a cardboard factory, but it's ours.

We're a tornado of energy, splitting tasks like we actually know what we're doing. Maci stakes out the reception area, hauling around boxes with surprising strength for someone who survives on a diet of kale and yoga. Her short blonde hair bounces with every move, and she looks entirely too cheerful for someone working this hard.

I head straight into my office, eyeing the mountains of work I've created for myself. My bookshelves, sturdy and about as big as a dinosaur, taunt me from the corner. I try to drag them across the room, barely budging them an inch. "Help, I've been trapped under a pile of my own ambition," I call out, flopping dramatically against the nearest stack of boxes.

Maci appears in the doorway, hands on hips, surveying my lack of progress. "Are you seriously stuck already?"

"No," I say, the picture of innocence. "Just testing gravity."

She tosses a wad of bubble wrap at my head. "It's working." She disappears back into the reception area, and I get serious about taming my unruly office.

I wrestle the bookshelves into submission, pausing every few minutes to catch my breath and shoot off a sarcastic remark about how child labor laws are unfairly keeping us from hiring tiny interns to do this work for us. Obviously, I don't condone child labor, don't come at me.

When I've managed to get everything more or less in place, I start unpacking books, stacking them on the shelves with no particular system other than they look pretty.

The office is slowly taking shape, though it's far from finished. My desk, an elegant fake antique when it's not in pieces, sprawls in the middle of the room like it just lost a fight with a giant wood chipper. I grab the instructions and squint at them like they're written in a foreign language. Who knew being the boss meant actual work?

"Maci," I yell, hoping she's not too buried in her own chaos.

"Why did we decide to be our own moving crew?"

Her voice drifts back, slightly muffled by the tower of boxes. "Because we're broke and ambitious?"

"One out of two isn't bad," I mutter, attacking the desk with renewed vigor.

Maci's working away, humming to herself as she turns the front office from a dump into a polished, professional-looking space. It's not too long before her progress shames me into productivity. I double down on the setup, finding an inner strength I didn't know existed—probably the spirit of some long-dead author—before dragging my desk into its rightful place. I collapse into the chair, covered in a fine layer of dust, just as Maci pokes her head in.

"You're still alive!" she exclaims with mock surprise.

"Barely," I say, but I'm grinning. My office may look like a mess, but it's a creative mess. I can already imagine it bustling with nervous first-time authors, boxes of newly printed books, and maybe even a few chairs.

Maci perches on one of the yet-to-be-assembled seat boxes, examining the pile of clutter and general chaos. "This place is going to be amazing," she says. I see her surveying her work with pride. She's put the reception desk in place, organized the chaos, and even started hanging some art on the walls. She's definitely winning in the unspoken competition to finish first.

I follow her gaze, trying to envision the chaos as a well-oiled machine of a publishing company. "This place is going to be amazing," I agree, with more conviction than breath.

"You know, after we met him the other day, I Googled him by the way," Maci says suddenly, unrolling a 'Girl Boss' poster that absolutely belongs in her office, not mine. "Ben Maddox. Harvard Business School. Featured in Forbes' 30 Under 40.

Apparently, he's some kind of financial genius."

"Sounds thrilling," I deadpan, digging through paint samples. "I've chosen 'Gentle Lavender' for my office. What do you think?"

A few hours later, I'm staring at walls that can only be described as 'offensive.' The lavender I'd carefully selected has somehow transformed into a violent purple that assaults my eyeballs. My hair is pulled into a messy bun; paint splattered across my cheeks and old Columbia t-shirt.

I'm horrified at the mess that screams "unicorn massacre purple." The paint, which looked perfectly lavender in the can, has dried into something that would make Barney the dinosaur say, "That's a bit much."

"What the hell?" I groan, dropping my roller into the paint tray with a splash that decorates my already paint-splattered jeans with more purple polka dots.

"So much for my vision of a sophisticated, professional office," I mutter, running a hand through my hair and promptly streaking it with purple. "Maybe we can tell people it's an artistic statement."

Maci pokes her head in, takes one look at the walls, and bursts into laughter. "Oh my God, Lex. It looks like Grimace threw up in here!"

"Thanks for the support," I say dryly. "I was going for 'understated creative genius.' I got 'five-year-old with a crayon collection.'"

"We could always repaint," Maci suggests, stepping fully into the room and examining my disaster. Her own office, I note with mild irritation, looks perfect with its crisp white walls and tasteful gray accents.

"No, we can't." I say, resigned. "I need to hire a professional.

Someone handsome and charming." I say, the author in me taking over.

We're both laughing when a throat clears behind us. I whip around, grabbing the paint roller, raising it like a weapon, only to find myself face-to-face with Ben Maddox. He stands in my doorway like he owns the entire building, not just the office next door. His crisp navy suit is a stark contrast to my paint-splattered ensemble, and his eyes flick over the purple monstrosity behind me with barely concealed disdain.

"I see the circus has come to town," he says, his voice as cool as his gaze.

I lower my paint roller, but only slightly. "Funny, I don't recall sending you an invitation."

"My assistant has informed me that you two have been distracting her with your noise." He says in a tone that is both formal and arrogant.

"Ahh yes, Angel." I say in my best innocent voice. "Awful personality, that one. Tell her she would get more work done if she removed the stick stuck up her-"

"—her ass." Maci finishes for me, which is shocking since she never swears. She actually blushes after saying it.

Ben's eyebrows shoot up, but I swear I catch the tiniest twitch at the corner of his mouth before his face settles back into its default setting: Corporate Robot.

"How eloquent," he says, adjusting his perfectly knotted tie. "Is that the literary genius that's made you a bestseller?"

Huh, he's researched me. Color me surprised. And purple.

"Of course. Do your best not to fawn all over my greatness." I reply in a pompous voice meant to mirror his own.

His eyes narrow, and I can almost hear the gears turning in his perfectly styled head. "I'd like to remind you that some of us are trying to run legitimate businesses here."

I gasp dramatically, pressing a paint-covered hand to my chest. "As opposed to our illegitimate book trafficking ring? I'm wounded, Maddox."

"What I mean," he says, jaw clenching, "is that your… redecorating… is creating a disturbance."

I glance at the purple walls, then back at him, and something mischievous takes over. I step closer, paint roller still in hand. "You know, this color would look amazing in your office. Really brighten up all that corporate drabness."

His eyes widen slightly as he takes a step back, like I'm wielding a weapon instead of home decor. "Stay away from me with that."

"What's wrong, Ben? Afraid of a little color in your life?" I take another step toward him, the roller dripping ominously.

Maci clears her throat. "Lex, maybe don't threaten the neighbor with paint on day one?"

I sigh and lower my weapon of mass decoration. "Fine. But only because you asked so nicely." I turn back to Ben. "Is there anything else we can help you with? Perhaps a personality transplant?"

"For Angel's sake," he starts in a resigned tone, "please keep it down."

"Listen, you know damn well that we weren't making loud noises or causing any disturbance whatsoever." I say, beginning to lose my temper. "Angel has been on us all day; from the moment we arrived. Do not make me take this to the building management. They will not take kindly to your business bullying my own. I hear they take harassment seriously. Keep her away from us."

For a moment, Ben actually looks surprised, like he wasn't

expecting me to stand up to him so directly. His gray eyes narrow slightly, and I can practically see him reassessing me.

"Fine," he says finally, his voice clipped. "I'll speak with Angel."

"Thank you," I say, managing to sound both gracious and smug at the same time. It's a talent.

Ben turns to leave but pauses in the doorway. "By the way," he says, glancing back at my purple walls, "they make color-correcting primers for… mistakes like that."

And then he's gone, leaving me standing there with a dripping paint roller and the distinct feeling that I've just been insulted by a walking Brooks Brothers catalog.

"Well," Maci says after a beat of silence, "that was… intense."

I snort, turning back to my purple nightmare. "That wasn't intense. That was just Ben being Ben—insufferable and annoyingly right about my paint choice."

"I don't know," Maci says thoughtfully, tilting her head. "There was definitely something there."

"Yeah, mutual hatred," I mutter, dropping my roller into the tray with a splash.

"If you say so," Maci sings, retreating back to her perfectly painted office.

I stare at my purple walls, sighing heavily. I hate to admit it, but Ben's right—I need a color-correcting primer. And probably professional help. For the walls, I mean. Definitely just for the walls.

"Maci!" I call out. "Do you think the building allows exorcisms? Because I think my office is possessed by the ghost of Prince!"

Her laughter floats back to me, and I can't help but smile despite my paint disaster. We may have the neighbor from corporate hell, but at least we have each other. And soon, hopefully, an office that doesn't look like it was decorated by a color-blind kindergartner.

I spend the next hour trying to salvage what I can of my office, but eventually admit defeat. The purple walls mock me with their vibrance, and I decide they can stay for now. After all, I'm a creative professional. This is just… expressing my unique vision. Or something.

By the time we finish setting up the essentials—desks, chairs, and enough coffee-making equipment to fuel a small army—it's well past dinnertime. My stomach grumbles loudly enough that Maci hears it from across the room.

"Food?" she suggests, already reaching for her phone. "I'll order Chinese."

"You're a lifesaver," I say, collapsing into my newly assembled chair. It wobbles precariously, threatening to dump me onto the floor. "And maybe add 'functional furniture' to our shopping list."

While Maci orders enough food to feed us for the next three days, I stare out the window at the Chicago skyline. The lights are starting to come on, twinkling like stars against the darkening sky. Despite the chaos, the purple walls, and the uptight neighbor, I feel a sense of pride swelling in my chest. We did it. We're actually here, in a real office, with our names on the door and everything.

"Hey," I call out to Maci, "we should celebrate."

She pokes her head in, phone still pressed to her ear. "Twenty minutes for the food," she says, covering the mouthpiece. "And celebrate how? I'm pretty sure my body is 90% paint fumes and sweat right now."

"I have fruit punch," I declare, pulling a bottle from my oversized tote bag. Don't judge. I'm on a tight budget thanks to our new office space. "I came prepared."

"Of course you did," Maci laughs, ending her call and joining me by the window. "Glasses?"

I pull out two paper cups from our earlier coffee run. "Only the finest dinnerware for us."

"Classy," she says, taking one of the cups. "Just like our publishing house."

I manage to open the fruit punch without taking spilling any on me—a personal victory—and pour generous amounts into our paper cups. Because I have the coordination of a toddler, the juice threatens to overflow, just like my emotions right now.

"To us," I say, raising my cup. "To surviving purple walls and corporate assholes."

"To us," Maci echoes, tapping her cup against mine. "And to bestsellers and bigger offices."

We sip our fruit punch as the city lights flicker on below us. For a moment, everything feels perfect. We've made it this far, against all odds. What's a little paint disaster and an annoying neighbor in the grand scheme of things?

The sound of a door closing down the hall reminds me that we're not alone in the building. Most of the financial firm's employees have left for the day, but I wonder if Ben is still there, working late, being all serious and corporate in his perfectly tailored suit.

"Do you think they ever have fun over there?" I ask, nodding toward the wall we share with the financial firm.

Maci shrugs, taking another sip of champagne. "Maybe their idea of fun is different from ours. Like, spreadsheet parties or dividend celebrations."

I snort, nearly choking on my drink. "Stop, you're killing me."

"I'm serious! Maybe they get really wild and use colored tabs in their binders."

We're both giggling now, the stress of the day melting away with each sip of cheap bubbly. By the time our food arrives, we're sprawled on the floor of the reception area, surrounded by empty paint cans and assembly instructions.

"This is the life," I sigh, digging into my lo mein. "Five-star dining in our five-star office."

Three

Champagne, Compliments, and Confusion

By the following month, we are officially up and running. My office, now the correct shade of lavender complete with white Victorian trim, showcases everything that is posh and trendy. For once, I am pleased with the way it looks thanks to the professionals I hired at an astronomical price.

Our online presence has helped us garner huge attention, so we are taking advantage of the moment and hosting an open house. A way for potential authors, agents- don't get me started, and bookstores all to come together.

The team- there's only four of us total- is out in full force, bustling around to make everything perfect. Maci is in her element, directing the caterers with military precision while somehow managing to look effortlessly chic in her navy blue dress. She's got this whole professional-yet-approachable vibe going that I'm still trying to master.

I, on the other hand, am hiding in my office, pretending to arrange books while actually having a minor panic attack. My hair is cooperating for once, cascading down my back in loose waves, and I've even put on a dress—a fitted emerald number that makes me look like I actually know what I'm doing with my life.

"Lexie!" Maci calls, poking her head into my sanctuary. "People are arriving in fifteen minutes. Are you ready?"

I gesture vaguely at myself. "As ready as I'll ever be to schmooze with people who think we're legitimate business owners."

"We are legitimate business owners," she reminds me, adjusting a stack of our latest releases on my desk. "Bestselling ones."

"Right," I nod, smoothing down my dress. "Just keep reminding me of that when I start talking about my collection of mismatched socks instead of our publishing goals."

I'm standing in the middle of our main space, surrounded by the buzz of literary energy and the click of camera shutters. The air smells of expensive perfume, ambition, and the catered hors d'oeuvres that cost more than my first car. Our logo—a sleek, modern take on an open book—gleams from the wall behind me, and I can't help but feel a little surge of pride.

"Ms. Phillips, can I get a quote for my blog?" A young woman with curly hair and thick-rimmed glasses appears at my elbow, recorder in hand.

"Sure," I say, flashing my most professional smile. "At Bound Books Publishing, we believe every story deserves to be told—especially the ones that keep you up at night, either because they're too steamy or too scary."

She blinks, then laughs. "That's perfect, thank you!"

As she disappears into the crowd, Maci slides up next to me, looking like a million dollars in her blue cocktail dress. "We're trending on X," she whispers, showing me her phone screen. "#BoundBooksLaunch is blowing up."

"No kidding?" I say trying and failing not to do a happy dance. "That's amazing.

I scan the room, taking in the diverse crowd of industry professionals, local authors, and book lovers who've shown up to support us. There's a buzz in the air, an electricity that feels like the start of something big. Or maybe that's just the champagne hitting my bloodstream.

"Did you see who just walked in?" Maci asks, nodding toward the door.

I follow her gaze and nearly choke on my drink. Ben Maddox, his business partner Eli Davis, and a few other men from the business whose names escape me are standing in our doorway looking like they just took a wrong turn on their way to the boardroom.

Ben's dark suit is impeccable as usual, but there's something different about him tonight—maybe it's the slight loosening of his tie or the fact that his hair isn't quite as severely styled.

"What are they doing here?" I hiss, instinctively smoothing down my dress.

Maci shrugs, a mischievous glint in her eye. "I may have sent invitations to the whole floor. You know, being neighborly and all that."

"You did what?" I whisper-shriek.

Before Maci can respond, Ben's gaze locks with mine across the room. For a split second, I swear I see something that isn't pure disdain in those steely gray eyes—curiosity, maybe? But then his usual mask of indifference slides back into place, and he whispers something to Eli that makes his friend smirk.

"I'm going to kill you," I mutter to Maci, plastering on a smile that feels more like a grimace. "Slowly and painfully, with papercuts from rejection letters."

"Oh, come on," she says, nudging me with her elbow. "It's good business to play nice with the neighbors. Besides, they look almost human tonight."

"Almost being the operative word," I reply, downing the rest of my champagne in one gulp.

Maci grins, already backing away. "That's the spirit! Now, I need to go check on the caterers. Act natural."

"Natural for me is sarcasm and inappropriate jokes. Are you sure that's what you want?" I call to her retreating back.

I take a deep breath, straighten my shoulders, and make my way through the crowd toward our unexpected guests. Each step feels like I'm walking to my own execution, but I'm determined to be professional. Or at least, professional-adjacent.

"Well, well," I say as I approach them, my voice dripping with fake enthusiasm. "If it isn't the fun police. To what do we owe this pleasure?"

Ben's eyes do a quick sweep of my dress before meeting my gaze. "Ms. Phillips," he acknowledges with a slight nod. "Quite the gathering you've assembled."

"We publisher types know how to party," I say, waving a hand at the buzzing crowd. "No spreadsheets required."

Eli, Ben's much more personable business partner, steps forward with a genuine smile. "The place looks great," he says, extending his hand. "I'm Eli Davis, by the way. I don't think we've been formally introduced."

I shake his hand, surprised by his warmth. "Lexie Phillips.

And thanks. It only took three coats of primer to fix the purple disaster."

Ben's mouth twitches at that, which I'm counting as a win.

"So," I continue, rocking back on my heels, "don't tell me you are actually interested in our company?"

"Actually," Eli jumps in before Ben can respond, "we came to be supportive neighbors. And maybe network a bit. You've got quite the impressive guest list."

"Networking at a publishing party?" I raise an eyebrow. "Let me guess, you're hoping to convince some bestselling author to let you manage their newfound wealth?"

"Something like that," Ben finally speaks up, his voice soft.

I glance back, taken off guard by his tone. "Well," I begin, the first time in forever at a loss for words. "I really appreciate you guys stopping in and offering your support."

I catch a hint of surprise in Ben's eyes, like he wasn't expecting civility from me. Well, that makes two of us.

"Your company has generated quite the buzz," Ben continues, his voice still holding that strange softness. "Three bestsellers in a year is impressive by any standard."

"Why, Benjamin Maddox," I gasp, pressing a hand to my chest. "Was that almost a compliment? Should I check if pigs are flying outside?"

His jaw tightens, but there's something like amusement hiding in the corners of his mouth. "I can acknowledge success when I see it, Ms. Phillips. Even when it comes in… unconventional packages."

"Like purple offices and champagne in paper cups?" I ask, remembering our first day.

"Precisely," he says, and I swear his eyes actually crinkle at the corners.

Before this bizarre moment can continue, a server passes with a tray of hor dourves. I grab one, needing something to do with my hands before I do something stupid like notice how the dim lighting softens Ben's sharp features.

"So," Eli jumps in, clearly sensing the strange tension, "Ben tells me you're not just the owner but also an author yourself?"

"Guilty," I nod, taking a sip of my drink. "Though tonight I'm wearing my publisher hat. Less comfortable but more professional."

"What kind of books do you write?" Eli asks, seeming genuinely interested.

"Fantasy, Romance," I answer, watching Ben's reaction from the corner of my eye. "You know, magic, relationships, happily ever after's."

"She's being modest," a voice chimes in, and suddenly Maci is at my side, all smiles and social grace. "Lexie's latest novel spent twelve weeks on the New York Times bestseller list. You know the three bestsellers Ben mentioned earlier? All hers."

"Impressive," Eli nods, while Ben remains suspiciously silent.

"What's it about?" one of the other financial guys asks, speaking up for the first time.

"Oh, you know," I shrug, feeling a wicked smile spread across my face. "Girl meets boy, boy is insufferably arrogant, girl contemplates murder, they fall in love instead. The usual."

Ben's eyes narrow slightly, and I can practically hear the gears turning in his head. "Sounds… intriguing."

"Does it?" I ask innocently. "Pure fiction, I assure you."

Maci, bless her heart, chooses this moment to intervene. "Can I offer you gentlemen a tour of our space? It's come a long way since the purple incident."

As Maci leads Eli and the others toward our main conference

room, Ben lingers, his gaze still fixed on me with an intensity that makes me want to fidget.

"What?" I finally ask, uncomfortably aware of how close we're standing.

"You surprise me," he says, his voice low enough that only I can hear it.

"Is that a good thing or a bad thing?" I counter, trying to keep my tone light despite the sudden flutter in my stomach.

Ben tilts his head slightly, studying me like I'm a particularly complex investment portfolio. "I'm still deciding."

Before I can come up with a suitably snarky response, someone calls my name from across the room. I turn to see one of Chicago's top literary agents waving me over.

"Duty calls," I say, oddly reluctant to end our bizarre exchange. "Try not to scowl at any of my guests while I'm gone. It might scare them."

"I'll do my best," he replies, and I swear there's the ghost of a smile playing on his lips.

I navigate through the crowd, greeting authors and industry professionals with handshakes and air kisses, but my mind keeps drifting back to Ben's unexpected appearance and even more unexpected almost-compliments. What game is he playing?

The rest of the evening passes in a blur of networking, champagne, and increasingly loud conversations. Our open house is, by all accounts, a roaring success. The who's who of Chicago's literary scene mingle with local media, bookstore owners, and aspiring authors, all buzzing about Bound Books Publishing's meteoric rise.

I'm in the middle of explaining our submission process to an eager young writer when I notice Ben and his colleagues preparing to leave. Eli catches my eye and gives me a friendly wave, which I return. Ben, however, simply nods in my direction, his expression unreadable before he turns to follow his friends out the door.

"And that's how you submit your manuscript," I finish automatically, my attention still split between the hopeful author and Ben's retreating back.

"Thanks so much, Ms. Phillips," the young woman gushes. "I can't wait to send it in!"

"Looking forward to it," I reply with a smile that I hope doesn't look as distracted as I feel.

As the crowd finally begins to thin around midnight, Maci finds me collapsed in my office chair, heels kicked off and a half-empty champagne flute dangling from my fingers.

"We did it!" she exclaims, flopping onto the small sofa I'd crammed into the corner. "We're officially legit!"

"Were we ever not legit?" I ask, swiveling lazily in my chair.

"Well, remember when we used to meet authors at that coffee shop and pretend the bathroom was our conference room?"

I snort, nearly spilling my champagne. "Oh God, those were the days. 'Please excuse the hand dryer, it's our printer.'"

We both dissolve into giggles, the stress of the evening melting away with each laugh. I kick my feet up on my desk, not caring that it's probably unprofessional. My emerald dress bunches around my thighs, but I'm too tired to care.

"So," Maci says, her voice taking on that tone she uses when she's about to dig for gossip. "What was that about?"

"What was what about?" I ask innocently, though I know exactly what she means.

"You and Mr. Wall Street having an actual conversation that didn't end in bloodshed."

I roll my eyes dramatically. "We were being civil. It's a special occasion."

"Mmm-hmm," Maci hums, clearly unconvinced. "And I'm secretly a unicorn."

"If you were, you'd have told me by now," I quip, draining the last of my champagne. "Seriously, it was nothing. He said our success was impressive, I nearly had a heart attack from shock, end of story."

Maci studies me for a moment, her blue eyes narrowed. "He couldn't take his eyes off you all night."

"Probably planning my murder," I suggest. "Or wondering how someone so unprofessional could run a successful business."

"If you say so," Maci sings, clearly unconvinced. "But I saw the way you kept tracking him around the room."

"I was making sure he wasn't scaring off potential clients with his resting finance face," I defend, but even I can hear how weak that sounds.

Maci just smirks, too tired to push it further. "Whatever helps you sleep at night, bestie."

I throw a pen at her, which she dodges easily. "Don't even start with that. The man is insufferable."

"Insufferably hot," she corrects.

"I'm too tired and too buzzed to have this conversation," I declare, standing up and stretching. My back pops in three places, and I groan. "Can we please just celebrate our amazing night instead of psychoanalyzing my hostile relationship with the neighbor?"

Maci raises her hands in surrender. "Fine, fine. Consider it dropped. For now."

We spend the next hour cleaning up the worst of the mess,

leaving the rest for tomorrow's problem. By the time we lock up, it's nearly 2 AM, and the city has quieted to a gentle hum outside our windows.

Her Uber arrives before mine, and I wave her off, watching as she disappears into the night. My own ride is still five minutes away, so I lean against the building's glass entrance, enjoying the cool night air on my flushed skin.

The city is never truly quiet, but there's a softness to it at this hour—the distant hum of traffic, the occasional burst of laughter from late-night revelers, the gentle whoosh of wind between buildings. I close my eyes for a moment, soaking it all in. This is what success feels like, I think. Not just the party or the bestseller list, but this moment of pure contentment.

"Long night?"

I nearly jump out of my skin at the sound of Ben's voice. My eyes fly open to find him standing a few feet away, his tie now completely loosened around his neck, suit jacket draped over one arm.

"Jesus, Maddox!" I press a hand to my chest. "Do you always lurk in shadows waiting to give people heart attacks?"

"Only on special occasions," he replies, the ghost of a smile playing at his lips. "Waiting for a ride?"

I nod, trying to regain my composure. "What about you? Don't tell me the Wall Street boys actually know how to party past midnight."

"Dinner with clients," he explains, gesturing vaguely down the street. "Just wrapped up."

An awkward silence falls between us, neither of us quite sure what to do with this unexpected moment of privacy. I shift my weight from one foot to the other, suddenly aware of my bare feet on the cool pavement—I'd stuffed my torture devices (otherwise known as heels) into my bag the moment I stepped outside.

"Your event seemed successful," Ben offers finally, his voice softer than I've ever heard it.

"It was," I agree, unable to keep the pride from my voice. "Turns out people actually want to read the books we publish. Who knew?"

He chuckles—actually chuckles—and the sound is so unexpected that I find myself staring at him. In the dim glow of the streetlights, with his hair slightly mussed and his collar unbuttoned, he looks almost… human.

"What?" he asks, catching me staring.

"Nothing," I say quickly. "Just trying to figure out if you've been body-snatched. The Ben Maddox I know doesn't laugh at my jokes."

"Maybe you've never been funny before," he counters, but there's no real bite to it.

My phone buzzes with a notification, my Uber canceled my ride.

I sigh, dropping my phone back into my purse. "Great. Just great."

"Problem?" Ben asks, his eyebrows lifting slightly.

"My ride canceled," I explain, trying not to sound as annoyed as I feel. "Screw it, I'll walk."

He looks genuinely alarmed. "It's late; you can't walk alone at this hour. Which way are you going? I will walk with you."

Oddly touched by his offer but not wanting to put him out. "Oh, you don't have to. It's not too far down Orleans."

"I live off of Orleans as well, I'll walk with you," he says, his tone leaving no room for argument.

I open my mouth to protest but quickly realize I'm too tired to fight. Plus, there's something weirdly comforting about not walking alone at 2 AM, even if my companion is usually my nemesis.

"Fine," I concede, adjusting my bag on my shoulder. "But if this is an elaborate plot to murder me and hide my body in the river, just know that Maci has detailed files on all my enemies. You're in folder one."

Ben actually smiles at that—a real smile that transforms his face completely. "Noted. Though I think murdering a bestselling author would draw too much attention."

We fall into step beside each other, the quiet hum of the city surrounding us. The night air is cool against my skin, and I'm suddenly aware of how close we're walking. Close enough that I can smell his cologne—something expensive and woodsy that definitely doesn't scream cheap.

"So," I say, breaking the silence before it gets awkward, "do you actually read books, or is that against the finance bro code?"

He glances at me, one eyebrow raised. "I read quite a bit, actually. Though I doubt my taste aligns with your publishing catalog."

"Let me guess," I tap a finger against my chin dramatically. "Self-help books about crushing the competition? 'How to Make a Million Before Breakfast'? 'The Art of Looking Down on Creative Types'?"

"Classics, mostly," he replies, ignoring my jabs with surprising grace. "Some historical non-fiction. The occasional thriller."

"Huh," I say, genuinely surprised. "I wouldn't have pegged you for a classics guy."

"There's a lot you don't know about me, Ms. Phillips."

"Lexie," I correct automatically. "If you're walking me home at 2 AM, you might as well use my first name."

He nods, the hint of a smile playing at his lips again. "Lexie, then."

We walk another block in surprisingly comfortable silence. The streets are nearly empty, just the occasional cab whizzing by or late-night reveler stumbling home. Chicago feels different at this hour—less frantic, more intimate.

"You know," I say, unable to help myself, "I still can't figure you out, Ben Maddox."

"Is that so?" he asks, glancing down at me with those intense gray eyes.

"One minute you're the human embodiment of a spreadsheet, and the next you're offering to walk a damsel in distress home."

"I wouldn't exactly call you a damsel in distress," he says dryly. "More like a tornado in heels."

I chuckle despite myself. "Not anymore," I say, glancing down at my bare feet. He follows my gaze, pausing when he spots my shoeless toes.

"You're walking barefoot in downtown Chicago?" Ben asks, looking as if I'd just told him I moonlight as a mime.

"My feet were staging a rebellion," I explain, grimacing at the blister on my heel. "And honestly, these sidewalks are cleaner than my kitchen floor, so…"

Ben shakes his head, but there's something like amusement in his eyes. "You're full of surprises, aren't you?"

"That's what it says on my business cards," I quip, wiggling my toes against the cool pavement. "Lexie Phillips: Publisher, Author, Professional Surprise Machine."

We turn down a quieter street, the buildings casting long shadows across our path. Without the heels, I'm even more aware of our height difference—he towers over me by at least half a foot, his long strides slowing to match my pace.

"So," I say, because apparently, I can't handle comfortable silence, "was that an actual compliment earlier? About our success being impressive?"

Ben glances down at me, his expression unreadable in the dim light. "It was. Three bestsellers in a year is objectively impressive, regardless of how I feel about your… management style."

"What's wrong with my management style?" I ask, feigning offense.

"Where should I start?" he replies dryly. "The purple office incident? The impromptu dance parties I can hear through the wall? The fact that your idea of professional attire includes t-shirts with literary puns?"

"Hey, 'You had me at Cello' is a classic," I defend, referring to my favorite shirt. "And those dance parties are team-building exercises, I'll have you know."

"Of course they are," he says, but his voice lacks its usual edge.

We walk another block in companionable silence, and I find myself stealing glances at him. In this light, away from the office, he looks younger somehow. Less like the uptight finance guy next door and more like… well, just a guy.

As we arrive at my apartment building—a converted warehouse that screams "aspiring hipster" with its exposed brick, industrial chic vibe, and a lobby packed with far too many plants—I slow my pace and come to a stop. "This is me," I announce, hoping my breathlessness sounds more from exertion than anything else. "Thanks for the escort service." The words leave my mouth before I have a chance to stop them, but I barely pause to breathe before trying to explain. "Not that kind of escort service, obviously."

Ben raises an eyebrow, the corner of his mouth threatening

to betray his usual composure. "You're welcome."

I shift awkwardly, suddenly unsure how to end this strange interlude. Do I shake his hand? Wave? Pretend this never happened and go back to snarking at him across the hallway tomorrow?

"Well," I say, clutching my purse to my chest like some kind of bizarre security blanket. "See you around, I guess."

Ben nods, his eyes meeting mine with unexpected intensity. "Congratulations again on your event. It was… illuminating."

"Thanks," I reply, genuinely touched. "That's… surprisingly nice of you to say."

"Don't get used to it," he says, but there's no malice in his tone.

"I wouldn't dream of it," I reply with a smirk.

For a moment, we just stand there, caught in some weird limbo between enemies and… something else. The streetlight casts shadows across his face, softening his usually sharp features. Without thinking, I reach up and straighten his already loose tie.

"There," I say, my voice coming out softer than intended. "Can't have you walking around looking disheveled. What would the other finance bros think?"

His eyes widen slightly at the contact, but he doesn't pull away. "Probably that I've been corrupted by my creative neighbor."

"The horror," I whisper dramatically, letting my hand fall back to my side.

He clears his throat, taking a small step back. "Goodnight, Lexie."

"Goodnight, Ben," I reply, fumbling for my keys.

I watch him walk away, his tall figure disappearing into the shadows of the Chicago night. Only when he's completely out of sight do I let out the breath I didn't realize I was holding.

What the hell was that?

Four

Charity, Coffee, and Conflicting Feelings

I'm knee-deep in manuscript edits when Maci bursts into my office the next morning, coffee in one hand and a pastry bag in the other. Her eyes are wide with excitement, like she's about to spill the juiciest gossip in the publishing world.

"So," she says, dragging out the word as she plops the coffee on my desk, "I just ran into Ben in the hallway."

I keep my eyes firmly on my computer screen, pretending to be engrossed in a particularly challenging paragraph. "And this is newsworthy because…?"

"Because he asked about you," she replies, perching on the edge of my desk. "Specifically."

My fingers freeze over the keyboard, but I force my face to remain neutral.

"He was probably just checking if I'm plotting my next attack on his precious corporate atmosphere," I say, finally looking up at her. "What did he want to know, my weakness so he can exploit it?"

Maci rolls her eyes so hard I'm worried they might get stuck. "He asked if you got in okay this morning."

My treacherous heart does a little flip, which I promptly ignore. "That's… oddly considerate."

"Almost like he's a human being and not a corporate robot," Maci says, unwrapping her pastry with surgical precision. "So? Did something happen after I left that I should know about?"

"Nothing worth mentioning," I say, reaching for my coffee. "My Uber canceled, he walked me home. No bloodshed, minimal insults. The end."

Maci's eyebrows shoot up so high they nearly disappear into her blonde bangs. "He walked you home? At 2 AM? In the dark? Just the two of you?"

"Don't make it sound like the beginning of a rom-com," I warn, pointing my pen at her. "It was purely practical. He lives in the same direction."

"Interesting," Maci says, drawing out each syllable like she's savoring it. "Very interesting."

"It's really not," I insist, turning back to my computer. "Can we please focus on actual work? Like the fact that Bethany's latest manuscript has more plot holes than my shower drain has hair?"

Maci sighs dramatically but allows the subject change. "Fine. But this conversation isn't over."

"It absolutely is," I counter, already scrolling through the document. "Now, can you please tell Bethany that her protagonist can't suddenly know how to fly a helicopter in chapter twelve when she was afraid of heights in chapter three?"

Maci slides off my desk, pastry in hand. "On it, boss."

But first, one more thing." She reaches into her bag and pulls out a copy of this morning's Tribune. "Check this out."

I take the paper, eyes scanning the headline in the arts section: "Bound Books Publishing: Chicago's Hottest New Literary Force." There's even a photo from our launch party—me in my emerald dress, surrounded by Chicago's literary elite, looking like I actually belong there.

"Holy shit," I breathe, coffee forgotten. "We're in the Tribune."

"Not just in it," Maci says, tapping the byline. "Written by Caroline Winters. She's like, the literary critic in Chicago."

I skim the article, my eyes catching phrases like "fresh perspective," "revolutionary approach," and "breathing new life into publishing." Each word feels like validation, like maybe we aren't just faking this whole business owner thing after all.

"We should frame this," I say, carefully folding the paper. "Put it right in the reception area so everyone can see it."

"Already ordered three copies," Maci says with a grin. "One for each office and one for your ego."

I throw a paperclip at her, which she dodges easily. "My ego and I thank you."

After Maci leaves, I try to focus on work, but my mind keeps drifting back to last night—the walk home with Ben, the strange moment outside my building. It was… nice. Which is exactly why it's so unsettling. Ben Maddox isn't supposed to be nice. He's supposed to be the uptight neighbor who scowls at our existence and complains about our music being too loud.

I'm deep in thought, absently chewing on the end of a pen, when there's a sharp knock at my door. I look up, expecting Maci, but instead find myself staring at the bane of my existence. Angel is back, cruel smirk and all, as she stands in my doorway like she owns the place.

"Can I help you?" I ask, setting down my pen and straightening my shoulders.

Angel's eyes sweep across my office, lingering on the slightly crooked picture frames and the stack of manuscripts teetering on the edge of my desk. "I have asked you repeatedly to keep the noise to a minimum," she says, her voice dripping with disdain.

This bitch. Only Maci and I are in the office today and neither one of us have spoke in well over an hour, so I know this ish is up to no good, and I'm not in the mood for it today.

I lean back in my chair, crossing my arms. "Funny, because the only noise I've heard all morning is the sound of my own thoughts, which—unless you've developed telepathy—shouldn't be bothering you."

Angel's perfectly painted lips purse. "Mr. Maddox has meetings with very important clients today. We can't have any… distractions."

"By distractions, do you mean us existing? Because that's going to be tough to fix." I stand up, suddenly tired of being looked down on—literally and figuratively. "Listen, Angel. We run a legitimate business here, just like you do. We're not throwing raves or hosting drum circles. We're editing books. Quietly."

She sniffs, adjusting her already immaculate blazer. "Perhaps you don't understand the caliber of clients Mr. Maddox deals with."

"Perhaps you don't understand that I don't care," I reply sweetly. "Now, is there anything else I can help you with, or did you just come here to practice your disapproving schoolmarm impression?"

Angel's face flushes an impressive shade of crimson. "This is exactly the kind of unprofessional behavior I'm talking about."

"No, unprofessional would be me telling you exactly where you can shove your complaints," I say, my smile never wavering. "This is me being remarkably restrained. Now, if there is nothing else, see yourself out and do not come back."

She leaves in a graceful huff. I should have known yesterday was a fluke. Ben's back to his superiority complex today; sending his little minion over here to make sure we stay in line.

For a fleeting moment, I consider marching over to his office and confronting him directly, but I resist the urge. That's probably exactly what Angel wants—me causing a scene that she can use as ammunition later. Instead, I take a deep breath and return to my editing, attacking the manuscript with renewed vigor.

By lunchtime, I'm so engrossed in work that I barely notice when Maci pokes her head in.

"Earth to Lexie," she says, waving a sandwich in front of my face. "Food break. You've been staring at that screen for three hours straight."

I blink, suddenly aware of the stiffness in my neck. "Sorry, I was in the zone."

"I could tell," Maci says, setting the sandwich on my desk. "You had your 'murder face' on."

"My what?"

"Your murder face. The one you get when you're either deeply focused or plotting someone's demise." She plops down in the chair across from me. "So, which was it?"

"Both," I admit, unwrapping the sandwich. "Angel stopped by earlier."

Maci groans. "Again? What did Her Royal Highness want this time?"

"Same old song and dance. We're too noisy, too unprofessional, too everything." I take a bite of my sandwich, suddenly realizing how hungry I am. "I swear, that woman has it out for us."

"Maybe she's jealous," Maci suggests, opening her own lunch. "I mean, we're young, successful, and we don't have to wear panty hose to work."

I snort, nearly choking on my food. "I don't think Angel's capable of emotions that complex. Pretty sure she runs on spite and expensive coffee."

After she heads back to her office, I sit glancing at the afternoon sun streaming through my office windows. Despite Angel's visit, I can't help but feel a sense of contentment. We've come so far from our days working out of my parents' garage, scraping together enough money to print our first book. Now we're in the Tribune, hosting successful launch parties, and—

My thoughts are interrupted by another knock at my door. I look up, expecting Angel round two, but instead find Eli Davis standing there, a hesitant smile on his face.

"Sorry to interrupt," he says, looking genuinely apologetic. "Is this a bad time?"

"Not at all," I say, setting down my sandwich. "What can we do for you, Eli?"

He steps into the office, his tall frame making the space feel suddenly smaller. Unlike Ben, who seems perpetually annoyed by our existence, Eli radiates an easy warmth. "I wanted to apologize for Angel," he says, surprising me. "She can be a bit... intense."

"That's one word for it," I mutter.

"We don't really like having her around, but she's the daughter of mine and Ben's business partner and, unfortunately, majority owner.

So, we're stuck with her," he finishes with a grimace.

I blink, processing this unexpected information. "That… actually explains a lot."

"Well, I won't keep you, I just wanted to come over and apologize for Angel." He rubs the back of his neck, looking slightly embarrassed. "She's been particularly difficult lately."

"I appreciate the apology, but you're not responsible for her behavior," I say, surprised by my own diplomacy. Maybe I'm growing as a person. Or maybe I'm just too tired to be snarky.

"Actually, I also wanted to ask you about something else," Eli continues, shifting his weight. "Your launch party was impressive. Really impressive."

I can't help the small surge of pride. "Thanks. We clean up nice when we have to."

"I was wondering if you might be interested in collaborating on something."

This catches me off guard. "Collaborating? With the finance guys? On what, a guide to passive-aggressive office etiquette?"

Eli laughs, a genuine sound that makes it hard not to like him. "Nothing like that. My sister runs a literacy nonprofit for underprivileged teens in the city. We're always looking for authors to come speak, donate books, that sort of thing."

"Oh," I say, feeling a twinge of guilt for my automatic snark. "That actually sounds amazing."

"Great!" His face lights up. "Maybe you could stop by our office later? We can talk details."

I hesitate for a moment, the thought of voluntarily entering the finance lair making me nervous. But the cause is good, and I've never been one to turn down an opportunity to help kids discover reading.

"Sure," I say, pushing aside my reservations. "Let me just wrap up a few things here. Would thirty minutes work?"

"Perfect," Eli says with a warm smile. "And don't worry about Ben. He's in meetings most of the afternoon."

I try not to look relieved at this information. "I wasn't worried," I lie, poorly.

After Eli leaves, I spend a few minutes fixing my hair and reapplying my lip gloss. For professional reasons, obviously. Not because I might run into a certain irritating neighbor with stormy gray eyes.

"Where are you off to?" Maci asks as I pass her office.

"Meeting with Eli about a literacy program," I explain, smoothing down my blouse. "Apparently, they do charity work when they're not counting gold coins like dragons."

Maci's eyes light up. "Ooh, fraternizing with the enemy!"

"It's for underprivileged kids," I remind her. "I'm being altruistic, not treasonous."

"Sure, sure," she says with a knowing smile. "Just remember – if you see Ben, try not to start a war. We share a wall with them."

"Your faith in me is touching," I say dryly, heading for the door. "If I'm not back in an hour, send a search party. Or at least a strongly worded email."

The finance firm's office is exactly what I expected – sleek, modern, and so aggressively neutral it hurts my eyes. Gone are the colorful book displays and cozy reading nooks of our space, replaced by chrome accents and minimalist furniture that probably costs more than my car.

Angel sits at the reception desk, and her eyes narrow when she spots me. "Can I help you?" she asks, her tone suggesting she'd rather help me off a cliff.

"I'm here to see Eli," I say, plastering on my most professional smile. "He's expecting me."

Before Angel can respond (presumably to tell me to take a hike), Eli appears from one of the conference rooms. "Lexie! Perfect timing. Come on back."

I follow him past Angel's desk, resisting the urge to stick out my tongue at her. I'm a professional, after all. A professional with the maturity of a twelve-year-old, but still.

Eli leads me through a maze of identical-looking offices, each more sterile than the last. I catch glimpses of serious-looking people staring at multiple computer screens, their faces illuminated by the glow of financial data.

"So, this is where fun comes to die," I mutter under my breath taking a seat as he closes the door to his office.

Eli chuckles, closing his office door behind us. "We prefer to call it 'focused productivity,' but I see your point."

His office is less sterile than the others, with a few personal touches—a framed photo of him with an adorable fluffy puppy, a small plant that's actually alive, and a collection of colorful paperweights that look out of place among all the gray and white.

"So," I say, settling into a chair that's probably worth more than my monthly rent, "tell me more about this literacy program."

Eli's face lights up as he launches into an explanation of "Words for Tomorrow," the nonprofit his sister Olivia founded three years ago. They work with teens in underserved communities, providing books, writing workshops, and mentorship opportunities. It's impressive, meaningful work—exactly the kind of thing I'd want our company involved with.

"We're always looking for authors to come speak to the

kids," Eli explains, leaning forward in his chair. "Someone like you—young, successful, with a non-traditional path—would be incredibly inspiring."

"I'm flattered," I say, genuinely touched. "And definitely interested. When were you thinking?"

We dive into logistics, discussing dates and what kind of presentation would resonate most with the teens. I'm so caught up in the conversation that I don't notice the door opening behind me.

"Eli, do you have the Peterson file—" The voice stops abruptly.

I don't need to turn around to know who it is. The air in the room shifts instantly, like someone cranked up the tension dial to eleven.

"Ben," Eli says, glancing over my shoulder. "I thought you were in meetings all afternoon."

"Wrapped up early," Ben replies, his voice carefully neutral. "I didn't realize you had company."

I spin in my chair, meeting those stormy gray eyes with what I hope is casual indifference. "Hey, neighbor. Fancy running into you in your natural habitat."

Ben's gaze flicks between Eli and me, his expression unreadable. "Ms. Phillips."

"Back to 'Ms. Phillips,' are we?" I ask, raising an eyebrow. "And here I thought we'd made progress with first names."

A muscle twitches in his jaw. "Lexie, then. What brings you to our side of the building?"

"Plotting world domination," I reply automatically. "One financial firm at a time."

Eli jumps in before Ben can respond. "Lexie and I were just discussing her involvement with Words for Tomorrow," Eli explains quickly. "The literacy program Olivia runs."

Ben's expression shifts almost imperceptibly. "I see."

"It sounds like an amazing program," I say, turning back to Eli. "I'd be honored to participate."

Ben moves further into the room, his presence somehow making the spacious office feel smaller. "Words for Tomorrow is an excellent initiative," he says, surprising me with what sounds like genuine approval. "The impact they've had on literacy rates in the city is impressive."

I blink at him, momentarily thrown by his supportive tone. "You're… familiar with the program?"

"Ben's one of our biggest donors," Eli explains with a grin.

"Well," I say, standing up and smoothing down my blouse, "I should get back to my side of the building. Those books won't publish themselves."

"I'll email you the details," Eli promises, rising as well. "And I'll let Olivia know you're on board. She'll be thrilled."

"Looking forward to it," I say, meaning it.

I head for the door, but Ben doesn't move from his position, forcing me to squeeze past him. As I do, I catch a whiff of that same woodsy cologne from last night, and something flutters in my stomach that I refuse to acknowledge.

"See you around, neighbor," I say, pausing briefly beside him.

His eyes meet mine, and for a moment, I swear I see something soften in that steely gaze. "I'm sure you will," he replies, his voice low enough that only I can hear it.

Time stretches between us, taut with something I can't—or won't—name, before Angel barges into our moment. "Mr. Maddox, the Murphy clients are here." Eli lets out a low whistle. "Damn, Maddox, the Murphy's? You get them and you're set for life."

"Yes, well, they will be tricky to land. Very traditional values, very strict in their *needs*." He responds, apprehension leaking into his voice. It sounds weird coming from him.

I don't know what any of this means, but I know that now would be a good time to make my escape. I nod and slip past them, making my exit as graceful as possible while practically sprinting away from the finance bros and their big-deal clients. The whole interaction leaves me feeling oddly unsettled. Ben Maddox, secret charity supporter? The man who sends Angel to harass us about noise that doesn't exist actually cares about underprivileged kids? It doesn't compute with the image I've built of him in my head.

As I push open the door to our office, I nearly collide with Maci, who's carrying a stack of manuscripts so high she can barely see over them.

"Whoa there!" I grab the top few before they topple. "Where's the fire?"

"Bethany sent over her ideas for revisions," Maci explains, her face flushed with excitement. "And they're actually good. Like, really good."

"No way," I say, following her to the conference room where she dumps the manuscripts onto the table. "She's gonna fix the helicopter scene?"

"Better," Maci says, flipping pages until she finds what she's looking for. "She's thinking of redoing the entire third act. The protagonist doesn't suddenly know how to fly a helicopter. She explains how she will already know about it and get this—she hijacks one with a pilot already inside."

I scan the pages, a smile spreading across my face. "This… actually works. Damn."

"I know, right?" Maci beams. "So, how was your trip to enemy territory? Did you make it out alive?"

I settle into one of the conference chairs, kicking my feet up on the table. "Barely." I confirm, flopping into the chair across from her desk. "Though Angel did try to murder me with her eyes."

"That's just her face," Maci says dismissively. "So? How'd it go with Eli?"

I fill her in on the literacy program, trying to sound casual when I mention Ben's surprise appearance and his connection to the charity.

Maci's eyebrows shoot up. "No way. Mr. Wall Street cares about something other than profit margins?"

"Apparently," I shrug, still trying to reconcile this new information with my mental image of Ben. "Though he was back to his usual charming self when he saw me in Eli's office."

"Interesting," Maci says, drawing out the word like she's savoring it. "Very interesting."

"Don't start," I warn, pointing a finger at her. "Whatever you're thinking, stop it."

"I'm not thinking anything," she says innocently. "Just finding it curious that the uptight neighbor who supposedly hates us is also secretly philanthropic. It's like finding out Darth Vader volunteers at animal shelters on weekends."

I snort at the image. "I doubt he's personally reading to children or anything. Probably just writes a check once a year for the tax deduction."

"Mmm-hmm," Maci hums, clearly unconvinced. "If you say so."

Five

Bestselling Author, Secondhand High

Friday morning at the office is a big deal for me. We have managed to get one of the biggest authors on the planet to come by for a talk. Turns out he is looking for a new publisher, one more open to creative expression, so naturally, he thought of us. Having been one of the top authors since the early 90s, this would be a freaking gold mine for us.

By the time he arrives in my office, 23 minutes late, I'm a bundle of nerves. I expected to meet the well-groomed man whose photo adorns the back of countless best sellers. What comes through my door is the embodiment of Leo the hippy from That 70s Show. I have to say, I did not see that coming.

"Lexie Phillips," I say, extending my hand. "Such an honor to meet you."

The living legend, Zephyr McKnight, grasps my hand with both of his, giving it an enthusiastic shake that threatens to dislocate my shoulder. His gray hair is pulled into a messy man-bun, his Hawaiian shirt is at least three sizes too big, and the scent of patchouli wafts off him in waves strong enough to make my eyes water.

"Zephyr McKnight," he announces, striding into my office like he owns the place. "You must be the infamous Lexie Phillips."

"Mr. McKnight!" I greet enthusiastically. "Such an honor to meet you. I'm a huge fan of your work."

He waves away my formality with a flick of his wrist. "Zephyr, please. 'Mr. McKnight' makes me sound like someone who pays taxes on time."

I laugh, probably a bit too enthusiastically. "Zephyr it is. Please, have a seat."

He flops into the chair across from my desk, immediately stretching out his legs and making himself at home. "Nice digs," he says, glancing around my office. "Very… trippy."

"Uh, thank you, sir." I say, fumbling for the right words to say. Smooth, Lexie.

"It's got personality," he says with a grin. "Just like your books."

My heart does a little somersault. Zephyr McKnight has read my books? I try to keep my cool, but inside I'm doing cartwheels.

"So," I say, attempting to sound professional despite the internal screaming, "you mentioned you're looking for a new publisher?"

Zephyr leans forward, suddenly all business despite his hippie appearance. "Here's the deal, kid. I've been with Pinnacle for twenty years. They've made me rich, I've made them richer. But lately, they've been… restrictive."

"Restrictive how?" I ask, already mentally calculating what our budget could handle for an advance.

"They want me to stick to what works," he sighs, running a

hand through his messy ponytail. "Another thriller series with the same damn detective solving the same damn crimes. But I've got other stories to tell."

I nod, understanding completely. "And they're not interested in those stories?"

"They're interested in money," Zephyr says bluntly. "Which is fine—publishing is a business. But I'm at a point in my career where I want to write what speaks to me, not what speaks to their bottom line."

"What kind of stories are you looking to tell?" I ask, genuinely curious.

Zephyr's eyes light up. "I've been working on a fantasy series. Completely different from anything I've done before. Dark, complex, bit of romance thrown in. The kind of books that make readers think, you know?"

I try not to visibly drool. I have to sign this author. Okay, think Lex, think. "That sounds incredible, Zephyr. I know the world would want to hear that story as much as I do."

"That's what I wanted to hear." He says, pulling a joint out of his pocket and lightening it up right there in my office.

Okayyyy. He takes a long drag, and I can practically see the smoke entering his lungs. He flicks a tiny ash onto the floor of my very professional office, and my very professional mind races. Is this even legal here? Am I going to have to bail him out before he fires us for having no chill?

This has to be a test. It must be his way of separating the corporate suits from the true artists. A writer like Zephyr would totally pull something like this. Well, I'm an artist, too. And we need this client more than I need my dignity.

When he passes me the joint, the challenge is clear in his eyes. I hesitate for half a heartbeat before accepting it, trying to channel my inner carefree bohemian.

Hell, why not?

I take a small puff, trying not to embarrass myself with a coughing fit. The smoke burns my lungs, but I hold it together, passing it back to him with what I hope is casual grace.

"So," I say, my voice only slightly strained, "at Bound Books, we're all about creative freedom. We want our authors to write the stories they're passionate about."

Zephyr nods appreciatively, taking another hit. "That's what I've heard about you. Young, hungry, not afraid to take risks."

I'm trying to focus on his words, but my head is already feeling lighter. Note to self: Do not smoke with literary legends before lunch.

"We may be small," I continue, "but that means we can give our authors more personal attention. More input on covers, marketing strategies, creative direction."

Zephyr's eyes sparkle with interest. "And what about advances? My agent mentioned you might not be able to match what Pinnacle offers."

I take a deep breath, preparing for the make-or-break moment. "You're right. We can't match their numbers." His face falls slightly, and I rush to continue. "But we can offer higher royalty percentages, especially on digital sales. And complete creative control. No one telling you what to write or how to write it."

He considers this, stroking his beard thoughtfully. "Money isn't everything at this point in my career. I've got enough to keep me in Hawaiian shirts for life."

I laugh, feeling more relaxed now. Whether it's the weed or the fact that Zephyr seems genuinely interested, I'm not sure. "Plus, we're nimble. We can get books to market faster than the big houses."

"I like that," he says, nodding. "Speed is good. The world moves fast these days."

We chat for another hour, passing the joint back and forth, discussing everything from his new fantasy concept (which sounds incredible) to the state of modern literature (which he thinks is "too sanitized"). By the time we stand up to shake hands, I'm feeling confident—and slightly buzzed.

"I'll talk to my agent," Zephyr says, giving my hand another enthusiastic shake. "But I've got a good feeling about you, Lexie Phillips. You've got moxie."

"Thank you," I say, hoping I don't sound as giddy as I feel. "It was an honor to meet you, Zephyr."

He winks at me. "The honor's all mine, kid. Not every publisher would smoke with me in their office. You're a risk-taker. I like that."

After he leaves, I throw open my window, frantically waving a folder to disperse the lingering smell. The last thing I need is for the uptight finance bros to catch a whiff of this. I can just imagine Ben's disapproving scowl. I light all seven of the decorative scented candles, turn on the wax melt thingy, and start spraying perfume all around my office. Within 20 minutes, there's no pot smell, and I'm still high as a kite.

I'm half-wondering if I should cancel my afternoon meetings when Maci barges in, then stops dead in her tracks. She takes one look at my glassy eyes and the array of scented candles and narrows her eyes.

"Why does your office smell like a Bath & Body Works had a fight with a perfume counter?" she asks, sniffing suspiciously.

"No reason," I say, trying to look innocent and failing miserably. "Just… freshening up the place."

"Uh-huh." She crosses her arms. "And the fact that your eyes are redder than that time you binge-read the entire 'Throne of Glass' series in one weekend is also just a coincidence?"

"Allergies?" I offer weakly.

"Lexie Phillips," she says, using my full name like a disappointed mother, "did you just get high with Zephyr McKnight in our office?"

I slump back in my chair, giving up the charade. "Maybe? But in my defense, he started it. He just pulled out a joint like it was a business card. What was I supposed to do?"

"Say no?" Maci suggests, but she's fighting a smile.

"To Zephyr McKnight? I think not." I reach for my water bottle, suddenly aware of how dry my mouth is. "Besides, I think it helped. He's going to talk to his agent."

Maci's eyes widen. "Are you serious? You might have actually landed him?"

"Maybe," I say, trying not to get too excited. "He seemed to like our vibe. And our 'trippy' office."

"I bet he did," Maci laughs, perching on the edge of my desk. "So, how was it? Meeting your literary hero?"

I lean back, a goofy smile spreading across my face. "Surreal. He's like this weird combination of profound literary genius and your uncle who's always telling conspiracy theories at Thanksgiving dinner."

"And now you're stoned out of your mind in the middle of a workday," Maci observes, shaking her head. "You know we have that meeting with the cover designer at two, right?"

I glance at my watch and groan. "Crap. That's in forty-five minutes."

"Don't worry," Maci says, patting my arm. "I'll handle it. You just… sit here and contemplate the universe or whatever it is you're doing."

"You're the best," I say, grabbing her hand and squeezing it a bit too enthusiastically. "Have I told you that lately? Because you are. The absolute best. Like, if there was a contest for best business partners, you'd win. Gold medal. Blue ribbon. Trophy with your name on it—"

"Okay, okay," she laughs, extracting herself. "I'll come back in to check on you once the meetings done."

Left alone with my own thoughts, I try to focus on editing my next novel, but all I can think about is my desire to eat. A lot. I pull up my Uber Eats app, searching for what I want. Problem is, I want everything…I forgot about the munchies.

I order everything I can think of: a burger, fries, a milkshake, two different kinds of tacos, mozzarella sticks, and a side of mac and cheese that I'm definitely going to regret later. The delivery estimate says thirty minutes, which feels like an eternity in my current state.

I type out a quick text to Maci in the other room: "Ordered enough food to feed a small nation. Contemplating the meaning of lavender. The usual."

She replies with a laughing emoji and "Hang in there. Be done in 20."

While waiting for my feast to arrive, I spin in my chair, watching the ceiling fan go round and round. It's hypnotic. When did we get a ceiling fan? Has it always been there? These are the deep questions I'm pondering when there's a knock at my door.

I freeze mid-spin. "Come in," I call, trying to sound professional despite the room still rotating slightly.

The door opens, and I blink several times, convinced I'm hallucinating. But no—Ben Maddox is actually standing in my doorway, a folder in his hand and his perpetually perfect tie knotted at his throat.

"Bad time?" he asks, one eyebrow raised as he takes in my disheveled appearance.

"No, no," I say, straightening up so fast I nearly topple out of my chair. "Just, um, brainstorming. Creative process. Very intense."

He steps into my office, and I suddenly become hyper-aware of everything—the excessive number of scented candles, my red eyes, the fact that I'm wearing mismatched socks. One has teddy bears on it.

"What brings you to the creative side of the building?" I ask, trying to sound casual while frantically hoping the pot smell is completely gone.

"I have the information about Words for Tomorrow," he says, holding up the folder. "Eli asked me to drop it off since he's in meetings all afternoon."

"Oh! Great. Thanks." I reach for the folder, hoping my hand doesn't visibly tremble. Our fingers brush briefly, and I pull back like I've been shocked.

Ben's eyes narrow slightly as he studies my face. "Are you feeling alright?"

"Never better," I say with a smile that feels too wide. "Just, you know, Friday energy."

He looks skeptical but doesn't press it. Instead, he glances around my office, taking in the lavender walls (now a proper shade thanks to professional painters), the bookshelves crammed with colorful spines, and the framed Tribune article above my desk.

"Your office is… different," he observes.

"Different good or different bad?" I challenge, feeling oddly defensive.

The corner of his mouth twitches. "Just different. Mine doesn't have quite so many… candles."

"You should try it," I suggest, gesturing to the flickering array. "Ambiance is important for creativity."

"I'll take your word for it," he says dryly, but his tone isn't harsh.

An awkward silence falls between us, and I'm acutely aware that I should say something professional and coherent. Instead, thanks to my stoner brain, what comes out is: "Do you ever think about how weird office buildings are?" I blurt out. "Like, we're all just in these little boxes, separated by walls, doing completely different things."

Ben looks at me like I've grown a second head. "I… can't say I've given it much thought."

"You should," I nod earnestly. "It's fascinating. You're over there moving money around, and I'm over here making up stories about people who don't exist."

A flicker of something—amusement? concern?—crosses his face. "Are you sure you're alright?"

"I'm fantastic," I assure him, spinning once in my chair for emphasis. "Just… contemplating the universe."

There's another knock at my door. My Uber Eats has arrived - all six bags of it.

"Ms. Phillips?" The delivery guy looks overwhelmed by the sheer volume of food he's carrying. "I've got your, uh… everything?"

Ben's eyebrows shoot up as I jump to my feet, nearly knocking over my chair in the process.

"Yes! That's mine. All mine. Thank you so much," I babble, taking the bags and practically throwing my tip at the poor guy.

When the delivery guy leaves, I'm left standing there with enough food to feed a small army and Ben Maddox's questioning gaze.

"Hungry?" he asks mildly.

"Starving," I admit, setting the feast on my desk. "I, uh, couldn't decide what I wanted."

"So you ordered the entire menu?"

"Not the entire menu," I defend, pulling out containers. "They were out of egg rolls."

To my surprise, Ben doesn't leave. Instead, he watches with what might be amusement as I arrange my impromptu buffet.

I'm caught in this awkward moment, standing with an obscene amount of food while Ben Maddox watches me with that infuriating eyebrow raised. There's something about the way he's looking at me—less judgmental than usual, more… curious.

"Want some?" I offer impulsively, holding out a container of mozzarella sticks. "I clearly ordered enough for the entire floor."

He hesitates, and for a second I think he's going to decline and retreat back to his sterile office. But then something unexpected happens—he loosens his tie slightly and takes a step forward.

"Sure," he says, the word sounding foreign on his lips. "Why not?"

I blink at him, certain I'm hallucinating. "I'm sorry, did Ben Maddox just agree to eat junk food in my office? Should I check if the sky is falling?"

A small smile—an actual smile—tugs at the corner of his mouth. "I do eat, you know. Not just the souls of creative types."

I snort, nearly choking on my first bite of burger. "Could've fooled me."

He takes the container I offer and sits down in the chair across from my desk, looking oddly at ease for someone so out of place. I notice his suit jacket is slightly rumpled, his hair not quite as perfectly styled as usual.

"Rough day?" I ask, pushing the fries toward him.

He shrugs, the gesture so casual it seems alien coming from him. "Just… complicated. These clients we're trying to land are very traditional. Old money, old values."

"Ah," I nod, taking a massive bite of my burger. "The Murphy's, right?"

His eyebrows shoot up. "You remember that?"

I tap my temple with my free hand. "Elephant's memory. Also, Angel mentioned they're a big deal on one of her many trips over here to complain about our existence."

"They are," he confirms, biting into a mozzarella stick with surprising enthusiasm. "Landing them would be a significant win for our firm."

"So, what's the problem?" I ask, genuinely curious. "Aside from them being stuck in 1952."

Ben hesitates, and I can almost see the internal debate: how much to reveal to the chaotic publisher who's clearly high as a kite? Finally, he says, "They're very… image-conscious. Traditional family values and all that."

"Ah," I say knowingly, even though I don't really know at all. "And they want to make sure their money manager is equally traditional?"

He nods, looking slightly surprised at my perception. "Something like that."

I study him for a moment, taking in the perfectly tailored suit, the expensive watch, the carefully controlled demeanor.

"Well, you're practically the poster child for tradition. Clean-cut, successful, probably have a 401(k) that doesn't make you want to cry. What's the issue?"

Ben's expression shifts, something unreadable. "I'm a 29 year old bachelor. They see it as a weakness."

"Kinda archaic, but I guess if you got the money, people do what you want?" I muse as my mind wanders back into stoner land. I wonder what deserts I could order.

I'm pulled back to reality when Ben's eyes narrow slightly. "Are you sure you're alright, Lexie?"

"Mmhmm," I say around a mouthful of fries. "Why do you ask?"

"Your eyes are red, you ordered enough food for a small army, and you just asked if clouds get lonely." He pauses. "I don't think you realized you said that last part out loud."

Did I? Oh God. I swallow hard, feeling my cheeks heat up. "I'm fine. Just… tired. Creative brain, you know how it is."

Ben's gaze is entirely too perceptive as he takes another mozzarella stick. "Right. And it has nothing to do with the lingering smell of marijuana beneath all those candles?"

I choke on my milkshake, nearly spraying it across my desk. "I don't know what you're talking about," I sputter, unconvincingly.

"Lexie," he says, his voice surprisingly gentle, "I'm not completely obtuse, I know what weed smells like."

For a moment, I consider continuing the charade, but the combination of being high and being caught makes me burst into giggles instead. "Fine. You caught me. But in my defense, Zephyr McKnight started it."

"*The* Zephyr McKnight?" Ben asks, looking genuinely impressed for the first time since I've known him.

"The one and only," I confirm, feeling a small burst of pride at his reaction. "He came in for a meeting about potentially signing with us, pulled out a joint, and, well… what was I supposed to do? Say no to a literary legend?"

To my utter shock, Ben laughs. Not a chuckle or a smirk, but an actual laugh that transforms his usually stern face. "That's… not what I expected to hear today."

"Yeah, well, welcome to publishing," I say, waving a fry for emphasis. "It's not all tweed jackets and grammar debates."

"Clearly," he says, his eyes still crinkled with amusement. "Did you at least sign him?"

"Maybe," I say, unable to keep the excitement from my voice. "He's talking to his agent, but it sounds promising. He likes our 'vibe.'"

"I can see why," Ben remarks, glancing around my colorful office. "It's very… you."

"Is that a compliment or an insult?" I ask, narrowing my eyes.

"Observation," he replies, but there's no bite to it. "Your company reflects your personality. That's rare in business."

I'm momentarily speechless, both from the unexpected almost-compliment and from the bizarre surreality of sitting in my office, high as a kite, sharing a feast with Ben Maddox—the man I've been mentally feuding with for weeks.

"So," I say, desperate to change the subject before I do or say anything else stupid. "What are you gonna do about the Murphy dilemma?"

"They prefer someone who embodies 'family values,'" he adds, making air quotes with his fingers. The gesture looks so out of place coming from him that I almost laugh.

"So, they want you married with 2.5 kids and a golden retriever?" I ask, dunking a fry in ketchup. "That's ridiculous."

"That's business," he says with a shrug, but I can tell it bothers him. There's a tightness around his eyes that wasn't there before.

I'm not sure if it's the pot making me bold or just my natural lack of filter, but I blurt out, "Why not just fake it? Pretend to have a fiancé for the meetings and dinners or something."

Ben looks at me like I've suggested he commit securities fraud. "Excuse me?"

"You know, like in those romantic comedies. Hire someone to pretend to be your adoring lover." I take another bite of my burger, chewing thoughtfully. "Though I guess that only works in movies."

"That would be completely unprofessional," he says, but there's a thoughtful look in his eyes that wasn't there before. "Not to mention dishonest."

"Hey, sometimes we do crazy things to get what we want." I say, "Like getting high with famous authors to close a deal."

Ben shakes his head, but there's the faintest hint of a smile playing at his lips. "I suppose we all have our methods." He reaches for another mozzarella stick, then hesitates. "I should get back. I have a conference call in fifteen minutes."

"Sure, sure," I say, waving my hand dismissively. "Go back to your spreadsheets and serious phone voice."

As he stands to leave, I notice something shift in his expression—a softening around the eyes, maybe, or a slight relaxation of his perpetually rigid posture. "Thanks for the food," he says, gesturing to the feast spread across my desk.

"Anytime," I reply, surprising myself with how much I mean it. "My door's always open for anyone willing to help me tackle this mountain of calories."

He pauses at the doorway, turning back with an expression

I can't quite read. "Good luck with Zephyr McKnight," he says, his voice sincere. "It would be a significant win for your company."

"Thanks," I say, momentarily thrown by his genuine support. "And good luck with your stuffy rich clients. Maybe consider my fake fiancé idea. I hear it works out well in the end."

A genuine laugh escapes him, brief but real. "I'll take that under advisement."

When he's gone, I slump back in my chair, staring at the door like it might explain what just happened. Did I really just have a civil—almost friendly—conversation with Ben Maddox? While high? And did he actually laugh at something I said?

I reach for my phone, texting Maci: "I think I'm hallucinating. Ben just ate mozzarella sticks in my office and didn't judge me for being high."

Her response is immediate: "??!!!! WHAT???? Coming back RIGHT NOW."

Before I can reply, my office door flies open, and Maci bursts in, eyes wide with disbelief. "Explain. Everything. Now."

I gesture to the spread of food still covering my desk. "Want some?"

"Don't change the subject," she says, but she grabs a taco anyway. "Ben Maddox was in your office? Willingly?"

"He came to drop off some information about that literacy program," I explain, reaching for my milkshake. "Then my food arrived, and I offered to share, and he… accepted?"

"And he knew you were high?" Maci asks, eyes growing even wider.

"Called me out on it directly," I confirm, feeling a strange mix of embarrassment and amusement. "But he was cool about it. Almost like a normal human being."

Maci drops into the chair Ben just vacated, looking stunned. "Who is this man, and what has he done with our uptight neighbor?"

"I don't know," I admit, "but we actually had a decent conversation. He even wished me luck with landing Zephyr."

"Maybe he's been body-snatched," I suggest, wiggling my fingers mysteriously. "Or maybe this is just what happens when you get him away from Angel's evil influence."

Maci takes another bite of taco, chewing thoughtfully. "Or maybe he just likes you."

I nearly choke on my milkshake. "Please. The man can barely tolerate my existence."

"Then why did he spend his lunch break eating junk food in your office?" she counters, raising an eyebrow in a perfect imitation of Ben. "When he could have just dropped off the folder and left?"

"Because…" I search for a reasonable explanation. "Because I have food and he was hungry?"

"Uh-huh," Maci says skeptically. "And I'm sure he regularly eats mozzarella sticks with all his neighbors."

"Can we please change the subject?" I beg, feeling my cheeks heat up. "I'm still too high for this conversation."

Maci grins like she's just won a major victory but mercifully drops it. "Fine. Tell me more about Zephyr. Do you really think we might sign him?"

I latch onto the change of topic with relief. "I think we have a shot. He seemed genuinely interested in what we're offering—creative freedom, higher royalty percentages. And he liked that we're not stuffy corporate types."

"Clearly," Maci laughs, gesturing to my red eyes.

We spend the rest of the afternoon strategizing about Zephyr, finishing off my feast, and pointedly not discussing Ben Maddox. By the time five o'clock rolls around, I'm coming down from my high and feeling the onset of a food coma.

"I'm heading out," Maci announces, gathering her things. "You coming?"

"In a bit," I say, stifling a yawn. "I want to finish this chapter first."

After she leaves, the office falls into a peaceful quiet. I turn to my laptop, determined to make some progress on my current manuscript despite the lingering fog in my brain. I finally decide to call it quits, packing up my laptop and locking up the office before heading for the elevator.

Once I get outside, I pull out my phone to call an Uber, but a voice calling my name stops me in my tracks. It's Eli, sitting in the outside patio area at the local Mexican restaurant adjacent from our office building and he looks well past drunk. Looks like their whole financial gang is all there, Ben included.

"Hey, Lexie!" Eli waves me over with a little too much enthusiasm, nearly toppling his margarita in the process. "Join us for happy hour!"

I hesitate, glancing at the group of finance bros in various states of inebriation. Ben sits at the end of the table, his tie gone and sleeves rolled up to his elbows, nursing what looks like whiskey. He catches my eye, and I swear there's a flicker of something—invitation? curiosity?—before he looks away.

"Oh, I don't want to intrude on your work thing," I say, taking a step back.

"Nonsense!" Eli insists, patting the empty chair beside him. "We're celebrating. Or drowning our sorrows. I'm not sure which yet."

"The Murphy meeting?" I guess, remembering Ben's earlier

concerns.

"How'd you know?" Eli asks, looking genuinely surprised.

I shrug, feeling oddly self-conscious. "Just a guess."

"Well, come on, sit down," Eli urges. "First round's on me."

Against my better judgment—or maybe because of the lingering effects of my earlier high—I find myself sliding into the empty chair. It happens to be right across from Ben, who watches me with those stormy gray eyes that seem to see too much.

"So," I say, trying to sound casual, "celebration or wake?"

"Too early to tell," Eli says, signaling the waitress. "The Murphy's are… deliberating."

"They're toying with us," another guy—I think his name is Derek—slurs slightly. "Making us sweat."

"That's business," Ben says, his voice controlled as always, though I notice his glass is nearly empty.

The waitress arrives, and Eli orders me a margarita before I can protest. When she leaves, he turns to me with a grin that's a little too wide. "So, Lexie, how was your meeting with the famous author? Did you sign him?"

I feel Ben's eyes on me and fight back a blush. "We're still in talks," I say diplomatically. "But it's looking promising."

"She got high with Zephyr McKnight," Ben says matter-of-factly, a hint of amusement in his voice.

The table erupts in exclamations and questions, and I shoot Ben a look that's half-murderous, half-impressed that he actually made a joke. He merely raises his glass in a silent toast, the ghost of a smile playing on his lips.

"It was a business strategy," I defend, feeling my cheeks heat up. "Sometimes you have to meet clients where they are."

"And where he was," Ben adds dryly, "was approximately ten

thousand feet in the stratosphere."

I can't help but laugh at that. "Exactly. Very high-level negotiations."

Eli and the others roar with laughter, and I find myself relaxing despite the strange company. My margarita arrives, frosty and inviting, and I take a generous sip.

"So that's how publishing works," Derek says, looking impressed. "Maybe I chose the wrong career."

"Trust me," I say, licking salt from the rim of my glass, "most days it's less 'smoking with celebrities' and more 'explaining to authors why their 200,000-word vampire romance needs editing.'"

The table laughs again, and I catch Ben watching me with an expression I can't quite decipher. There's something different about him here, outside the office—a slight loosening of that perpetual control, perhaps.

"What about you guys?" I ask, genuinely curious. "Is finance really all spreadsheets and serious meetings?"

"And client dinners," Eli adds, raising his glass. "Endless client dinners where you can't order what you want because you're too busy calculating the appropriate price range that says 'successful but not wasteful.'"

"Don't forget the golf," another guy chimes in. "So much golf."

"I hate golf," Ben mutters into his drink, so quietly I almost miss it.

I look at him in surprise. "The great Ben Maddox, finance extraordinaire, hates golf? Isn't that against the Wall Street code or something?"

His eyes meet mine, a challenge in them. "I contain multitudes."

"Clearly," I say, holding his gaze a beat too long before turning back to the group.

Six

Accidentally Engaged

We talk for a bit longer before we all say our goodbyes for the evening. Ben follows me out, sticking close to my side. I didn't realize it while we were sitting, but he is drunk. That Murphy ordeal must be getting to him.

"Need some company walking home?" he asks, his voice slightly less crisp than usual. There's a subtle slur to his words that I find oddly endearing.

"Are you offering to be my knight in shining Armani?" I ask, unable to help myself.

He runs a hand through his usually perfect hair, making it stand up in places. "Something like that," he admits. "Though I'm not sure how effective I'd be against dragons right now."

I laugh, surprised by this looser version of Ben. "I think I can handle myself, but I wouldn't mind the company."

We fall into step beside each other, the evening air cool against my skin. The city is alive around us, people rushing home from work or heading out for dinner, the streetlights just starting to flicker on in the dusk. The further we go, the more drunk he seems. He stumbles every so often, causing me to reach out and steady him more than once.

"Ben, hun," I say after the third save, "you're drunk."

"Am not," he mutters, but the way he sways slightly betrays him. "Just… feeling relaxed."

"Uh-huh," I say, grabbing his arm to steady him as he stumbles over a crack in the sidewalk. "And I'm secretly a queen."

He looks down at me, his gray eyes softer than I've ever seen them. "You'd make a very pretty queen."

My heart does a stupid little flip that I immediately blame on the margarita. "Wow, you really are drunk. The Ben Maddox I know would rather eat glass than compliment me."

He frowns, his forehead creasing adorably. "That's not true. I compliment you. In my head."

"Oh, well, that's super helpful," I laugh, adjusting my grip on his arm. "How am I supposed to know about your secret brain compliments?"

"They're not secret," he insists with the earnestness only drunk people can manage. "They're just… professional."

"Professional compliments," I repeat slowly. "Like what? 'Nice spreadsheet, Phillips'?"

"Like… your company is impressive," he says, staring straight ahead. "And your books are good. Really good."

I nearly trip over my own feet. "You've read my books?"

He nods, looking almost sheepish. "After the launch party. I was curious."

"And?" I prompt, suddenly desperate to know what he thought.

"And they're good," he repeats. "Smart. Funny. Not what I

expected."

"What did you expect? Sparkly vampires and heaving bosoms?"

His lips twitch. "Something like that."

We walk another block in silence, my mind racing. Ben Maddox read my books. And liked them. The universe has officially gone sideways.

"So," I say, desperate to break the silence, "what's the deal with these Murphy clients? Why are they so important?"

Ben sighs, running a hand through his hair again. "They're one of the wealthiest families in Chicago. Old money. Very traditional. Landing them would put our firm on a different level."

"And they care about your marital status because…?"

"They believe in stability," he explains, his words slightly less slurred now. "A man who can't commit to a family can't be trusted with their money. Or so their logic goes."

"That's ridiculous," I say flatly. "What century are they living in?"

"The one where they have fifty million dollars to invest," Ben replies dryly.

Before I can respond, an elderly sounding voice calls out to Ben from behind us. "Mr. Maddox, is that you?"

I feel Ben stiffen beside me as I turn to see a rich, stuffy looking couple making their way towards us. All of a sudden, I feel like chaos is about to take over. I should be used to it by now.

"Mr. and Mrs. Murphy, what a pleasant surprise." Ben says, adopting his formal voice, though still slightly slurred. The Murphy's? Oh shit.

I'm frozen in place, panic rising in my chest as I watch Ben try to straighten his rumpled appearance. The Murphy's are exactly what I expected—white-haired, impeccably dressed, with expressions that suggest they've just caught us doing something scandalous rather than simply walking down the street.

"And who might this young lady be?" Mrs. Murphy asks, her eyes scanning me from head to toe.

Before I can introduce myself, Ben's arm slides around my waist, pulling me against his side. I nearly yelp in surprise.

"This is Lexie Phillips," he says, his voice suddenly much more sober than it was seconds ago. "My fiancé."

Wait, what?

I manage not to choke on air, but it's a close call. My eyes dart to Ben's face, but he's looking at the Murphy's with a practiced smile, his arm tightening around me in what I can only assume is a silent plea not to contradict him.

"fiancé?" Mr. Murphy's bushy eyebrows shoot up. "You didn't mention you were engaged during our meeting."

"It's… recent," Ben says smoothly. "We were waiting for the right moment to announce it."

Mrs. Murphy's stern expression softens slightly as she extends a hand toward me. "How lovely to meet you, dear. Benjamin has been quite the mystery to us."

"The pleasure is mine," I reply automatically, shaking her hand and trying to look like someone who regularly gets engaged to uptight financial advisors. "Ben has told me so much about you both."

"Has he?" Mr. Murphy looks pleased. "All good things, I hope."

"The best," I assure him, leaning into Ben's side like we do this every day. His body is warm against mine, solid and surprisingly comfortable. "He's very excited about the possibility of working with you."

"How did you two meet?" Mrs. Murphy asks, clearly settling in for the full story.

"We're neighbors," I reply truthfully, my mind racing. "Our offices are right next to each other in the Wacker building."

"Office romance," Mr. Murphy says with a knowing nod. "Classic."

"And when's the wedding?" Mrs. Murphy asks, eyes twinkling as she looks between us.

I feel Ben tense beside me, and I realize he hasn't thought this far ahead. Time to improvise.

"Next spring," I say, sliding my hand up to rest on Ben's chest in what I hope looks like an affectionate gesture. "We want cherry blossoms. Right, honey?"

"Right," Ben agrees, his voice strained. His hand finds mine and squeezes—whether in thanks or warning, I'm not sure. "Lexie has it all planned out."

"A woman who knows what she wants," Mr. Murphy says approvingly. "That's what you need, Benjamin. Someone to keep you grounded."

"Oh, she definitely keeps me grounded," Ben says, and I swear I detect a hint of genuine amusement in his voice.

Mrs. Murphy beams at us, all traces of her earlier frostiness gone. "You must join us for dinner next week. We'd love to get to know the woman who captured our Benjamin's heart."

"We'd be delighted," Ben says before I can formulate a polite refusal.

"Wonderful!" Mrs. Murphy clasps her hands together. "How about Thursday at The Aviary? Seven o'clock?"

"Perfect," Ben says, his smile looking increasingly pained.

After a few more excruciating minutes of small talk, during which I learn more about Mrs. Murphy's hip replacement than I ever wanted to know, they finally bid us goodbye and continue on their way. We remain entangled in one another, both frozen in the unexpected turn of events. Finally, the silence stretches too long and I can't stand it any longer. "I thought you said my fiancé suggestion was dishonest, and essentially a bad idea." I ask, unable to keep the wonder out of my voice.

"It was a momentary lapse in judgment," Ben says, finally dropping his arm from my waist. The sudden absence of his warmth leaves me feeling oddly bereft. "The Murphy's caught me off guard."

"So your solution was to spontaneously propose to me?" I ask, raising an eyebrow. "I'm flattered, really, but I usually prefer dinner first."

He runs a hand through his already disheveled hair, looking more frazzled than I've ever seen him. "I panicked, okay? They were right there, and you were right there, and I just… said it."

"Implementing my brilliant fake fiancé plan after all," I say, unable to hold back my smirk. "I told you it works in the movies."

"This isn't a movie, Lexie," he groans, looking around like the Murphy's might still be lurking nearby. "This is my career."

"Which apparently hinges on your marital status," I point out. "Not exactly progressive of them."

Ben sighs heavily, suddenly looking exhausted. "Look, I'm sorry I dragged you into this. I'll call them tomorrow, tell them the truth."

I should feel relieved. This is clearly the sensible solution to this ridiculous situation. But instead, I hear myself saying, "Or we could just go to dinner."

His head snaps up, eyes wide with surprise. "What?"

"The dinner," I clarify, wondering if I've lost my mind. "We could go, play the happy couple for one night, help you land your stuffy rich clients, and then stage a heartbreaking but amicable breakup after you've secured their business."

"You'd do that?" he asks, sounding genuinely bewildered. "Why?"

It's a good question, and one I'm not entirely sure I have an answer for. "Because it's hilarious?" I offer. "Because I'm an excellent actress? Because I'm curious to see what Ben Maddox looks like when he's not scowling at my existence?"

He studies me for a long moment, his gray eyes intense even through his drunken haze. "You realize this would involve spending an entire evening pretending to be madly in love with me."

A flutter of something dangerous stirs in my stomach. "I think I can manage," I say dryly. "I am a writer, after all. I make up stuff for a living."

"And what do you get out of this arrangement?" he asks, narrowing his eyes suspiciously.

I pretend to consider this, tapping my chin thoughtfully. "How about unlimited mozzarella sticks for a year? And you have to be nice to me in the office. No more sending Angel to complain about our music."

"Done," he says immediately, then adds, "Though for the record, I never sent Angel to complain. She does that entirely of her own volition."

"Yeah, well, she's annoying. And pretentious. And if she comes over again, I'm getting her high. She needs to chill out."

Ben actually laughs at that, a full-bodied laugh that catches me off guard. "As entertaining as that would be, please don't.

Her father would have my head."

"Fine," I sigh dramatically. "I'll restrain myself. For your sake."

We stand there on the sidewalk, the absurdity of the situation hanging between us. Ben Maddox just introduced me as his fiancé to important clients, and I've somehow agreed to continue the charade. What is happening to my life?

"So," I say, breaking the silence, "if we're doing this, we should probably get our story straight. How did you propose? Was it romantic? Did you cry? I bet you cried."

"I did not cry," he says indignantly, but there's a hint of a smile playing at his lips. "And for the record, it was very romantic. Sunset on the lakefront, champagne, the works."

"Wow," I say, impressed despite myself. "Who knew you had it in you? I would have guessed a PowerPoint presentation on the financial benefits of marriage."

"You underestimate me, Phillips," he says, and there's something in his tone that makes my heart skip a beat.

"Apparently so," I murmur, suddenly aware of how close we're standing. "Though you might want to start calling me by my first name if we're engaged."

"Lexie," he says, my name sounding different in his voice. Softer. Almost reverent.

A shiver runs down my spine that has nothing to do with the evening breeze. "That's better…"

Ben clears his throat, taking a small step back. "We should exchange numbers. For… planning purposes."

"Right," I say, pulling out my phone. "Planning purposes. Very important."

We swap phones, and I find myself typing my number into Ben Maddox's contacts. The universe has officially gone mad.

"I'll text you," he says, pocketing his phone. "About dinner details."

"Looking forward to it," I reply, trying to sound casual despite the butterflies suddenly taking flight in my stomach. "It's a date. I mean, not a date-date. A fake date. For your clients."

"Right," Ben nods, looking as uncomfortable as I feel. "A fake date."

"Well," I say, gesturing vaguely down the street, "I should probably get going. Long day of doing nothing ahead of me tomorrow."

Ben seems to hesitate, swaying slightly on his feet. "I'll walk you the rest of the way."

"You can barely walk yourself," I point out, gesturing to his unsteady stance. "I think I can manage the last few blocks without your drunken protection."

"I'm not that drunk," he insists, and then promptly stumbles over absolutely nothing.

I catch his arm again, rolling my eyes. "Right. And I'm not that sarcastic. How about this," I propose holding onto him to keep him steady, "How about I walk you home in case you decide to propose to anyone else."

He chuckles, and the sound is warmer than I expected. "Fair point. But I think I can manage, besides, I'm supposed to take care of you."

"Fine," I sigh, adjusting my grip on his arm. "But if you propose to anyone else on the way, I'm calling off our fake engagement."

"I promise to save all my fake proposals exclusively for you," he says solemnly, placing a hand over his heart.

We walk in comfortable silence for a few blocks, the city humming around us. Ben seems to be sobering up slightly with each step, his gait becoming steadier. I'm acutely aware of his arm linked with mine, the expensive fabric of his suit jacket soft beneath my fingers.

"So," I say, trying to fill the silence, "is this a common occurrence for you? Getting drunk and proposing to random women on the street?"

Ben's lips quirk upward. "Only on Fridays. And only to publishers with purple offices."

"I'm honored to be your first, then," I reply, then immediately feel my cheeks heat up at the unintended double entendre.

Ben either doesn't notice or kindly pretends not to. "The Murphy's seemed to like you," he says, his voice thoughtful.

"Of course they did. I'm delightful," I respond automatically. "Plus, I think Mrs. Murphy was just relieved you're not secretly a serial killer."

"The bar for success was admittedly low," he agrees, and I catch a glimpse of that elusive smile again.

When we get to my building, I all of a sudden have no idea how to not make this awkward.

"Will you be okay getting home? I can call you an Uber."

"I'll be fine," he insists, then ruins it by stumbling slightly. "It's only a few blocks."

I sigh, pulling out my phone. "I'm calling you an Uber. Consider it my first act as your fake fiancé."

"So bossy," he murmurs, but doesn't protest further.

While we wait for the car, we stand in awkward silence, neither quite sure how to end this bizarre evening. The streetlights cast a golden glow over Ben's features, softening his usually sharp angles. Without his perpetual scowl, he's annoyingly handsome.

"So," I say, because I can't handle silence, "Thursday night. Fancy dinner with the Murphy's. Should I wear white to really sell the bride thing, or is that too on the nose?"

Ben chuckles, the sound warm in the cool evening air. "Maybe save the wedding dress for the actual wedding."

"You mean our fake wedding that will never happen because this is just a business arrangement?" I clarify, raising an eyebrow.

"Exactly," he nods, looking relieved that I understand. "Just wear something… nice."

"Define 'nice,'" I challenge. "Because my definition might be very different from yours."

He considers this, eyes traveling over my current outfit—jeans and a t-shirt that reads "I like big books and I cannot lie."

"Something formal," he says finally. "The Aviary is very upscale."

"So no graphic tees about literature? You're crushing my spirit, Maddox."

His lips twitch. "I'm sure you'll manage."

The Uber pulls up, saving us from further awkwardness. Ben takes a step toward it, then pauses, turning back to me.

"Thank you," he says, his voice surprisingly sincere. "For agreeing to this ridiculous plan."

"Don't thank me yet," I warn him. "I might still ruin everything by telling the Murphy's about your secret passion for boy bands."

"I do not—" he starts, then sees my smirk. "Very funny."

"I thought so," I say innocently. "Goodnight, fake fiancé."

"Goodnight, fake fiancé," he replies, and there's something in his voice that makes my heart do a little flip. "I'll text you."

"You better," I say, backing away. "We've got a wedding to plan, after all. I'm thinking doves. Hundreds of them."

He groans, but he's smiling. "Goodnight, Lexie."

"Goodnight, Ben." I watch as he smoothly slides into the car despite his inebriated state. I stand there staring long after the car disappears around the corner.

As I walk to my apartment, my phone buzzes in my pocket, and I pull it out to find a text from Ben:

"No doves. -B"

I laugh out loud, before quickly typing a response:

"Fine. Flamingos it is. -L"

His reply comes almost instantly:

"You're impossible."

I grin at my phone like an idiot, feeling a warmth spread through my chest that has nothing to do with the lingering effects of my earlier high.

As I climb the stairs to my apartment, I can't help but wonder what I've gotten myself into. One minute Ben Maddox is my uptight, judgmental neighbor, and the next I'm pretending to be engaged to him. This is either the best or worst idea I've ever had—and I once tried to cut my own bangs after three glasses of wine.

I unlock my door and flop onto my couch, my mind still reeling from the evening's events. My phone buzzes again:

"For the record, I did not agree to flamingos either. Get some sleep. We have a lot to discuss."

I smile despite myself, typing back:

"Fine. Trained squirrels it is. Goodnight, Ben."

I set my phone down, staring at the ceiling. What have I done? And more importantly, why does the thought of pretending to be in love with Ben Maddox make my heart race in a way that has nothing to do with anxiety?

Seven

Dress to Deceive

"You agreed to WHAT?" Maci nearly spits out her coffee, staring at me like I've just announced my plans to move to Mars.

"It's not a big deal," I insist, though the way my voice squeaks suggests otherwise. "It's just one dinner. I help him land his stuffy clients, he owes me a lifetime supply of mozzarella sticks, everyone wins."

We're sitting in my office Monday morning, the weekend having passed in a blur of text messages with Ben—surprisingly normal ones about our "backstory" and what to expect at dinner, not the snarky exchanges I would have anticipated.

"Not a big deal?" Maci repeats incredulously. "Lexie, you're pretending to be engaged to a man you've been at war with since day one!"

"We haven't been at war," I protest weakly. "Just… strongly opposed."

Maci raises an eyebrow, unimpressed. "You once said, and I

quote, 'If Ben Maddox was on fire and I had a glass of water, I'd drink it.'"

"That was before I knew he was good at picking restaurants," I say with a shrug. "People change."

"In two days?" Maci asks skeptically.

I busy myself with my computer, avoiding her knowing gaze. "Look, it's just a favor for a… colleague. That's all."

"A colleague," Maci repeats slowly. "Right. And I suppose the fact that he's gorgeous and you've been weirdly obsessed with him since we moved in has nothing to do with it?"

"I have not been obsessed!" I squawk, feeling my cheeks heat up. "I've been annoyed. There's a difference."

"Mmm-hmm," Maci hums, clearly unconvinced.

"Admit it," she presses, leaning forward with that look she gets when she knows she's right. "There's a thin line between hate and—"

"If you say 'love,' I will fire you," I threaten, pointing my pen at her.

"You can't fire me. I'm co-owner," she reminds me cheerfully. "And you're avoiding the question."

I groan, dropping my head onto my desk with a thud. "Can we please focus on work? Like the fact that Zephyr's agent called this morning and wants to set up a formal meeting?"

Maci's eyes widen, momentarily distracted. "Seriously? That's huge!"

"I know," I say, relieved to change the subject. "They're coming in Wednesday to discuss terms."

"Wednesday…" Maci repeats, her eyes narrowing. "Isn't your fake date with Ben on Thursday?"

"Yes," I sigh, accepting that I won't escape this conversation. "Which means I need to focus on Zephyr now and worry about the Murphy dinner later."

"Or," Maci suggests with a sly smile, "you could tell me what you're wearing to seduce your fake fiancé."

"I'm not trying to seduce anyone!" I protest, perhaps a bit too loudly. "It's a business arrangement. Plain and simple."

"Right," Maci nods, her expression skeptical. "So you haven't picked out a dress yet?"

I hesitate just a beat too long. "That would be ridiculous."

"You totally have!" she crows triumphantly. "Show me."

"There's nothing to show," I insist, but my phone is already in my hand, betraying me as I pull up the photo of the dress I ordered yesterday after spending three hours scrolling through online boutiques.

Maci snatches my phone before I can change my mind. "Oh. My. God." She stares at the screen, eyes wide. "This is not a 'business arrangement' dress, Lex. This is a 'please rip this off me later' dress."

"It is not!" I grab my phone back, glancing at the glossy black silk slip dress that admittedly does hug every curve I possess. It cost me $1,000 but who's counting? "It's sophisticated. The Aviary is fancy."

"Uh-huh," Maci says, clearly not buying it. "And the slit up to your thigh is for… ease of movement during business discussions?"

I feel my cheeks burn. "I'm trying to look the part of a woman engaged to a successful financial advisor. That's all."

"And what part is that? Trophy wife?"

"No!" I protest, then reconsider. "Well, maybe a little. The Murphy's seem very traditional. I figured they'd expect Ben to be with someone… polished."

Maci's expression softens. "Lex, you don't need to change

who you are for this guy or his clients. If this is just a business arrangement, be yourself."

I fidget with my pen, suddenly finding the cap fascinating. "It's not about changing myself. It's about… playing the part convincingly." I look up at her. "Besides, maybe I want to see his face when he realizes I can clean up pretty well."

"Now we're getting somewhere," Maci says, triumphant. "You want to impress him."

"I want to shock him," I correct her. "There's a difference."

"If you say so." She stands, heading for the door. "Just be careful, okay? This whole fake engagement thing is straight out of a rom-com, and we both know how those end."

"With someone running through an airport?" I suggest innocently.

She points a warning finger at me. "With people falling in love when they least expect it."

After she leaves, I stare at my computer screen without really seeing it. This is just a favor for a colleague. A handsome, occasionally funny colleague who smells amazing and reads my books. Nothing to worry about.

My phone buzzes with a text from Ben: "Angel just asked why Mrs. Murphy called to congratulate me on my engagement. What have we done?"

I can't help but smile as I type back: "Created chaos, obviously. Isn't that what neighbors are for?"

His response comes quickly: "I've created a monster. Dinner details confirmed for Thursday. I'll pick you up at 6:30."

"I'll be the one in white with the veil," I reply, then add: "Kidding. Mostly."

"You're enjoying this too much," he texts back, and I can almost hear his exasperated tone.

"One of us has to," I respond. "See you Thursday, fiancé."

I set my phone down, trying to ignore the flutter in my stomach. It's just dinner. One night of pretending to be in love with Ben Maddox. What could possibly go wrong?

Eight

Fake It Don't Feel It

Wednesday flies by in a whirlwind of meetings with Zephyr and his agent. By some miracle, we manage to sign him—his fantasy series will be published exclusively by Bound Books, starting next spring. It's the biggest deal we've ever landed, and I should be ecstatic. I am ecstatic. But as Wednesday turns into Thursday, I find myself increasingly distracted by thoughts of the evening ahead.

I leave the office early, ignoring Maci's knowing smirk, and spend an ungodly amount of time getting ready. Hair, makeup, the works. By the time 6:25 rolls around, I barely recognize myself in the mirror. The black silk dress hugs every curve, my hair falls in soft waves down my back, and I've applied makeup with more precision than I typically use for anything short of a photo shoot. My doorbell rings exactly at 6:30, because of course Ben Maddox would be precisely on time.

I take a deep breath, smoothing down the silk of my dress

one last time before opening the door. The moment I do, I'm rewarded with the sight of Ben freezing mid-knock, his eyes widening as they travel from my face down the length of my body and back up again.

"Hi," I say, suddenly feeling shy despite my bold outfit choice.

Ben clears his throat, adjusting his already perfect tie. "Lexie. You look… different."

"Different good or different bad?" I challenge, echoing our conversation from weeks ago.

The corner of his mouth twitches upward. "Different good," he admits, his voice slightly rougher than usual. "Very good."

My heart does a stupid little flutter that I promptly ignore. "You clean up pretty well yourself," I say, taking in his impeccably tailored black suit and crisp white shirt. He's always well-dressed, but tonight he's taken it to another level entirely.

"Are you ready?" he asks, offering me his arm like we've stepped into some alternate reality where we're actually a couple and not just playing pretend for one night.

I grab my clutch and nod, slipping my arm through his. "As I'll ever be. Let's go convince some stuffy rich people we're madly in love."

The car ride to The Aviary is filled with last-minute strategy discussions. We've spent the past few days texting about our "relationship"—how we met (offices next door, obviously), our first date (dinner at a little Italian place in Lincoln Park), how long we've been together (eight months), and the proposal (sunset by the lake, just as Ben improvised that night). We've got the basics covered, but I still feel woefully unprepared.

"What if they ask something we haven't discussed?" I whisper as we pull up to the restaurant, an ultra-modern glass structure that screams expensive. that screams expensive.

Ben's hand covers mine briefly, surprisingly warm and reassuring. "Then we'll improvise. We're both good at thinking on our feet. Oh, here, before I forget." He reaches into his pocket, pulling out a ring box. "We need to sell it, don't we?"

My heart leaps into my throat as he flips open the box, revealing a stunning emerald-cut diamond ring that catches the light from the restaurant's exterior and practically blinds me.

"Holy—" I breathe, staring at it. "That looks real."

"It is real," Ben says matter-of-factly. "Family heirloom. My grandmother's."

I blink at him, momentarily speechless. "You're letting me wear your grandmother's ring for a fake engagement?"

Something flickers across his face too quickly for me to identify. "It's the only engagement ring I have access to on short notice. The Murphy's would notice if it wasn't… substantial."

"Substantial is one word for it," I murmur as he slides it onto my finger. It fits perfectly, which I decide not to read into. "This thing probably costs more than my apartment."

"Probably," he agrees, his fingers lingering on mine a moment longer than necessary. "Ready?"

No, not even slightly. But I nod anyway, plastering on my best "madly in love" smile as the valet opens my door.

The Aviary is even more intimidating on the inside—all sleek lines and modern art, with waitstaff dressed better than I am on my best day. The maître d' leads us to a private table where the Murphy's are already seated, looking like they stepped out of a Ralph Lauren catalog for the retirement set.

"Benjamin!" Mrs. Murphy exclaims, rising to greet us. "And Lexie! So wonderful to see you both again."

Ben's arm slides around my waist, pulling me close to his side.

The gesture is so natural it almost scares me. "Mr. and Mrs. Murphy, thank you for inviting us."

"Please, call us Margaret and Richard," Mrs. Murphy insists, her eyes twinkling as she takes my hands in hers. "Let me see the ring, dear."

I extend my hand, letting the massive diamond do its job. Margaret gasps appreciatively, turning my hand this way and that to catch the light.

"His grandmother's," she says, clearly recognizing it. "How wonderful, Benjamin. I knew you were a traditionalist at heart."

Ben's smile is perfectly calibrated—proud but humble. "Some traditions are worth keeping."

We sit down, and I find myself hyperaware of Ben beside me—the brush of his leg against mine under the table, the subtle cologne that I'm starting to associate exclusively with him, the way his hand rests protectively on the back of my chair.

"So," Richard says, after we've ordered drinks, "Benjamin tells us you're a publisher as well as a bestselling author, Lexie. That must be fascinating work."

"It is," I say, grateful for a topic I can discuss with genuine enthusiasm. "Every day is different. One minute I'm editing a thriller, the next I'm negotiating rights for a fantasy series."

"She's being modest," Ben interjects, "Her latest novel was on the New York Times bestseller list for twelve weeks."

I glance at him, surprised by the genuine pride in his voice. "It was a lucky break."

"Nonsense," Richard says, sipping his scotch. "Success like that doesn't happen by accident. You must be very talented."

"Oh, yes," Margaret agrees. "What kind of books do you write, dear?"

I hesitate, suddenly aware that my usual genre might not align with the Murphy's' traditional values. "Contemporary fiction," I say vaguely. "With romantic elements."

"She writes beautiful love stories," Ben interjects smoothly, his eyes meeting mine with unexpected warmth. "Actually, I first read her work before we even started dating. I was... captivated."

My heart does a strange little flip. We never discussed this part of our backstory.

"How romantic," Margaret sighs, clearly charmed. "Reading her words before knowing her heart."

"It was quite the surprise when I discovered my new neighbor was the author I'd been admiring," Ben continues, his thumb tracing small circles on my shoulder that are entirely too distracting. "Though she wasn't exactly thrilled with me at first."

"Oh?" Richard raises an eyebrow, clearly interested in this twist.

I decide to play along. "He was a bit... standoffish," I explain, giving Ben a look that's half-teasing, half-genuine. "Always complaining about the noise from our office."

"In my defense," Ben says with a chuckle that sounds startlingly natural, "her team was having dance parties at 10 AM on Tuesdays."

"Team building exercises," I correct primly, making the Murphy's laugh.

"So how did you go from bickering neighbors to engaged?" Margaret asks, leaning forward eagerly.

Ben's eyes meet mine, and for a moment, I forget this is all pretend. "I asked her to dinner," he says simply. "To apologize for being, as she put it, 'a corporate robot with a spreadsheet for a soul.'"

I nearly choke on my wine. I definitely called him that once, but never to his face. How did he know?

"And the rest is history," I manage, recovering quickly. "Turns out he's not all spreadsheets and frowns."

"I've never seen Benjamin smile so much as he has tonight," Richard observes, his eyes twinkling. "You've clearly been a good influence."

The waiter arrives with our appetizers, saving me from having to respond. The next hour passes in a surprisingly pleasant blur of excellent food and even better conversation. I find myself relaxing into the role of Ben's fiancé more easily than I expected, laughing at his dry jokes and finishing his sentences like we've been together for years instead of pretending for a night.

Ben, for his part, is a revelation. Gone is the uptight neighbor who scowls at my existence. In his place is a charming, attentive man who looks at me like I'm the center of his universe. It's all an act, I remind myself firmly. A very convincing act.

"Tell me about the proposal," Margaret says as dessert arrives, her eyes sparkling with romantic interest. "Benjamin mentioned the lakefront, but I want all the details."

Ben's hand finds mine on the table, our fingers intertwining with practiced ease. "It was sunset," he begins, his voice taking on a soft quality I've never heard before. "We'd been walking along the shore after dinner, and Lexie was telling me about this new book she was working on—a story about two people who couldn't stand each other at first but slowly realized they were perfect together."

I stare at him, momentarily speechless. This is definitely not what we rehearsed.

"The sky was this incredible shade of pink," he continues, his eyes never leaving mine, "and suddenly I knew I couldn't wait another day. I had the ring in my pocket—I'd been carrying it around for weeks, waiting for the perfect moment."

"He got down on one knee right there in the sand," I jump in, finding my voice. "With people walking by and everything. It was so unlike him to do something so… public."

"When you know, you know," Ben says simply, his thumb brushing over my knuckles in a way that sends shivers up my arm.

Margaret sighs dreamily. "How wonderful. Young love is so beautiful to witness."

"Indeed," Richard agrees, raising his glass. "To Benjamin and Lexie. May your future together be as bright as that rock on her finger."

We all raise our glasses, and I catch Ben's eye over the rim of mine. There's something in his gaze I can't quite decipher—something warm and almost vulnerable that makes my heart stutter in my chest.

The rest of dinner passes in a pleasant haze. By the time we say our goodbyes, with promises to have the Murphy's over for dinner at "our place" soon, I'm feeling slightly dizzy from the combination of expensive wine and Ben's constant, convincing affection.

"That went well," Ben says as we slide into the back of his car. "Really well, actually. Richard mentioned setting up a formal meeting next week to discuss their portfolio."

"Mission accomplished, then," I say, feeling an unexpected hollowness at the prospect of our fake engagement being over.

I twist the ring around my finger, already feeling strange about giving it back. "So, I guess this is the end of our whirlwind romance?"

Ben is quiet for a moment, his profile illuminated by the passing streetlights. "Not quite yet," he says finally. "The Murphy's invited us to their charity gala next weekend. It would be... suspicious if we broke up before then."

"Oh." I try not to sound too pleased. "Well, I suppose I can tolerate being engaged to you for another week."

"Your sacrifice is noted," he says dryly, but there's a hint of a smile playing at his lips.

We ride in comfortable silence for a while, the city sliding by outside our windows. I'm acutely aware of Ben beside me, his arm occasionally brushing against mine when the car turns. The evening feels unfinished somehow, hanging suspended between us.

"You were good tonight," he says suddenly, his voice low. "Very convincing."

"I'm a writer," I shrug, trying to sound casual. "Making up stories is what I do."

"Is that all this was?" he asks, his eyes finding mine in the dim light. "A story?"

My heart speeds up traitorously. "Isn't that what we agreed on? A business arrangement?"

He holds my gaze for a beat too long before looking away. "Right. Of course."

When we reach my building, Ben insists on walking me to my door, ever the perfect gentleman. We stand outside my apartment in awkward silence, neither quite sure how to end this non-date.

"So," I say, fiddling with my keys, "that was... interesting."

"Indeed," he agrees, hands in his pockets. "Thank you again, Lexie. The Murphy's were clearly charmed by you."

"What can I say? I'm a treat when I want to be." I attempt a smile that feels wobbly around the edges. "And hey, you weren't half bad yourself. Almost human, even."

The corner of his mouth quirks up. "High praise, coming from you."

Another silence falls, heavier this time. I'm suddenly aware of how close we're standing, close enough that I can feel the warmth radiating from him, smell that intoxicating cologne that's become oddly familiar.

"I should give this back," I say reluctantly, slipping his grandmother's ring from my finger.

Ben's hand closes over mine before I can remove it completely. "Keep it for now," he says, his voice oddly rough. "For the gala next weekend. It would be suspicious if you weren't wearing it at work, too."

"Right," I nod, trying to ignore the flutter in my stomach. "Can't have Angel catching on to our scheme."

"Exactly," he says, but he doesn't let go of my hand. "Goodnight, Lexie."

"Goodnight, Ben," I whisper, reaching up and kissing him on the cheek. Where did that come from?

I pull back quickly, my cheeks burning. What possessed me to do that? The spot where my lips touched his skin tingles, and I find myself staring at his mouth, wondering what it would feel like to…

No. Absolutely not. This is a business arrangement. Nothing more.

Ben seems equally thrown, his gray eyes darkening as he stares at me with an intensity that makes my knees weak. For a heart-stopping moment, I think he might lean in and kiss me properly.

Instead, he takes a deliberate step back, clearing his throat.

"I'll text you about the gala details."

"Perfect," I say, my voice higher than normal. "Looking forward to it."

It's a lie. I'm not looking forward to it—I'm dreading it. Because tonight made one thing painfully clear: pretending to be in love with Ben Maddox is dangerously easy.

"Goodnight, then," he says again, backing toward the elevator.

"Night," I mumble, fumbling with my keys and practically falling into my apartment.

Once inside, I lean against the door, letting out a long, shaky breath. What is happening to me? This is Ben Maddox—uptight, argumentative, perpetually disapproving Ben Maddox. Not someone I should be thinking about kissing.

And yet.

My phone buzzes with a text, making me jump. It's from Ben:

"You were amazing tonight. The Murphy's are completely convinced. Thank you."

I stare at the message, trying to ignore the disappointment that washes over me. Of course that's all he's thinking about—the clients, the business deal. This is just a transaction for him.

"All part of the service," I text back, aiming for breezy. "Though you owe me big time for that story about our first date. Very creative."

His response comes quickly: "Of course, whatever you wish. See you tomorrow?"

Tomorrow. Right. We work in the same building. How am I supposed to face him after tonight? After I kissed him on the cheek like some lovesick teenager?

"Sure thing."

I toss my phone onto the couch, not waiting for his reply. I need a shower, a glass of wine, and possibly a lobotomy to remove all thoughts of Ben Maddox from my brain.

As I step into the shower, letting the hot water wash away the evening, I can't help but replay every moment—the way his hand felt in mine, the pride in his voice when he talked about my books, the intensity in his eyes when he described our fake proposal. It felt so real.

That's the problem, isn't it? For a few hours tonight, I forgot we were pretending.

By the time I crawl into bed, I've convinced myself that it was just the atmosphere—the fancy restaurant, the expensive wine, the romantic stories we were spinning. Anyone would get caught up in that. It doesn't mean anything.

By morning, I've decided there is no way I can go into the office today. I can't face him after last night. I am officially playing the part of the Cowardly Lion. A day of vegging on the couch is exactly what I need.

I text Maci first thing, claiming a migraine, which isn't entirely a lie—my head is pounding, though more from confusion than actual pain. She responds with a string of concerned emojis, promising to handle everything at the office. I feel guilty for the deception, but not guilty enough to change my mind.

My day of vegging quickly devolves into obsessively checking my phone, waiting for… what? A text from Ben? Some sign that last night affected him as much as it affected me? Pathetic.

By noon, I've cycled through every streaming service I subscribe to and eaten an entire bag of chips. My phone remains stubbornly silent except for work emails and a text from Maci asking if I need anything. Nothing from Ben.

"This is ridiculous," I mutter to myself, tossing my phone aside for the hundredth time. "It was fake. All of it. Get it together, Phillips."

I force myself to open my laptop and work on my manuscript—the one thing that usually calms my chaotic mind. But instead of focusing on my fictional characters' love story, I keep replaying moments from last night. The way Ben looked at me when he first saw me in that dress. How his hand felt on the small of my back, guiding me through the restaurant. The unexpected warmth in his voice when he talked about my books.

My phone buzzes, and I lunge for it embarrassingly fast.

It's him.

"Noticed you weren't at the office today. Everything okay?"

My heart does a stupid little flip. He noticed I wasn't there? I stare at the message, trying to decipher hidden meanings that probably don't exist.

"Just feeling under the weather," I type back, aiming for casual. "Nothing serious."

Three dots appear immediately, then disappear, then reappear. Finally: "Need anything?"

The question throws me. Since when does Ben Maddox offer to help when I'm sick? I hesitate before responding.

"I'm good, thanks. Just resting."

This time his response comes quickly: "Okay. Feel better. The Murphy's called this morning. They're moving our meeting up to Monday."

And there it is—the reminder that this is all business. He's only checking on me because he needs his fake fiancé in working order for the next performance.

"I'll be back Monday," I assure him. "Wouldn't want to let down our adoring fans."

Before I put my phone back down, it rings—Maci's face

lighting up my screen.

"Hey," I answer, trying to sound appropriately under-the-weather. "What's up?"

"Don't 'what's up' me with your fake sick voice," Maci says immediately. "I just ran into Ben in the hallway, and he asked about you with actual concern in his eyes. What happened last night?"

I groan, sinking deeper into my couch cushions. "Nothing happened."

"Lexie Phillips, you are the worst liar in Chicago. Spill. Now."

"Fine," I sigh, knowing resistance is futile. "Dinner was… weird."

"Weird how? Did he embarrass you? Was he rude? Do I need to go next door and threaten him with office supplies?"

"No, no," I say quickly. "He was… perfect. That's the problem."

There's a pause on the other end of the line. "I'm going to need more details than that."

I launch into the whole story—the dress, his reaction, the way he looked at me all night, the stories he told about our relationship, the ring, the almost-kiss at my door.

"Holy shit," Maci breathes when I finish. "This is straight out of a movie."

"It's straight out of a disaster," I correct her. "I kissed him on the cheek, Mace. Like some lovesick teenager. And now I can't face him because I'm afraid I'm going to do something even more embarrassing, like actually kiss him for real."

"Would that be so terrible?" Maci asks gently.

"Yes!" I exclaim, then lower my voice even though I'm alone in my apartment. "He's… Ben. Mr. Spreadsheet. The guy who probably irons his underwear."

"The guy who couldn't take his eyes off you all night," Maci points out. "The guy who said he read your books and loved them. The guy who let you wear his grandmother's ring."

"For business purposes," I remind her. "This whole thing is just to land the Murphy account."

"If you say so," Maci says, in a tone that clearly indicates she doesn't believe me. "But for what it's worth, he looked genuinely worried when I told him you were sick."

My traitorous heart flutters again. "That's just because he needs me for the gala next weekend."

"Right," Maci says dryly. "Keep telling yourself that. Anyway, I called because we just heard back from Zephyr's publicist. They want to do a joint announcement about the deal next week. Can you pull yourself together enough to approve the press release I'm sending to your email?"

Work. Right. The thing I should be focusing on instead of my confusing feelings for my fake fiancé.

"Of course," I say, grateful for the distraction. "I'll look at it right now."

"Good. And Lex? Maybe stop hiding from your feelings. Just a thought."

"I'm not hiding from anything except a migraine," I mumble, knowing she doesn't believe me for a second.

After we hang up, I force myself to focus on the press release, making a few small edits before sending it back to Maci. Work is good. Work makes sense. Work doesn't make me question everything I thought I knew about myself and my irritatingly handsome neighbor.

I spend the rest of the day alternating between actual productivity and pathetic phone-checking. By evening, I've convinced myself that Monday will be fine. I'll be professional. Distant but friendly. I'll wear my most businesslike outfit and keep any interactions with Ben brief and to the point. Can't let him know he got to me.

As I prepare for bed, I try to put all thoughts of Ben out of my mind.

My phone buzzes just as I'm about to turn off the light. Another text from Ben:

"The Murphy's mentioned how much they enjoyed meeting you. Mr. Murphy specifically said you're 'refreshing.' I think that's a compliment."

Despite myself, I smile at the screen. "Of course it's a compliment. I'm marvelous."

His response comes quickly: "You were. More than I expected."

My heart does that stupid flutter again. What does he mean by that? Before I can overthink it, another text arrives:

"Get some rest. See you Monday."

I set my phone down, staring at the ceiling. Monday. Right. When I'll have to face him and pretend that nothing has changed. That I haven't spent the entire day thinking about him. That my heart doesn't race every time his name appears on my phone.

This is going to be a disaster.

Nine

Congratulations on the Emotional Crisis

The next morning arrives with the subtlety of a freight train. I stand in front of my closet, discarding outfit after outfit. Too casual. Too formal. Too "trying too hard." Too "not trying hard enough."

I finally settle on a navy-blue pencil skirt and cream blouse—professional but not stuffy. I wear the diamond ring, of course. Can't blow our cover. The weight of it on my finger feels both foreign and strangely right. My thoughts are a jumbled mess as I ride the elevator up to our floor. We agreed to keep up appearances until after the gala, which means wearing it at work. Which means everyone will see it. Including Maci, who's going to have a field day with this.

I'm so distracted by my own thoughts that I almost crash into Angel as I step off the elevator.

"Oh," she says, her perfect nose wrinkling slightly. "You're back."

"Miss me?" I ask sweetly.

Her eyes drop to my left hand, widening almost comically when she spots the ring. "What is that?"

"A hand," I reply, wiggling my fingers. "Most humans have them. Two, actually."

"You know what I mean," she hisses, grabbing my wrist to examine the ring more closely. "Is this some kind of joke?"

I gently extract my hand from her grip. "No joke. Though your reaction is pretty amusing."

She looks like she's about to have an aneurysm. "You're engaged? To whom?"

Before I can answer, a familiar voice cuts in from behind me. "To me."

Ben steps off the elevator, looking irritatingly perfect in a charcoal suit. His hand slides around my waist with practiced ease, as if we've been doing this for years rather than one dinner.

Angel's jaw actually drops. "You and… her?" She points between us like she's witnessing some bizarre circus act.

"Hard to believe, isn't it?" I say cheerfully. "Love works in mysterious ways."

Ben's arm tightens slightly around my waist. "Angel, would you mind giving us a moment? I'd like to speak with my fiancé privately."

The word 'fiancé' in Ben's mouth does something strange to my insides. Angel looks between us once more before stalking off, already pulling out her phone—no doubt to spread the gossip as quickly as possible.

"Well," I say, turning to face Ben, "that cat's out of the bag."

"Indeed," he agrees, his expression unreadable. "Are you

feeling better?"

"Much," I nod, suddenly aware of how close we're standing. His hand is still on my waist, warm through the thin fabric of my blouse. "Just needed a day of rest."

"Good." His eyes search mine for a moment before he steps back, breaking contact. "The Murphy's moved our meeting to this afternoon, but I will check in with you after; let you know how it goes."

"Okay," I say, trying to hide my disappointment at his businesslike tone. "Good luck with the meeting."

"Thank you," he says formally, and for a moment I glimpse the old Ben—stiff, professional, distant. Then his expression softens slightly. "You look nice today."

The compliment catches me off guard. "Thanks. I figured I should dress the part of a fancy fiancé."

A ghost of a smile touches his lips. "You don't need to change your style for me, Lexie."

"I know," I say quickly. "It's just… for appearances."

"Right," he nods. "Appearances."

We stand there awkwardly for a moment, neither quite sure what to say next. The hallway feels too small suddenly, the air between us charged with something I can't—or won't—name.

"Well," I finally say, gesturing vaguely toward my office, "I should get to work. Lots of catching up to do after my sick day."

"Of course," Ben agrees, taking another step back. "I'll text you after the meeting."

I watch him walk away, his shoulders straight, his stride confident. Only when he disappears into his office do I let out the breath I've been holding.

"Holy shit," Maci's voice makes me jump. She's standing in our doorway, eyes wide as saucers. "Was that… affection I just witnessed? From the robot?"

"Shh!" I hiss, dragging her inside our office. "It's for show, remember? The whole building probably knows by now, thanks to Angel."

"Uh-huh," Maci says skeptically, following me into my private office. "And the way he was looking at you? Was that for show too?"

"How was he looking at me?" I ask before I can stop myself.

Maci's grin is downright predatory. "Like he was mentally undressing you."

"He was not," I protest, my cheeks burning. "He was being polite."

"Polite doesn't make your pupils dilate like that," Maci says, plopping into the chair across from my desk. "Trust me, I took a psychology class once."

"Can we please focus on work?" I beg, opening my laptop. "We have the Zephyr announcement going out today, remember?"

"Fine," Maci sighs dramatically. "But this conversation isn't over."

The morning passes in a blur of emails, phone calls, and pointedly ignoring Maci's knowing looks whenever I glance at my phone. By lunchtime, I've made decent progress on my to-do list, but my mind keeps drifting to Ben and his meeting with the Murphy's.

I'm just about to order lunch when my office door flies open and Eli barrels in, looking like he's won the lottery.

"You!" he exclaims, pointing at me with unbridled enthusiasm. "You beautiful, magnificent woman!"

"Um, thanks?" I say, slightly alarmed by his exuberance. "Is this about my hair? Because I tried something new with the curling iron."

"This is about you being the best fake fiancé in the history of fake fiancés!" Eli announces, practically bouncing on his toes. "The Murphy's just committed their entire portfolio to us. All fifty million dollars of it!"

"They did?" I sit up straighter, genuinely surprised. "That's… wow."

"It's more than wow," Eli corrects, dropping into the chair across from me. "It's career-making. And it's all because of you."

"I doubt that," I say, feeling oddly pleased despite myself. "I just had dinner with them once."

"Once was enough," Eli insists. "They wouldn't stop talking about how perfect you are for Ben. How you've 'softened his edges.' Their words, not mine."

I try to ignore the warmth spreading through my chest. "Well, I'm glad the performance was convincing."

Eli studies me for a moment, his enthusiasm dimming slightly. "Is that all it was? A performance?"

"Of course," I say, too quickly. "We had a deal. I help him land the clients, he… owes me mozzarella sticks."

"Mozzarella sticks," Eli repeats slowly. "Right."

"Where is Ben, anyway?" I ask, trying to sound casual. "I figured he'd be the one sharing the good news."

"Still in the meeting, hammering out details," Eli explains, rising from his chair. "But he'll be done soon. Just wanted to come thank you myself."

"No need for thanks," I say, waving him off. "I'm glad I could help," I say, feeling oddly touched. "Even if all I did was eat expensive food and make up stories about our fake relationship."

Eli's grin falters slightly. "About that… the Murphy's are

pretty excited about your engagement. Mrs. Murphy is already talking about attending the wedding."

"Oh," I say, a knot forming in my stomach. "That might be… complicated."

"Yeah, well," Eli shrugs, standing up, "that's a problem for future Ben. Right now, we're celebrating. Drinks after work? The whole finance team is going to Murphy's Pub—ironic, I know—and you and Maci should join us."

"I'll check with her," I promise, though the thought of spending more time pretending with Ben makes my stomach do funny things.

After Eli leaves, I sit staring at my computer screen, not really seeing it. The Murphy's signed because of me. Because they thought Ben and I were in love. The deception worked—maybe too well.

My phone buzzes with a text from Ben: "Meeting successful. The Murphy's signed. Thank you."

I stare at the message, trying to decode any hidden meaning. It's so formal, so… Ben. I type back: "So I heard. Eli just burst into my office like a town crier. Congrats!"

His response comes quickly: "Couldn't have done it without you. Eli mentioned drinks tonight?"

"He invited us. Not sure if I can make it though. I'm working on a new novel and the plot twist it giving me fits."

"I understand. Rain check?"

I stare at his text, trying to decipher any disappointment. Is he just being polite? Does he actually want me there? I'm overthinking this, as usual.

"Definitely. Enjoy celebrating your big win."

I set my phone down, determined to actually focus on work for the rest of the day. The Zephyr announcement goes live at three, and I still need to approve the final press release.

My resolve lasts approximately forty-five minutes before my office door opens again. This time, it's Ben himself, looking slightly rumpled but triumphant.

"Hey," I say, my voice coming out softer than intended.

"Hey," he echoes, closing the door behind him. "I wanted to thank you in person."

"No need," I say, gesturing for him to sit. "Just fulfilling my end of our bargain."

Ben sits across from me, loosening his tie slightly. "The Murphy's are very impressed with you."

"So I've heard," I reply, trying to sound casual. "Eli mentioned Mrs. Murphy is already planning our wedding."

Ben winces slightly. "About that. They're… quite invested in our relationship."

"I gathered," I say dryly. "So what's the plan? Fake breakup after the gala?"

"That would be the logical next step," he agrees, but there's something hesitant in his tone.

"But?" I prompt, my heart rate picking up.

Ben leans forward, resting his elbows on his knees. "The Murphy's are significant clients. They've committed their entire portfolio to us, with the understanding that I'm… settling down."

"And if you suddenly break up with your fiancé, they might reconsider," I finish for him, understanding dawning.

"Exactly," he nods, looking relieved that I get it. "It's complicated."

"How long?" I ask, tapping my pen against my desk. "How long would we need to keep this charade going?"

Ben hesitates. "A few months, at least. Until their accounts are fully established with our firm."

"Months?" I repeat, my voice rising slightly. "Ben, that's… that's a lot to ask."

"I know," he says quickly. "And I wouldn't ask if it wasn't important. But this account could change everything for our firm. For my career."

I study his face, noting the genuine concern in his eyes. This matters to him—really matters. And despite all my better judgment, I find myself wanting to help.

"What exactly would this entail?" I ask cautiously. "More dinners? Public appearances?"

"Some, yes," he nods. "The gala this weekend, obviously. Perhaps a dinner or two with the Murphy's. And we'd need to maintain appearances at the office."

"So basically, we'd be dating. Without the… benefits."

A hint of color appears on Ben's cheeks. "I wouldn't phrase it quite like that, but essentially, yes."

I lean back in my chair, trying to process this request. Months of pretending to be engaged to Ben Maddox. Months of his arm around my waist, his hand in mine, his eyes meeting mine across dinner tables. Months of trying to convince myself it's all an act.

"What's in it for me?" I ask, not because I need incentive but because I need time to think.

"Name your price," he says simply.

I'm surprised by his directness. "You're that desperate?"

"I'm that serious about my career," he corrects, holding my gaze. I don't know why that particular comment felt like a stab to the chest. I guess that it was yet another reminder that it's all an act. To him. I wish I could say the same.

"I'll have to get back to you on that." I say after hesitating too long.

Ben watches me carefully, his gray eyes searching mine. "Take your time. I know it's a lot to ask."

"It is," I agree, twirling a pen between my fingers. "But I'll think about it."

His face brightens slightly. "Thank you. That's all I can ask for."

An awkward silence falls between us. I'm painfully aware of him sitting across from me, looking rumpled and relieved and unfairly attractive.

"So," I say, desperate to break the tension, "I guess congratulations are in order. Landing a fifty-million-dollar client is pretty impressive."

"Thank you," he says, a genuine smile spreading across his face. "It's a significant win for us."

"I bet Angel is thrilled," I say, unable to resist. "Though probably not about the reason for your success."

Ben chuckles, the sound warming something in my chest. "She's... adjusting to the news. I believe her exact words were 'What could you possibly see in her?'"

"Charming," I mutter. "What did you tell her?"

"That it's none of her business," he replies simply.

I blink at him, surprised by the firmness in his tone. "Well. That must have gone over well."

"About as well as you'd expect." He shrugs, loosening his tie further. "But she'll have to get used to it if we're going to continue this arrangement."

Right. The arrangement. The fake engagement that's starting to feel less fake by the minute.

"I should let you get back to work," Ben says, rising from his chair. "Just... think about what I said? About extending our agreement?"

"I will," I promise, watching as he heads for the door.

He pauses with his hand on the doorknob. "And Lexie? The offer for drinks still stands. If you change your mind."

After he leaves, I sit staring at my computer screen, not seeing a single word. Months of pretending to be engaged to Ben Maddox. Months of fighting these inconvenient feelings that keep bubbling up whenever he's near. Months of lying to everyone around us.

What could possibly go wrong?

Everything. Everything could go wrong.

I spend the rest of the afternoon trying to focus on work, but my mind keeps circling back to Ben's proposal—and not the romantic kind. Months of pretending. Months of his hand in mine, his arm around my waist, his lips occasionally brushing my cheek for show. The thought makes my stomach flip in a way that has nothing to do with dread and everything to do with anticipation.

By six o'clock, I've made exactly zero progress on my manuscript and answered approximately three emails. Productivity at its finest.

"You're still here?" Maci pokes her head into my office, already wearing her coat. "I thought you'd be at Murphy's by now, celebrating with your fake fiancé."

"I told him I couldn't make it," I say, closing my laptop with perhaps more force than necessary. "Novel problems."

Maci raises an eyebrow. "The same novel you haven't touched in three days?"

"I've been thinking about it," I defend weakly.

"Uh-huh." She leans against the doorframe, studying me. "What's really going on, Lex?"

I sigh, slumping back in my chair. "Ben wants to extend our arrangement."

"Extend how?" Maci asks, her eyes narrowing.

"Months," I reply miserably. "The Murphy's signed with his firm because they think he's settling down with me. If we suddenly break up…"

"They might take their business elsewhere," Maci finishes, understanding dawning. "So what did you tell him?"

"That I'd think about it." I twist the diamond ring on my finger, watching it catch the light. "It's a lot to ask."

Maci crosses the room, perching on the edge of my desk. "Is it, though? You're already wearing his grandmother's ring. You already convinced his clients you're in love. What's a few more months?"

"A few more months of pretending," I emphasize. "Of lying to everyone."

"Are you sure that's what's bothering you?" Maci asks gently. "Or is it that you're afraid it might stop being pretend?"

Bull's-eye. I glare at her. "That's ridiculous."

"Is it?" She shrugs. "Because from where I'm sitting, you two have more chemistry than most actual couples I know. Even when you're fighting, there's this… energy between you."

"That's called mutual irritation," I mutter.

"Keep telling yourself that." Maci stands, adjusting her purse. "Look, I'm heading to Murphy's. Eli invited me, and I never say no to free drinks. You should come."

"I can't," I insist, gesturing to my closed laptop. "Novel."

"Right," Maci says skeptically. "The novel. Well, if you change your mind, you know where to find us." She gives me a pointed look before heading out, leaving me alone with my thoughts.

I sit in the silence of my office, twisting Ben's grandmother's ring around my finger. It's too big of a decision to make while I'm emotionally compromised (and yes, I'm emotionally compromised—sue me). I need to clear my head.

After another twenty minutes of staring blankly at my computer, I give up. Maybe a walk will help. I grab my coat and purse, locking the office behind me.

Ten

The Hangover: Engagement Edition

The crisp evening air hits my face as I step outside, and I take a deep breath, letting it clear some of the fog from my brain. I find myself outside of a little piano bar, I've never seen before. warm and inviting—dim lighting, plush velvet booths along the walls, and a baby grand piano in the center where a woman with silver hair is playing something soft and jazzy. It's not crowded yet, just a few couples and small groups scattered around. I find a small table in the corner and order a glass of wine from a passing server. This is exactly what I needed—a neutral space to think without the distractions of work or Ben's too-attractive face clouding my judgment. The wine arrives, and I take a generous sip, letting rich flavor coat my tongue. The pianist shifts into something melancholy that matches my mood perfectly. I pull out my phone, intending to jot down some actual notes about my novel while I'm feeling contemplative, but my thumb hovers over my text messages instead.

No new messages from Ben. Why does that disappoint me?

I set my phone down, determined not to check it again for at least an hour. I need to think about this logically. Pros and cons. Like a proper adult.

Pro: Helping Ben secure his biggest clients ever. Con: Lying to everyone we know for months. Pro: More fancy dinners at restaurants I could never afford. Con: Having to pretend I'm in love with someone I'm definitely not in love with. Pro: Wearing a gorgeous diamond ring that makes other women jealous. Con: Eventually having to give said ring back. Pro: That look in Ben's eyes when he saw me in that black dress.

I stop, wine glass halfway to my lips. That last one shouldn't be on the list. That's not a logical reason to continue this charade. Grabbing my phone to check for the hundredth time; still no messages from Ben. I mindlessly scroll through my Facebook feed when I see Maci tagged in a group photo of Eli's. Everyone is there, smiling big, having a great time. Without me. Did I decide to avoid everyone and so I have no right to be mad? Yes. Am I mad? Hell, yes! I have a tendency to be dramatic at times.

I throw my phone into my purse, grab my things and stomp home like a petulant child. Once back in my apartment, I shut my phone off so I won't constantly pick it up to check it every 5 seconds but quickly turn it back on because I'm a masochist. I quickly take a shower, brush my teeth, and crawl into bed with my laptop ready for a late night writing session. Somewhere around 4 AM, I finally doze off as the thoughts in my mind continued to race.

I wake up to my phone buzzing on the nightstand, the vibration amplified by the wood surface until it sounds like a chainsaw to my pounding head. Groaning, I reach for it blindly, knocking over a glass of water I don't remember placing there.

"Perfect," I mutter, watching the water soak into my carpet. "Just perfect."

The phone continues its assault on my senses, and I finally manage to grab it, squinting at the too-bright screen. It's Maci. Of course it's Maci.

"What?" I answer, not bothering with pleasantries.

"Good morning to you too, sunshine," she says, far too cheerful for—I glance at the time—10:30 AM. "Just checking if you're alive since you disappeared last night. Also, are you planning to come in any time soon?"

"I didn't disappear," I grumble, sitting up and immediately regretting it as my head throbs in protest. "I told you I wasn't coming."

"Yes, but then you weren't answering texts, and then this morning, Ben was asking about you, and—"

I groan, shoving my face into my pillow. "I'm alive. Unfortunately."

"Late night?" Maci asks, and I can practically hear her smirk through the phone.

"Something like that," I mumble, rolling onto my back and wincing as the movement sends a fresh wave of pain through my skull. "I went to some piano bar and had a few too many glasses of wine while contemplating my life choices."

"Sounds healthy," she says. "Meanwhile, we were looking for you at Murphy's. Even your fake fiancé seemed disappointed you didn't show."

My heart does a stupid little flip at that. "Ben was disappointed?"

"Mmhmm," Maci hums knowingly. "Kept checking his phone

all night. Asked me twice if I'd heard from you."

"He did?" I sit up too quickly and immediately regret it, pressing a hand to my forehead. "Why didn't he just text me?"

"Why didn't you text him?" she counters. "You two are ridiculous, you know that? Anyway, are you planning to grace us with your presence today, or should I tell clients you've been abducted by aliens?"

I glance at the clock again. "Give me an hour. And coffee. Lots of coffee."

"Already got a latte with your name on it," she promises. "See you soon."

After we hang up, I drag myself to the shower, letting the hot water wash away some of the fog from my brain. Last night's wine-fueled writing session comes back to me in pieces—dramatic declarations of love, passionate kisses in the rain, all the romantic clichés I usually avoid in my work.

"Get it together, Phillips," I mutter to my reflection as I apply concealer to the dark circles under my eyes. I give up on the makeup and opt for Parada sunglasses. I'm opting for the mysterious author look today.

By the time I make it to the office, it's after one, and Maci is waiting with the promised coffee and a knowing smirk.

"You look like you had an interesting night," she observes, handing me the latte.

"I had an interesting bottle of wine," I correct her, taking a desperate sip. "Followed by some truly embarrassing writing that will never see the light of day."

"Drunk writing?" Maci perks up. "Is it sexy? Please tell me it's sexy."

"It's deleted," I lie, knowing full well the document is still open on my laptop at home. "And we are never speaking of it again."

Maci narrows her eyes at me. "Fine, keep your wine-soaked literary secrets. But we need to talk about the elephant in the building."

"Which is?" I take another long sip of coffee, pretending ignorance.

"Ben." She leans forward, lowering her voice. "He asked about you again this morning. When I passed him in the hallway."

My heart does that annoying little flip again. "What did you tell him?"

"That you were working from home. I didn't mention the likely hangover and emotional crisis."

"There is no emotional crisis," I insist, adjusting my sunglasses. "And I appreciate your discretion."

"Mmhmm." Maci crosses her arms. "So what's your plan? Are you going to agree to his extended fake engagement proposal?"

I fiddle with the diamond ring still on my finger. I'd forgotten to take it off last night—a detail I choose not to examine too closely.

"I think so," I admit quietly. "It means a lot to him, and it's not like it's hurting anyone."

"Except possibly you," Maci points out gently.

"I'm a big girl," I say, waving off her concern. "I can handle a few months of pretending."

"If you say so," Maci says, clearly unconvinced. "Just... be careful, okay? I don't want to see you get hurt."

"The only thing hurting right now is my head," I assure her, sipping my coffee. "Now, catch me up on what I missed this morning."

We spend the next hour going through emails and project updates. I'm just starting to feel human again when my office door opens without a knock. I look up, expecting Maci with more paperwork, but instead find Ben standing in my doorway.

My heart does an Olympic-level gymnastics routine in my chest.

"Hey," he says, his voice carefully neutral. "Got a minute?"

"Sure," I manage, grateful for the sunglasses hiding what I'm sure is panic in my eyes. "What's up?"

He steps in, closing the door behind him. I notice he's carrying a folder—always the professional, even when having potentially awkward conversations with his fake fiancé.

"I wanted to check in," he says, remaining standing. "You didn't make it last night."

"Yeah, sorry about that," I say, aiming for casual. "I got caught up in my writing and lost track of time."

It's not entirely a lie. I just leave out the part about drinking alone in a piano bar and writing embarrassingly sappy romance scenes based on us.

Ben nods, his expression unreadable. "Maci mentioned you were working from home this morning."

"Slight headache," I admit, tapping my sunglasses. "Hence the mysterious author look."

A hint of a smile touches his lips. "It suits you."

An awkward silence falls between us. I fidget with my coffee cup, suddenly very interested in the cardboard sleeve.

"Have you had a chance to think about what we discussed?" Ben asks finally, his voice carefully professional. "About extending our arrangement?"

I take a deep breath, meeting his gaze despite the sunglasses barrier. "I have. And I'll do it."

Something flickers across his face—relief? Gratitude? Something else? "You will?"

"Yes," I confirm, setting down my coffee. "I mean, what's a few more months, right? We've already convinced the Murphy's. Might as well see it through."

"Thank you," he says, and the sincerity in his voice makes my chest tight. "I know it's a lot to ask."

"It is," I agree, unable to resist a little jab. "But I'm nothing if not charitable."

That gets me a real smile, one that reaches his eyes. "Your generosity knows no bounds."

"I want something in return, though," I say, leaning forward.

He sits in the chair across from me, looking more relaxed than he has since this whole fake engagement began. "So, what's your price?"

"My price?" I echo, momentarily confused.

"For extending our arrangement," he clarifies. "You asked what was in it for you. I told you to name your price."

"Right." I tap my fingers against my desk, considering. What do I want from Ben Maddox? Besides the obvious, which I refuse to acknowledge even to myself. "First, unlimited access to your firm's box at the United Center. Hockey season's coming up."

Ben's eyebrows shoot up. "You're a hockey fan?"

"Die-hard," I confirm. "Second, you have to actually read my next manuscript before it goes to print and give me honest feedback."

"I'd be honored," he says, looking genuinely pleased by this request.

"And third…" I pause for dramatic effect. "You have to let me take you shopping for at least one outfit that doesn't scream 'I calculate tax deductions for fun.'"

He laughs, that real laugh that transforms his entire face. "Those are your demands? Sports tickets, manuscript feedback, and a shopping trip?"

"Take it or leave it, Maddox."

"Deal," he says without hesitation, extending his hand across my desk.

I shake it, trying to ignore the way my skin tingles where it touches his. "So, what's next on our fake engagement agenda?"

"The gala this Saturday," he reminds me. "Black tie. The Murphy's are honorary chairs."

"Right," I nod. "Fancy dress, fancy manners, fancy fiancé. Got it."

"So, what does this extended arrangement entail exactly? More fake dates? Public hand-holding? Should I start leaving toothbrushes at your place for authenticity?"

Ben's lips quirk upward. "The basics remain the same—maintaining appearances at work, occasional dinners with the Murphy's, the gala this weekend. As for toothbrushes..." His eyes try to meet mine through the sunglasses with an intensity that makes my stomach flip. "That might be overkill."

"Right," I say, withdrawing my hand perhaps a bit too quickly. "Just checking the parameters."

"Speaking of parameters," Ben says, shifting slightly in his chair, "we should probably discuss the... timeline."

"How long are we talking?" I ask, grateful for my sunglasses hiding whatever my eyes might reveal. "Weeks? Months? Years of blissful fake matrimony?"

"Three months," he says decisively. "By then, the Murphy's' accounts will be fully established with our firm, and we can stage an amicable breakup."

"Three months," I repeat, trying to ignore the hollow feeling in my chest. "Perfect. That gives us plenty of time to plan our tragic but mutual parting of ways. Oh, I got it. That hot barista who always remembers my complicated order and flirts with me whisked me away, perhaps?"

Ben's jaw tightens almost imperceptibly. "Let's keep it simple. Busy careers pulling us in different directions, mutual respect, no hard feelings."

"Boring but believable," I concede with a nod. "Though I like the Xander idea. He's hot as hell and he would definitely play along."

Ben's face darkens into something I've never seen before— almost like jealousy, which is ridiculous because this is all pretend.

"Who is Xander?" His voice is suddenly tight, all business-like formality evaporated.

I can't help the little thrill that runs through me at his reaction. "The barista at Grounded, that little coffee shop around the corner. You know, the one with the man-bun and the tattoo sleeve? Makes a mean oat milk latte?"

"I'm not familiar," Ben says coldly.

"Oh, you should be. He's quite memorable." I'm enjoying this way too much. "He always gives me extra caramel drizzle without charging me. And he writes little notes on my cup."

Ben's jaw clenches visibly. "I think our original plan will suffice. Career differences. Very clean, very believable."

"But much less dramatic," I sigh, leaning back in my chair. "Fine, have it your way. Boring breakup it is."

"Great." He stands abruptly, straightening his already perfect tie. "I should get back. I have a client call in ten minutes."

"Of course you do." I wave him off, fighting a smile. "Go make some money, honey."

He pauses at the door, his hand on the knob. "The gala is this Saturday. I'll pick you up at seven."

"I'll be the hot mess waiting for your arrival," I quip, unable to resist.

The corner of his mouth twitches. "You're impossible."

"Part of my charm," I reply sweetly.

After he leaves, I slump in my chair, removing my sunglasses to rub my tired eyes. What have I gotten myself into? Three more months of pretending to be in love with Ben Maddox. Three more months of fighting these inconvenient feelings that keep bubbling up whenever he's near.

Maci pokes her head in almost immediately, like she was hovering outside my door the whole time.

"Well?" she demands, closing the door behind her. "What happened?"

"I agreed to his proposal," I say, then wince at my poor choice of words. "The fake engagement extension, I mean."

"For how long?"

"Three months."

Maci whistles low. "That's a long time to pretend, Lex."

"I know," I groan, dropping my head into my hands. "But you should have seen his face when I said yes. He was so relieved, so grateful."

"And that matters to you because…?"

I glare at her. "Because I'm a nice person."

"Right," Maci says, clearly unconvinced. "And the fact that you nearly took my head off when I suggested he might be into you has nothing to do with it."

"He's not into me," I insist, though a flutter in my chest betrays me. "This is just business for him. The Murphy's are his biggest clients ever."

"And you're his biggest fake fiancé ever," Maci says, dropping into the chair Ben just vacated. "Did you see how he looked at you just now?"

"No, I missed that."

"He was looking at you like you hung the moon," Maci insists. "And don't think I didn't notice that little jealousy flare-up when you mentioned the hot barista."

I straighten in my chair, suddenly interested. "You heard that?"

"These walls are thin, and I have excellent hearing when it comes to gossip," she says unapologetically. "Ben was practically ready to hunt down poor innocent Xander and challenge him to a duel."

"He was not," I protest, but I can't help the little smile tugging at my lips. "He was just… concerned about the believability of our breakup story."

"Mmhmm," Maci hums, clearly unconvinced. "Well, whether you want to admit it or not, there's something very real happening between you two. And three months is a long time to pretend it isn't."

"Nothing is happening," I insist, putting my sunglasses back on. "It's all an act. For business."

"Keep telling yourself that," Maci says, rising from the chair. "But when you're ready to admit the truth, I'll be here with a bottle of wine and a giant 'I told you so' banner."

After she leaves, I stare blankly at my computer screen, trying to focus on work and not on the fact that I've just committed to three more months of emotional confusion.

Three months of Ben's hand in mine, his arm around my waist, his eyes meeting mine across dinner tables. Three months of pretending to be in love when I'm…

Not in love. Definitely not in love. Just… confused. And maybe a little attracted. But not in love.

Right?

Eleven

Retail Therapy (And Other Lies I Tell Myself)

The week passes in a whirlwind of work and carefully orchestrated "encounters" with Ben in the office—enough to maintain our cover story but not enough for any real conversation. By Friday afternoon, I've convinced myself that I have everything under control. My inconvenient feelings are just a product of the situation, nothing more.

I'm neck-deep in edits for Zephyr's manuscript when my phone buzzes with a text from Ben:

"Confirming tomorrow, 7pm. The gala is black tie. Do you need any details?"

I stare at the message, suddenly realizing I have no idea what one wears to a black-tie charity gala. The black dress from our dinner with the Murphy's was fancy, but probably not gala-level fancy. I mentally scan my closet and come up empty.

"What exactly does 'black tie' mean for women?" I text back.

"Asking for a friend who may be panicking that she has nothing appropriate to wear."

His response comes quickly: "Floor-length gown, typically. Don't panic. I'm sure you'll look beautiful in whatever you wear."

My heart does that annoying little flip again. Beautiful? Since when does Ben Maddox casually call me beautiful in text messages?

"That's the problem," I reply. "I don't own anything floor-length unless you count my shower curtain."

Three dots appear, disappear, then reappear. Finally: "Would you like help finding something suitable?"

I stare at my phone, trying to decipher his meaning. Is he offering to go shopping with me? To buy me a dress? To send his personal stylist (does he have a personal stylist?)?

"Are you volunteering to be my fairy godmother, Maddox?" I text back, aiming for lighthearted.

"Something like that. Are you free this afternoon? We could find you something appropriate."

My pulse quickens at the thought of shopping with Ben. "Aren't you working from home today?"

"Yes, but that doesn't matter. Is that a yes?"

I hesitate only briefly before responding: "Yes. When and where?"

"I'll pick you up at your office at 4. Wear comfortable shoes."

I set my phone down, a mix of excitement and nervousness bubbling in my stomach. Shopping with Ben Maddox. For a gown to wear to a fancy gala where we'll pretend to be engaged. This is fine. Totally normal Friday afternoon activity.

I spend the next hour alternating between halfhearted editing and obsessively checking the time. At 3:45, I give up all pretense of working and start packing up my things.

"Hot date?" Maci asks, appearing in my doorway with suspicious timing.

"Shopping expedition," I correct her, reaching for my purse. "With Ben."

Her eyebrows shoot up. "Shopping? With Mr. I-Own-Fifteen-Nearly-Identical-Suits? This I have to see."

"You're not invited," I say firmly. "He's helping me find something to wear to the gala tomorrow."

"How romantic," Maci sighs dramatically. "Your fake fiancé taking you shopping for a fancy dress. It's like Pretty Woman, but with less prostitution and more publishing."

"It's not romantic," I insist, checking my reflection in my compact mirror. "It's practical. I don't know what to wear to a black-tie event, and he does."

"Mmhmm," Maci hums skeptically. "And I'm sure his eagerness to see you try on evening gowns is purely professional."

Before I can respond with an appropriately withering comeback, there's a knock at my office door. Ben stands in the doorway, looking like I've never seen him dressed before. He's wearing jeans and a casual t-shirt and baseball cap on backwards. He's never looked so delicious. Am I drooling? I'm pretty sure I'm drooling.

My jaw literally drops. "What… are you wearing?"

Ben glances down at himself, as if he'd forgotten his own outfit. "Casual clothes? I do own them, contrary to popular belief."

"I'm sorry, I need a minute to process this," I say, holding up a hand. "Ben Maddox in jeans? And is that a Cubs hat? Backwards? Who are you and what have you done with my uptight neighbor?"

Maci is openly staring now, making no attempt to hide her shock. "I didn't know your programming allowed for casual mode, Ben."

He rolls his eyes, but there's a hint of amusement there. "Very funny. I thought it might be easier to shop without looking like I just stepped out of a board meeting."

"It's just… disconcerting," I admit, circling him like he's an exhibit in a museum. "Like seeing your elementary school teacher at the grocery store."

"If you're done analyzing my wardrobe," he says dryly, "we should get going. The stores won't stay open forever."

"Right." I grab my purse, still trying not to stare. The jeans fit him perfectly, and the simple gray t-shirt reveals arms that his suits usually keep hidden. Not that I'm noticing. "Ready when you are, Casual Ben."

"Have fun, kids," Maci calls after us, her voice laden with implication. "Don't do anything I wouldn't do!"

"That leaves the field wide open," I mutter as we head for the elevator.

Once we're alone in the elevator, I can't help stealing glances at this new version of Ben. He looks younger, more relaxed, almost approachable.

"You're staring," he says without looking at me.

"I'm observing," I correct him. "It's for research purposes. I might need to write a character who undergoes a shocking transformation someday."

His lips twitch. "Is it really that surprising that I own normal clothes?"

"Yes," I say emphatically. "Next you'll tell me you eat cereal straight from the box and leave wet towels on the bathroom floor."

"I do have some standards," he says, but he's definitely fighting a smile now.

The elevator doors open, and Ben places his hand lightly on the small of my back as we step out. It's such a natural gesture that I almost don't notice it. Almost.

We head to his car—a sleek black Audi that somehow matches both suited Ben and casual Ben equally well. He opens the passenger door for me, another gesture that feels oddly natural.

"So where are we going?" I ask as he slides into the driver's seat. "Please don't say Neiman Marcus. I'll feel like Julia Roberts in Pretty Woman, except without the obscene amount of money to spend."

"Not Neiman's," he assures me, pulling smoothly into traffic. "I have something else in mind."

"Mysterious," I comment, settling back against the leather seat. "I didn't take you for the surprise type."

"There are a lot of things you don't know about me, Lexie," he says, his eyes on the road but a small smile playing at his lips.

"Clearly," I agree, gesturing to his outfit. "The jeans alone have shattered my entire worldview."

He chuckles, the sound warm in the enclosed space of the car. "I'm glad I can still surprise you."

We drive in comfortable silence for a while, the radio playing softly in the background. I find myself stealing glances at his profile—the strong jaw, the usually perfect hair now slightly mussed under the baseball cap, the hint of stubble that suggests he hasn't shaved since a day or two. It's a good look on him. Too good.

"So," I say, desperate to break the silence before my thoughts wander into dangerous territory, "Congratulations again on the Murphy account."

"You underestimate your impact," he says quietly. "The Murphy's were on the fence before they met you. After dinner, they were convinced."

"Well, I am pretty charming," I concede with a grin. "Even when I'm high as a kite and covered in taco sauce."

Ben laughs, the sound startling me with its genuineness. "Yes, even then."

We pull up to a small boutique in Lincoln Park, nestled between a artisanal coffee shop and a bookstore. The storefront is elegant but understated, with a simple sign reading "Eleanor's" in flowing script.

"Here?" I ask, peering through the window at the beautiful gowns visible inside.

"A client recommended it," Ben explains, coming around to open my door. "Apparently, they specialize in evening wear that doesn't feel like costume."

"That's… thoughtful," I say, genuinely surprised by his consideration. "I was half-expecting you to drag me to some stuffy department store with salespeople who can smell my middle-class budget from a mile away."

"I do occasionally think about other people's comfort," he says with mock offense, holding the door open for me.

The interior of Eleanor's is even more beautiful than the storefront suggested—warm lighting, plush velvet seating areas, and racks of stunning gowns in every color imaginable. The space feels intimate and welcoming rather than intimidating.

A striking woman in her fifties with a silver bob and impeccable red lipstick approaches us with a warm smile. "Welcome to Eleanor's. I'm Eleanor. How can I help you today?"

"We're looking for a gown," Ben says, his hand finding the small of my back again. "For a charity gala tomorrow night."

Eleanor's eyes move between us, lingering on Ben's hand on my back and the diamond ring on my finger. "Ah, I see. And what sort of look are we going for, dear?" she asks, turning her attention to me.

"Something that says 'I belong here' but also 'I'm not trying too hard'?" I offer with a nervous laugh. "I've never been to a black-tie event before."

"First-timer," Eleanor says with an understanding nod. "Don't worry, we'll find you something perfect. Any color preferences?"

I glance at Ben, realizing I have no idea what he's wearing tomorrow. "What color is your tux?"

"Classic black," he replies, looking amused by my question.

"Of course it is," I mutter. "Um, no color preference, I guess? Just nothing that will make me look like I'm going to prom or auditioning for a Disney princess role."

Eleanor chuckles, already moving toward a rack of gowns. "I think I know exactly what you need. Why don't you have a seat, sir, while I get your fiancé started with some options?"

Ben raises an eyebrow at me as Eleanor bustles away. "Disney princess?"

"It's a legitimate concern," I defend. "I don't want to look like I'm playing dress-up."

"You could never," he says simply, and something in his tone makes my cheeks warm.

Eleanor returns with an armful of gowns in various jewel tones. "Let's start with these. The fitting rooms are just through there."

I follow her, throwing a nervous glance over my shoulder at Ben, who has settled into one of the velvet chairs with an encouraging smile.

The first dress is a deep emerald green with a plunging neckline and an open back. It's gorgeous and feels incredibly sexy.

"What do you think?" I ask Eleanor as she helps zip me up.

I stare at the woman in the mirror at a loss. I've never felt so sexy or beautiful as I do in this dress.

"You should definitely show your fiancé," Eleanor says with a knowing smile. "That color is magnificent with your complexion."

"I don't know," I hesitate, smoothing my hands over the silky fabric. "It's a lot more revealing than I usually wear."

"Trust me," Eleanor insists, "when a dress fits like this one does, you wear it. You don't let it wear you."

Taking a deep breath, I step out of the fitting room. Ben is scrolling through his phone, looking bored—until he glances up and sees me. His phone slips from his fingers, clattering to the floor. He doesn't even seem to notice.

"Wow," he says, his voice unusually husky. "That's… wow."

"Eloquent as always, Maddox," I tease, though my heart is racing at his reaction. "Is that a yes?"

He stands, approaching me slowly. "Turn around," he says softly.

I comply, turning in a slow circle. When I face him again, his eyes are darker than I've ever seen them, focused entirely on me.

"It's perfect," he says simply.

"I don't know," I hedge, suddenly self-conscious under his intense gaze. "It's pretty revealing."

"It's sophisticated," he corrects. "You look stunning."

Eleanor, hovering nearby, nods in agreement. "Your fiancé has excellent taste. That dress was made for you."

I glance at the price tag peeking out from under my arm and wince. "It's also made for someone with a trust fund."

Ben gently turns the tag to see the price. Without hesitation, he says, "We'll take it."

"What? No," I protest, stepping back. "It's way too expensive. I can't let you—"

"Consider it part of our arrangement," he says quietly, for my ears only. "You're helping me land the biggest client of my career. The least I can do is make sure you're properly dressed for the part."

"Ben," I start, torn between pride and practicality. The dress is gorgeous, and I know I'll never find anything like it in my price range.

"Please," he says, his eyes sincere. "Let me do this."

Something in his expression makes further argument impossible. "Fine," I concede. "But I'm buying my own shoes."

His lips quirk up in that almost-smile I'm starting to recognize. "Deal."

"Wonderful!" Eleanor claps her hands. "Let's get you back in your regular clothes, dear, and we'll get this wrapped up for tomorrow."

Back in the fitting room, I carefully step out of the emerald gown, unable to believe what just happened. Ben Maddox is buying me a designer dress. For a fake date. To impress his clients. This arrangement is getting more complicated by the minute.

As Eleanor helps me back into my regular clothes, she asks, "have you picked out your wedding dress yet? We have quite the selection to choose from."

"Oh, um, we haven't gotten that far in the planning yet," I stammer, feeling my cheeks heat up. "Still enjoying the engagement phase."

Eleanor's eyes twinkle knowingly. "Well, when you're ready, come back and see me. I do bridal consultations by appointment only."

"Thanks," I manage, wondering how many more awkward wedding-related conversations I'll have to navigate in the next three months.

When I emerge from the fitting room, Ben is waiting by the register, credit card already in hand. The emerald dress is being carefully wrapped in tissue paper by another saleswoman.

"Ready?" he asks, as if he hasn't just casually dropped several thousand dollars on a dress I'll wear exactly once.

"As I'll ever be," I reply, still feeling slightly dazed by the whole experience.

The drive back to my apartment is quieter than the drive to the boutique. I'm acutely aware of the expensive dress in its garment bag laid carefully across the back seat, and of Ben beside me, his profile illuminated by the passing streetlights.

"Thank you," I say finally, breaking the silence. "For the dress. It's beautiful."

"You're welcome," he says simply. "Though I think you're the one making it beautiful, not the other way around."

My heart does a ridiculous somersault in my chest. "Wow, that was smooth, Maddox. You practicing your lines for tomorrow night?"

The corner of his mouth quirks up. "Just stating facts."

We lapse into silence again, but it's comfortable rather than awkward. I find myself stealing glances at him, still thrown by Casual Ben in his jeans and backwards cap. He looks younger like this, more approachable. More… real.

When we reach my building, Ben insists on carrying the dress up to my apartment. I fumble with my keys, suddenly nervous about having him in my space—which is ridiculous, because this is just part of our arrangement. Nothing more.

"Thank you, again." I say, suddenly nervous. "I promise to be on my best behavior tomorrow."

"No need," Ben says, hanging the garment bag carefully on the hook behind my door. "Just be yourself."

"You sure? My 'self' tends to say inappropriate things and spill wine on expensive tablecloths."

His lips twitch with amusement. "I'm counting on it. The Murphy's find you refreshing, remember?"

We stand in my entryway, suddenly awkward. Ben's eyes scan my apartment, taking in the colorful throw pillows, overflowing bookshelves, and the half-empty wine glass I forgot on the coffee table this morning.

"Nice place," he says, his gaze lingering on the framed covers of my novels hanging on the wall. "Very you."

"Is that a compliment or an insult?" I ask, echoing our earlier conversation.

"Definitely a compliment," he says, his voice softening. "I like that your space reflects your personality."

"Chaotic and slightly disorganized?"

"Vibrant," he corrects. "Warm."

Something shifts in the air between us, a tension that wasn't there before. Ben takes a small step closer, close enough that I can smell his cologne—something woodsy and expensive that makes my heart beat faster.

"I should go," he says, though he makes no move toward the door.

His eyes drop to my lips for the briefest moment before returning to mine. "Seven tomorrow?"

"Seven," I confirm, my voice embarrassingly breathless.

Ben nods, finally taking a step back. "Goodnight, Lexie."

"Goodnight, Ben."

After he leaves, I lean against the closed door, my heart racing like I've run a marathon. What is happening to me? This is Ben Maddox—uptight, annoying, perpetually disapproving Ben Maddox. Not someone who makes my pulse quicken and my knees weak.

And yet.

I push away from the door and head straight for the bottle of wine in my kitchen. One glass to calm my nerves, and then I'm going to bed. Tomorrow is going to be a long day.

Twelve

Dressed to Impress—and Repress

By six o'clock Saturday evening, I've cycled through approximately seventeen emotional states, from excitement to dread to panic and back again. My hair and makeup are done—a sleek updo and smoky eyes that make me look far more sophisticated than I feel—and I'm just slipping into the emerald gown when my phone buzzes with a text from Maci:

"Good luck tonight! Remember: chin up, back straight, try not to fall in love with your fake fiancé. ❤"

I roll my eyes, typing back: "No danger of that. Though I might fall in love with this dress. It's RIDICULOUS."

I snap a quick mirror selfie and send it to her before I can second-guess myself.

Her response is immediate: "HOLY. SHIT. You look fire! Ben is going to swallow his tongue when he sees you!"

I laugh, setting my phone down to apply a final coat of lipstick. The woman in the mirror barely resembles me—she's elegant, sophisticated, the kind of woman who belongs at a black-tie gala with a handsome finance guy on her arm. The emerald dress hugs every curve, the deep v-neckline showing just enough skin to be daring without crossing into inappropriate territory. The open back, however, is downright scandalous.

My doorbell rings precisely at seven, because, again, Ben Maddox is always on time. I take a deep breath, smoothing down the silk of my dress one last time before opening the door.

The sight that greets me steals the air from my lungs. Ben in casual clothes was unexpected. Ben in a perfectly tailored tuxedo is devastating. The crisp black fabric accentuates his broad shoulders, the white dress shirt a stark contrast against his tanned skin. His hair is perfectly styled, and he's freshly shaved, his jaw sharp enough to cut glass.

"Hi," I manage, suddenly feeling shy despite my bold outfit.

Ben doesn't respond immediately. His eyes travel slowly from my face down the length of my body and back up again, darkening with each inch they cover. When he finally meets my gaze, there's an intensity there that makes my heart stutter.

"You look…" he starts, his voice rougher than usual. He clears his throat and tries again. "Stunning doesn't seem adequate."

A warm flush spreads across my cheeks. "Thank you. You clean up pretty well yourself."

"This?" He gestures to his tux. "Standard issue. You, on the other hand…" His eyes travel over me again, lingering on the neckline of my dress. "There will be nothing standard about you tonight."

I laugh, the sound a bit breathier than normal. "Careful, Maddox. Keep talking like that and I might start to think you actually like me."

The statement hangs between us, loaded with implications I'm not ready to examine. I reach for my clutch, breaking the moment. "We should probably get going. Don't want to be late for your big night."

Ben offers me his arm, a gesture so old-fashioned and charming it makes my heart do a silly little flip. "Ready when you are."

The car ride to the Palmer House Hilton is filled with small talk about the gala—who will be there, what to expect, which Murphy's' relatives I might meet. Ben briefs me on the charity the event is supporting (something about educational opportunities for underprivileged kids) and reminds me that the Murphy's are honorary chairs.

"So basically, they're a big deal," I summarize, fidgeting nervously with the clasp of my clutch. "And they're expecting to see their new favorite couple madly in love."

"Exactly," Ben says, his eyes briefly meeting mine in the dim light of the car. "Just be yourself. They already adore you."

"My authentic self would be at home in sweatpants watching Netflix," I remind him. "This version of me is definitely playing a part."

"Not entirely," he argues, his voice softening. "The woman who charmed the Murphy's—witty, intelligent, passionate about her work—that's the real you."

I blink at him, surprised by the insight. "I suppose," I concede. "Just with better posture and fewer taco stains."

He laughs, the sound warming me from the inside out. "The taco stains are part of your charm."

When we arrive at the Palmer House, I'm momentarily overwhelmed by the opulence of it all—the historic lobby with its elaborately painted ceiling, the sea of designer gowns and tuxedos, the champagne flowing freely. Ben's hand finds the small of my back, warm and reassuring through the thin fabric of my dress.

"Breathe," he murmurs close to my ear, sending a shiver down my spine. "You belong here."

"I really don't," I whisper back, accepting a flute of champagne from a passing waiter. "But I appreciate the vote of confidence."

We make our way through the crowd, Ben nodding at various acquaintances as we go. I notice several women giving me appraising looks, their eyes lingering on my dress, my ring, and then Ben. I straighten my spine, lifting my chin slightly. Maybe I don't belong here, but tonight I'm playing the part of a woman who does.

"Benjamin! Lexie!" Mrs. Murphy's voice cuts through the ambient chatter. She approaches us, resplendent in midnight blue chiffon, her husband following close behind. "Don't you both look absolutely marvelous!"

"Margaret," Ben greets her warmly, bending to kiss her cheek. "You look lovely tonight."

"Oh, this old thing," she dismisses with a wave of her bejeweled hand before turning her attention to me. "But you, my dear, are a vision in that color. Emerald suits you perfectly."

"Thank you," I say, genuinely touched by her enthusiasm. "Ben helped me pick it out."

"Did he now?" Richard raises an eyebrow, looking impressed. "Most men would rather walk over hot coals than go dress shopping."

Ben's arm slides around my waist, pulling me closer to his side. "It was my pleasure," he says, his eyes meeting mine with unexpected warmth. "Though I can't take credit for her looking beautiful. She manages that all on her own."

Mrs. Murphy clutches her heart dramatically. "Oh, you two are just precious. Young love is so magical."

The ballroom is a sea of black tuxedos and colorful gowns, crystal chandeliers casting a warm glow over the elegantly set tables. A string quartet plays softly in one corner, and waiters circulate with trays of champagne. Ben seems to know everyone, and they know him. It's like something out of a movie—the kind where the protagonist feels hopelessly out of place until her handsome escort whispers something encouraging in her ear.

Except Ben isn't just my handsome escort. He's my fake fiancé, I remind myself firmly. This is all pretend.

"There are some people I'd like you to meet," Ben murmurs close to my ear, his breath warm against my skin. "Important clients."

"Lead the way," I reply, taking a fortifying sip of champagne.

For the next hour, I play the part of the adoring fiancé to perfection—laughing at the right moments, squeezing Ben's hand when he talks about our "relationship," fielding questions about wedding plans with vague but enthusiastic responses. To my surprise, I'm actually enjoying myself. There's something liberating about being Lexie Phillips, Successful Author and fiancé of Ben Maddox, rather than just Lexie, the woman who sometimes eats cereal for dinner and binge-watches reality TV in her pajamas.

"You're a natural at this," Ben whispers as we move between conversation groups. "Everyone loves you."

"It's the dress," I demur, though I'm secretly pleased by the compliment. "Hard not to be confident when you feel like a million bucks."

"It's not the dress," he insists, his eyes meeting mine with an intensity that makes my heart skip. "It's you."

Before I can respond, the string quartet gives way to a full band, and couples begin migrating to the dance floor. Mrs. Murphy appears at our side, her eyes twinkling with mischief.

"Benjamin," she says, "surely you'll dance with your beautiful fiancé? I insist on seeing you two on the floor."

Ben's eyes find mine, a silent question in them. I nod slightly, ignoring the flutter in my stomach.

"We'd be delighted," he tells Mrs. Murphy, offering me his hand.

As he leads me to the dance floor, I lean in to whisper, "Fair warning: I have no formal dance training. The last time I danced was at a college party, and it involved a lot of jumping up and down to early 2000s hip hop."

Ben throws his head back and laughs, the sound sending a pleasant shiver down my spine. "Just follow my lead," he says, placing one hand on the small of my back and taking my other hand in his. "I won't let you fall."

The band is playing something slow and romantic, the kind of song that requires actual dancing rather than just swaying awkwardly. To my surprise, Ben is an excellent dancer, guiding me smoothly across the floor with confident steps.

"Where did you learn to dance like this?" I ask, genuinely impressed. "Let me guess—fancy prep school required ballroom dancing classes?"

"Close," he admits with a small smile. "My grandmother insisted. Said no grandson of hers would embarrass himself at formal functions."

"Smart woman," I comment, relaxing into his lead. "Was she the one who gave you the ring?"

Ben nods, his expression softening. "Yes. She was an

extraordinary woman. Strong-willed, sharp as a tack until the day she died." His thumb traces small circles on my back, sending tingles up my spine. "She would have liked you."

"Really?" I'm genuinely surprised. "Why?"

"Because you don't let me get away with anything," he says with a small smile. "She always said I needed someone who would challenge me."

The intimacy of the moment catches me off guard. This doesn't feel like pretending anymore. Ben's hand is warm against my back, his eyes focused entirely on me as we move across the dance floor. For a moment, I let myself imagine this is real—that I'm actually engaged to this complex, frustrating, occasionally wonderful man.

"You're thinking too hard," Ben murmurs, pulling me slightly closer. "Just feel the music."

I take a deep breath and allow myself to relax into his arms. "I'm surprised I haven't stepped on your toes yet."

"The night is young," he teases, expertly spinning me in a gentle twirl before bringing me back to his chest. "Though I should warn you—I've had compliments on my dancing."

"Shocking," I deadpan. "Ben Maddox, good at everything he attempts. The universe is so predictable."

He laughs softly, the sound rumbling through his chest where our bodies touch. "Not everything. I'm terrible at karaoke. And I can't cook to save my life."

"Now that I would pay to see," I say, grinning up at him. "Karaoke night with the financial advisors. Is that a regular thing? Please tell me it's a regular thing."

"Once a year at the holiday party," he admits, looking slightly embarrassed. "Highly classified information, of course."

"Of course," I agree solemnly. "I'll add it to the dossier of

"'Things That Make Ben Maddox Human.'"

His eyes find mine, unexpectedly serious. "And what else is in this dossier?"

The question hangs between us, heavier than it should be. "Well, there's the jeans from yesterday. The fact that you read my books. Your grandmother's dance lessons. The truth about your cooking skills." I pause, my heart racing for no good reason. "It's a work in progress."

The song changes to something even slower, and Ben's arm tightens around my waist, drawing me closer until there's barely space between us. My hand slides from his shoulder to the nape of his neck, and I swear I feel him shiver at the contact.

We sway together, and I'm hyperaware of every point where our bodies touch—his hand on my bare back, our clasped hands, his chest occasionally brushing against mine. This close, I can see flecks of silver in his gray eyes, the slight shadow of stubble along his jaw despite his clean shave. He's unfairly handsome in this light, all sharp angles and intensity.

"Everyone's watching us," I whisper, noticing the approving glances from surrounding couples.

"Let them," Ben says simply, his eyes never leaving mine. "We're giving them exactly what they expect to see."

"Which is?"

"A couple in love."

My breath catches in my throat. For a moment—just a moment—I let myself believe it's real. That the warmth in his eyes when he looks at me isn't just for show, that the gentle pressure of his hand on my back means something more than maintaining our cover.

The song ends too soon, breaking the spell. Ben reluctantly releases me, though his hand remains on the small of my back as we make our way off the dance floor.

"You two look absolutely perfect together," Mrs. Murphy gushes, appearing at our side with a knowing smile. "Richard and I were just saying how wonderful it is to see young people so in love these days."

"Thank you," Ben says smoothly, his hand still warm against my back. "It's easy when you find the right person."

I manage a smile, trying to ignore the way my heart constricts at his words. This isn't real, I remind myself. It's all for show.

"Lexie, dear," Mrs. Murphy continues, linking her arm through mine, "you simply must meet the Hendersons. They're tremendous supporters of the literary arts, and when I mentioned you're a published author, they were dying to meet you."

With an apologetic glance at Ben, I allow Mrs. Murphy to steer me toward an elegant older couple across the room. Ben mouths "I'll find you" before being pulled into conversation with a group of men in identical tuxedos.

The Hendersons turn out to be delightful—genuinely interested in my work and full of insightful questions about the publishing industry. Before I know it, I've spent nearly thirty minutes in animated conversation, almost forgetting I'm supposed to be playing a part.

"Your fiancé is quite the catch," Mrs. Henderson says, her eyes twinkling as she glances over my shoulder. "And clearly smitten with you."

I turn to find Ben watching me from across the room, a small smile playing on his lips. When our eyes meet, he raises his champagne glass in a silent toast.

"We're very happy," I say, surprised by how easily the words come. How true they feel in this moment.

"It shows," Mr. Henderson says kindly. "In both of you."

After excusing myself, I weave through the crowd, accepting another glass of champagne from a passing waiter. The room is warm, the alcohol creating a pleasant buzz under my skin. I scan the crowd for Ben, spotting him deep in conversation with Richard Murphy and another man I don't recognize.

Before I can reach him, I'm intercepted by a tall blonde woman in a sleek red dress, her smile sharp enough to cut glass.

"You must be Lexie," she says, giving me a once-over that feels distinctly judgmental. "I'm Vanessa Hargrove. Ben and I go way back."

Something in her tone sets off warning bells. "Nice to meet you," I say, keeping my voice neutral. "How do you know Ben?"

"Oh, we dated for a while in college," she says with a dismissive wave, though her eyes never leave mine. "And then on and off after graduation. Nothing serious, of course."

The emphasis on "nothing serious" feels pointed, as if she's trying to stake a claim or rattle me. I take a sip of champagne, buying time to formulate a response that won't involve dumping my drink on her perfect updo. I choose to channel my carefree snarky Lexie persona when I respond.

"How interesting," I smile brightly, channeling all my fake-sweetness. "Well, clearly nothing too serious if he's engaged to me now."

Vanessa's perfect smile falters slightly. "Yes, it was quite the surprise when I heard. Ben always said he wasn't the marrying type."

"People change when they meet the right person," I reply, twisting the diamond on my finger just enough to catch the light. "I guess I'm just special that way."

"Mmm," she hums, taking a delicate sip of her champagne.

"Special indeed. I must say, you're not his usual type."

"I'll take that as a compliment," I say with a wink. "Being unusual is my specialty."

Before Vanessa can respond with another thinly veiled insult, I feel a warm hand on my bare back. Ben appears at my side, his eyes flickering between us with barely concealed concern.

"I see you've met Vanessa," he says, his voice carefully neutral as his arm slides around my waist.

"We were just getting acquainted," I reply, leaning into his side. "Vanessa was telling me about your college days."

Something flashes in Ben's eyes—discomfort, maybe even embarrassment. "Ancient history," he says dismissively.

"Not that ancient," Vanessa purrs, her gaze lingering on Ben's face. "New Year's was only last year."

I feel Ben stiffen beside me, and my stomach does an unpleasant flip. Last year? That's not exactly ancient history.

"It was good seeing you, Vanessa," Ben says firmly, already guiding me away. "Enjoy the rest of your evening."

"You too," she calls after us, her voice dripping with false sweetness. "Lovely meeting you, Lexie. Hold onto that ring tight!"

Once we're safely across the ballroom, Ben leans down to murmur in my ear. "I'm sorry about that. Vanessa can be… difficult."

"Is that what we're calling it?" I ask, trying to keep my tone light despite the unexpected jealousy churning in my stomach. "She seemed quite determined to let me know about your history."

"There's not much to tell," he says with a sigh. "We dated briefly in college, then ran into each other at an industry event last year and had dinner. Once. It was a mistake I didn't repeat."

"You don't owe me an explanation," I remind him, though I'm embarrassingly relieved by his response. "This isn't real, remember?"

An awkward silence falls between us, heavier than any we've shared tonight. I take another sip of champagne, searching for something to say that will bring back the easy warmth we'd shared on the dance floor. My phone buzzes with a notification. I grab it quickly needing something to distract me from the awkwardness. It's from Xander.

The message reads: "Missing my favorite customer today! Your usual is waiting for you tomorrow. ;)"

What the hell? I look up to see Ben staring at my phone, expression stormy. Odd considering I just came face to face with his very real Ex.

I quickly shove my phone back in my clutch, feeling oddly guilty even though I've done nothing wrong. "Just the barista from my coffee shop," I explain, though I don't owe Ben an explanation any more than he owes me one about Vanessa.

"The one with the man-bun?" Ben asks, his voice tight. "Xander, was it?"

"That's the one," I confirm, surprised he remembered the name. "He's harmless."

"He doesn't sound harmless," Ben mutters, his jaw clenching visibly. "He sounds interested."

"And that bothers you because…?" I can't help myself from asking, eyebrow raised in challenge.

Ben's eyes meet mine, something fierce and possessive flashing in their gray depths. "Because tonight, you're with me." "Yeah," I say getting irritated. "But, it's all for show. In three months, you are going to go back to Vanessa. I should be able to date too!"

Ben's expression darkens, his posture stiffening. "I'm not going back to Vanessa," he says firmly.

"You don't know that," I counter, crossing my arms. "And anyway, it doesn't matter. This is pretend, Ben. You said it yourself."

Something shifts in his eyes, a vulnerability I've never seen before. "Is that what you want? To date the barista?"

"I don't know what I want," I admit, the champagne making me more honest than I intend. "But I do know I don't appreciate double standards. You can have an ex circling like a shark, but I can't get a text from a guy who makes my coffee?"

Ben runs a hand through his perfectly styled hair, messing it up in a way that somehow makes him even more attractive. Infuriating.

"You're right," he concedes, surprising me. "I apologize. It's none of my business."

"No, it's not," I agree, though the victory feels hollow. "Just like Vanessa is none of mine."

We stand in awkward silence, the gala swirling around us in a blur of laughter and music. I drain the last of my champagne, wishing it would wash away the complicated feelings churning inside me.

"Would you like to dance again?" Ben asks suddenly, extending his hand like a peace offering.

I hesitate, torn between pride and the undeniable desire to be back in his arms. "Are the Murphy's watching?"

Something flickers across his face—disappointment, maybe. "Does it matter?"

"Isn't that the point?" I challenge, keeping my voice low. "To convince them we're madly in love?"

Ben's eyes hold mine, intense and unreadable. "Maybe I just

want to dance with you."

My heart does a ridiculous somersault in my chest. Before I can respond, a man I've never met, appears at our side. Turns out the man-Jeffrey, needs Ben for a moment.

"There you are! Benjamin, I wanted to introduce you to Senator Collins. He's just arrived."

Ben hesitates, his eyes still locked with mine. "Can it wait a moment? Lexie and I were in the middle of something."

"Oh, I'm afraid not," Jeffrey says apologetically. "The Senator has to leave early. Political emergencies, you know how it is."

Ben looks torn, his gaze darting between Mrs. Murphy and me. "Lexie—"

"Go," I say, forcing a smile. "It's fine. We can talk later."

Thirteen

The Morning After the Masquerade

An hour later, he's still making the rounds while I stand to the side like a forgotten prom date. I've made small talk with everyone from elderly benefactors to catering staff, always keeping one eye on Ben as he works the room. He's in his element here—charming, confident, the perfect financial advisor. Everyone wants a piece of his time, and he gives it freely, though he occasionally catches my eye across the room and mouths "sorry" with an apologetic smile.

By my third glass of champagne, I'm feeling distinctly less charitable about the whole situation. This was supposed to be our night—our fake date to convince the Murphy's of our love. Instead, I'm standing alone by a potted palm while my fake fiancé networks his way across the ballroom.

"You look like you could use some fresh air," a kind voice says beside me. I turn to find Eli, resplendent in his own tuxedo, offering me a sympathetic smile.

"Is it that obvious?" I ask with a rueful laugh.

"Only to someone who knows Ben well enough to recognize when he's being an idiot," Eli replies, nodding toward a set of French doors. "There's a terrace out there. Much quieter."

I follow him gratefully, the cool night air a welcome relief after the stuffiness of the ballroom. The terrace overlooks a beautifully lit garden, strings of fairy lights twinkling among the trees. A few other guests mill about, enjoying the respite from the noise inside.

"Better?" Eli asks, leaning against the stone balustrade.

"Much," I sigh, kicking off my heels and flexing my aching toes. "These shoes are instruments of torture disguised as fashion statements."

Eli chuckles, his expression warm. "Ben's been caught up with the Senator for the last forty minutes. Political types never know when to stop talking."

"You don't have to make excuses for him," I say, perhaps more sharply than intended. "This is just business, after all."

Eli studies me for a long moment, his head tilted slightly. "Is it, though?"

I blink at him, caught off guard by the directness of the question. "What do you mean?"

"I've known Ben for fifteen years," Eli says, his voice thoughtful. "I've seen him with women before. It's never looked like this."

My heart speeds up traitorously. "Like what?"

"Like he can't take his eyes off you even when he's supposed to be listening to a U.S. Senator," Eli says simply. "Like he's constantly aware of exactly where you are in the room. Like he's actually happy."

I swallow hard, unsure how to respond. "You know about our arrangement, right? That this is all for the Murphy's' benefit?"

"I know what Ben told me," Eli nods. "But I also know what I see."

"Thanks, Eli." I say, happy to have him talk me down from my emotional high. He leaves me to my thoughts shortly after that. After about 20 minutes I decide to go back inside, but immediately regret it. Vanessa is hanging on Ben's arm acting like she belongs there. And he's doing nothing to shake her off.

I freeze, my heart plummeting to my stomach. Ben's leaning down, listening to whatever Vanessa is whispering in his ear, a polite smile on his face. Her red-nailed hand is possessively wrapped around his forearm, and they look... right together. Both tall, both stunning, both clearly from the same world of wealth and privilege.

I should leave. I should call an Uber and go home to my apartment, take off this borrowed-princess dress, and remember who I really am. This was always pretend, always temporary.

I turn on my heel, lift my chin and stroll out of there with far more gusto than I feel. Fuck Ben Maddox and his stupid account. I hope he loses it after tonight.

The cool night air hits me like a slap to the face as I burst through the main doors of the hotel. Tears prick at my eyes, but I refuse to let them fall. Not over Ben Maddox. Not over a fake relationship that was doomed from the start.

"Miss? Would you like me to call you a car?" a concerned valet asks, eyeing my slightly unsteady gait.

"Yes, please," I manage, fishing my phone from my clutch to order an Uber. My fingers are trembling too much to operate the app properly, and I curse under my breath.

The car arrives a few minutes later. Once I'm inside and the door firmly shut, I release a breath I didn't know I was holding.

The driver glances at me in the rearview mirror. "Rough night?"

"You could say that," I mutter, swiping angrily at a tear that's escaped despite my best efforts.

"Boyfriend troubles?" he asks sympathetically.

"Fake fiancé troubles," I correct him, then laugh at his confused expression. "It's a long story."

"I've got time," he shrugs. "Traffic's bad tonight."

I consider telling this stranger everything—about the deal with Ben, about the Murphy's, about Vanessa with her perfect hair and possessive grip. But what would be the point? Instead, I lean my head against the cool window and watch the city lights blur by.

My phone buzzes in my clutch. Then again. And again. I ignore it, knowing it's probably Ben wondering where I disappeared to. Let him wonder. Let him explain to the Murphy's why his fiancé suddenly vanished.

By the time I reach my apartment, I've received twelve texts and four missed calls. I kick off my heels the moment I'm through the door, not even bothering to turn on the lights as I make my way to my bedroom. The emerald dress suddenly feels like it's suffocating me, the fabric too tight, too expensive, too everything.

I struggle with the zipper for a full minute before giving up and simply shimmying out of it, leaving it in a pool of expensive silk on my bedroom floor. In just my underwear, I crawl into bed and pull the covers over my head.

My phone continues its assault from inside my discarded clutch. After the fifteenth buzz, I finally drag myself out of bed and retrieve it. Texts from Ben, Eli, and Maci. I ignore every one. I put myself out there to help someone who I didn't even really like. And what do I get as a thank you? Humiliated.

I force myself to put my phone on silent and toss it across the room. It lands with a soft thud on the armchair in the corner.

Sleep eludes me. Every time I close my eyes, I see Ben and Vanessa together—her hand on his arm, her lips at his ear, the way they just fit. Two beautiful people from the same world. Not like me, with my taco sauce stains and inappropriate jokes.

Around 3 AM, I give up on sleep entirely and drag myself to the kitchen. I make hot chocolate—the good kind with actual melted chocolate, not the powder—and curl up on my couch with a throw blanket. The city lights twinkle through my window, mocking me with their romantic glow.

"Stupid," I mutter to myself, blowing on my hot chocolate. "You knew it was fake."

But that's the problem, isn't it? Somewhere along the way, it stopped feeling fake to me. The hand-holding, the inside jokes, the way Ben looked at me on that dance floor—I'd started to believe my own fiction. Classic writer mistake.

By morning, my eyes are gritty from lack of sleep, and my head pounds with a combination of champagne hangover and emotional exhaustion. I finally retrieve my phone, bracing myself for the onslaught of messages.

Twenty-seven texts and nine missed calls. Most from Ben, some from Eli, a couple from Maci. I open Maci's first, knowing hers will be the least complicated.

"Hey, Eli just called me. Said you disappeared from the gala. Everything okay?"

And then an hour later: "Getting worried. Text me when you get this."

I quickly respond: "I'm fine. Just needed to leave. Call you later."

Next, I steel myself and check Eli's messages.

"Ben's looking for you. Everything okay?"

"Seriously, Lexie, Ben is freaking out. Where are you?"

"Just let someone know you're safe, okay?"

I send him a quick "I'm fine" text as well, not offering any further explanation.

Finally, I force myself to look at Ben's messages, starting from the earliest.

"Where are you?"

"Lexie, please answer your phone."

"Are you okay? I can't find you anywhere."

"Please just let me know you're safe."

"I'm worried. No one has seen you."

"Eli said you might have left. Did something happen?"

"Please call me."

"Lexie, I'm standing outside your apartment. Please let me know you're okay."

That last one was sent at 2:30 AM. I scroll through the rest—variations on the same themes of worry and confusion—until I reach the final message, sent just an hour ago.

"I don't know what happened last night, but I'm sorry. For whatever I did. Please call me when you're ready to talk."

He doesn't know what happened!? He can't be serious. I'm thinking now would be a good time to explore the whole Xander thing. I need a rebound. From a fake relationship. Man, I'm pathetic.

I toss my phone onto the coffee table and drag myself to the shower, letting the hot water wash away the remnants of makeup and the lingering scent of Ben's cologne that somehow clung to my skin. I scrub harder than necessary, as if I could physically remove the memory of his hands on my back, his eyes on my face.

Once dressed in my comfiest sweats and oversized t-shirt, I feel marginally more human. I make coffee, strong enough to strip paint, and curl up on my couch with my laptop. If there's one thing that can distract me from this emotional mess, it's work.

But the words won't come. Instead of my characters' voices in my head, all I hear is Ben's. "Maybe I just want to dance with you." The memory makes my chest ache in a way that has nothing to do with my hangover.

My phone buzzes again. Ben. This time I pick up.

"Hello?" My voice sounds raw, even to my own ears.

"Lexie." The relief in his voice is palpable. "Thank God. Are you okay?"

"I'm fine," I say flatly. "Just needed to leave."

"Without telling me?" There's genuine hurt in his voice. "I was worried sick. I thought something had happened to you."

"Something did happen," I snap, anger suddenly flaring. "I got tired of being humiliated by my fake fiancé in front of Chicago's most wealthy."

There's a long pause on the other end of the line.

"Humiliated?" Ben finally says, confusion evident in his voice. "What are you talking about?"

"Oh, please," I scoff, pacing my living room. "I saw you with Vanessa. You two looked very cozy while I stood alone on the terrace."

"Vanessa?" He sounds genuinely perplexed. "Lexie, she cornered me. I was trying to get away from her the entire time."

"Really? Because from where I was standing, you looked perfectly content to have her hanging all over you."

"I was being polite," Ben says, frustration creeping into his voice. "I was trying to extract myself from the conversation without causing a scene. You know how important last night was for the firm."

"Right," I say bitterly. "The firm. The clients. The account. That's all that matters, isn't it? Not how an author very much in the public eye looks getting embarrassed in front of everyone."

"That's not fair," he says quietly. "I looked for you everywhere. I was worried sick when I couldn't find you."

"Well, now you know I'm fine. Mission accomplished."

There's a long silence on the other end of the line, and for a moment I think Ben might have hung up.

"Lexie," he finally says, his voice softer now. "Can I come over? Please? I think we should talk about this in person."

"I don't think that's a good idea," I reply, wrapping my free arm around my middle. "I'm not exactly in the mood for company."

"I understand," he says, though the disappointment in his tone is unmistakable. "But for what it's worth, I'm sorry. I never meant to make you feel humiliated or abandoned. That was never my intention."

"It doesn't matter, Ben." I say feeling defeated. "I'm not doing any more of these events or whatever. I have my own reputation to uphold. If people ask, I will say we are engaged for the next three months, but I'm done being made to look like an idiot."

"Lexie, please—" Ben's voice takes on an urgent edge. "That's not what I want."

"What do you want, Ben?" I ask, exhaustion seeping into my bones. "Because from where I'm standing, this whole arrangement is about what you need for your career. My feelings, my image don't factor in."

There's a heavy pause. "That's not true," he says finally, his voice barely above a whisper. "Your feelings matter to me. More than you know."

I close my eyes, willing myself not to read too much into his words. "Look, I need some space. I'll keep up appearances at the office, but that's it."

"Okay," he concedes, though he sounds anything but okay. "Just… take care of yourself, Lexie."

"Always do," I reply, then end the call before I can say something I'll regret.

Fourteen

A Latte Confusion

I spend the rest of Sunday alternating between attempting to write, binge-watching mindless reality TV, and ignoring the ache in my chest that refuses to subside. By evening, I've convinced myself that some distance from Ben will be good for me. I need to remember what's real and what's not.

Monday morning arrives with cruel efficiency. I dress with particular care—a sleek black pencil skirt and crimson blouse that makes me feel armored. I even apply a bold red lipstick, like war paint. If I have to face Ben in the office, I'm going in with all my defenses up.

The diamond ring sits on my dresser where I left it Saturday night. I stare at it for a long moment before reluctantly slipping it back on my finger. I promised to maintain appearances, after all.

Maci is already at her desk when I arrive, her eyes widening as she takes in my carefully composed appearance.

"You look like you're dressed for battle," she observes, following me into my office. "Want to tell me what happened Saturday night?"

I sink into my chair, suddenly exhausted despite it being only 9 AM. "Not particularly."

"Eli called me," she says, closing my office door. "He was worried about you."

"I'm fine," I insist, powering up my computer to avoid meeting her eyes.

"Sure you are," Maci says skeptically. "That's why you're wearing your power outfit and enough mascara to supply a Broadway show."

I sigh, knowing she won't drop it. "I left early. That's all."

"Why?"

"Because I wasn't having fun," I say evasively.

Maci sits in the chair across from me, her expression softening. "Lex, come on. It's me. What happened?"

I fiddle with a pen on my desk, avoiding her gaze. "Ben was busy with clients. I got tired of standing around. His ex-girlfriend showed up and made it clear they have history. I looked like a fool. End of story."

"His ex?" Maci leans forward, suddenly interested. "What ex? Tell me everything."

"Her name is Vanessa. Tall, blonde, perfect. Apparently they dated in college and then again last year." I try to keep my tone casual, but the memory still stings. "She made sure to let me know about their history, then spent the rest of the night with her hand permanently attached to his arm."

"And Ben allowed this?" Maci asks, her brow furrowing.

"He didn't exactly push her away," I mutter, picking at my nail polish. "He was being 'polite,' according to him."

"Men," Maci scoffs, rolling her eyes. "They never understand these things. Did you confront him about it?"

"Not at the gala. I just left." I take a deep breath, focusing on keeping my voice steady. "We talked yesterday. He claims he was just being professional and didn't want to cause a scene."

"And you don't believe him?"

I shrug, trying to ignore the doubt creeping in. "It doesn't matter. This whole thing is fake anyway. I'm just tired of being made to look like a fool."

Maci studies me for a long moment. "Are you sure that's all this is about? Because from where I'm sitting, you seem awfully upset for someone who's just playing pretend."

"I don't want to talk about it anymore." I say, fidgeting with my pen. "You know what, I need coffee. I'm going to get coffee."

I grab my purse and practically run out the door before she can ask any more uncomfortable questions. The truth is, I'm not just upset about being embarrassed at the gala. I'm upset because somewhere along the way, I started wishing our fake relationship was real. And that realization terrifies me more than any humiliation.

Outside, the crisp autumn air hits my face, clearing some of the fog from my brain. I head straight for Grounded, the coffee shop around the corner where Xander works. Maybe some harmless flirtation is exactly what I need right now—a reminder that there are other men in the world besides Ben Maddox.

The coffee shop is bustling with Monday morning customers, but Xander spots me immediately, his face lighting up with a smile that would make most women weak in the knees. He really is ridiculously handsome, with his man-bun and sleeve of artistic tattoos.

"There's my favorite author!" he calls over the espresso machine. "The usual?"

"Please," I say, forcing a brightness into my voice that I don't feel. "Extra shot today."

"Rough weekend?" he asks, already preparing my complicated order with practiced ease.

"You could say that," I mutter, but putting on a fake smile for him.

Xander leans across the counter, lowering his voice conspiratorially. "Want to talk about it? I'm a great listener."

Before I can respond, the bell over the door chimes. I don't need to turn around to know who it is—the sudden tension in Xander's shoulders tells me everything.

"One oat milk latte with extra caramel for the lady," Xander says, sliding my drink across the counter with a wink that's a bit too familiar. "On the house, as always."

"Thank you," I say, reaching for my wallet anyway. "But I insist on paying."

"I insist harder," Xander grins, then glances over my shoulder, his smile cooling several degrees. "Can I help you, sir?"

I turn, already knowing what I'll find. Ben stands just inside the doorway, looking impossibly put-together in a charcoal suit that probably costs more than my monthly rent. His eyes move from me to Xander to the coffee between us, his expression darkening with each shift.

"No, thank you," he says coolly. "I was just passing by and saw Lexie through the window."

The lie is so obvious I almost laugh. Ben's office is in the opposite direction, and he's holding a coffee cup from the high-end place near our building.

"Well, now you've seen me," I say brightly, taking a deliberate sip of my free coffee. "Alive and well. Crisis averted."

Ben's jaw tightens almost imperceptibly. "Could I speak with you for a moment? Outside?"

"I'll be there in a second." I say, waving him off.

Ben's eyes narrow slightly, but he nods and steps outside, his shoulders rigid beneath his perfect suit.

"Thanks for the coffee," I tell Xander, offering him a genuine smile. "You're a lifesaver."

"Anytime," he replies, his eyes flicking to the window where Ben stands waiting. "That's the fiancé, huh?"

I glance down at the ring still on my finger. "Complicated situation."

"Aren't they all?" Xander says with a knowing grin. "Well, if uncomplicated ever sounds appealing, I get off at seven most nights."

I laugh despite myself. "I'll keep that in mind."

When I step outside, Ben is pacing a small section of sidewalk, his free hand shoved in his pocket. He stops abruptly when he sees me.

"Was that necessary?" he asks, nodding toward the coffee shop.

"Was what necessary? Getting coffee? It's a basic human need, Ben."

"You know what I mean," he says, his voice low. "The flirting. The free coffee. The man-bun barista looking at you like you're his next meal."

"Jealousy doesn't become you," I say coolly, taking another sip of my latte. "And anyway, why do you care who looks at me or gives me free coffee? It's not like we're actually engaged."

Ben runs a hand through his perfectly styled hair, messing it up in a way that makes him look frustratingly attractive. "I came to apologize," he says, changing tactics. "About Saturday night."

"You already did. Over the phone. Apology accepted, crisis averted, let's move on."

"Lexie," he says, and something in his voice makes me finally meet his eyes. "Please. Can we talk? Really talk?"

I sigh, glancing at my watch. "I have a meeting in twenty minutes."

"Then give me fifteen," he counters. "There's a bench in that little park across the street."

Part of me wants to refuse, to walk away and maintain the emotional distance I desperately need. But another part— the part that made me leave the gala in the first place—wants answers.

"Fine," I concede. "Fifteen minutes."

The park is more of a glorified median—a strip of green with a few benches between lanes of traffic. Not exactly peaceful, but at least semi-private. We sit side by side, neither speaking for a moment.

"I really am sorry about Saturday," Ben finally says, staring straight ahead. "I had no idea you felt abandoned. I thought you were enjoying yourself with the Hendersons when the Senator arrived."

"I was," I admit. "Until I wasn't."

"What happened?" he asks, turning to face me. "Was it just Vanessa-"

"Just Vanessa!?" I all but explode. "I am helping you out, because believe me, it's doing nothing for me, and you decide to flaunt your EX when trying to debut your fiancé. That was embarrassing."

Ben's expression shifts from confusion to realization, and

for a moment, he looks genuinely pained. "I wasn't flaunting anything," he says quietly. "Vanessa approached me. I was trying to be polite while extracting myself from the conversation."

"Well, you didn't try very hard," I snap, clutching my coffee cup like it's a lifeline. "She was practically draping herself over you, and you just stood there."

"What was I supposed to do? Cause a scene at a charity gala in front of all our clients? Her father is one of my top clients, I can't just rudely remove her from my person." He runs a hand through his hair again, making it stand up slightly. The disheveled look suits him, which only irritates me more.

"Ahh yes, it's all about business with you. You'd rather whore yourself out to Vanessa for her father's attention, then show any kind of respect for the woman who is giving up a lot, to help your business succeed." I say practically seething. "Put this ring on Vanessa's finger, you two would fit together far better than you and me."

Ben flinches as if I've slapped him. For a moment, he's completely silent, his gray eyes stormy with emotion.

"Is that what you think?" he asks finally, his voice dangerously quiet. "That I'm… 'whoring myself out' for business? That I have no respect for you?"

"What else am I supposed to think?" I throw my hands up in frustration. "You parade me around like some trophy when it's convenient, then ignore me when something more important comes along. Like Vanessa. Or the Senator. Or literally anyone else in that room."

"That's not fair, Lexie." Ben's voice has an edge I've never heard before. "I've never treated you like a trophy. And I certainly wasn't ignoring you for Vanessa's sake."

"I know you think that I'm some uneducated fool," I mutter,

looking away. "But, a man that truly holds respect for someone, would not ever humiliate them. You knew how it would look when she was all over you, but instead of upsetting the client, you allowed her to continue on, making me look like a fool. That is not respect for me."

I stand up and begin walking back towards work.

I feel Ben's hand on my elbow before I can get far, his grip firm but gentle.

"Lexie, wait." His voice sounds different—raw, almost desperate. "Please don't walk away again."

I stop but don't turn around, my eyes fixed on the sidewalk ahead. "What's the point, Ben? We clearly have different ideas about what this arrangement entails."

"Look at me," he says, moving to stand in front of me. "Please."

Reluctantly, I meet his gaze. The intensity in his gray eyes catches me off guard.

"You're right," he says, and the admission startles me into silence. "I wasn't thinking about how it looked to you. I was thinking about the client, about maintaining professional relationships. And that was wrong."

"Listen, I have to get back to work." I say needing sometime to clear my mind. "I told you that I would keep up appearances around the office if approached. I won't jeopardize your deal. But, I also won't be set up to be humiliated again."

He nods looking crestfallen, but says nothing.

Back at my office, I throw myself into work with a vengeance. Maci keeps shooting me concerned glances throughout the day, but I wave her off with forced smiles and vague assurances that I'm fine. I'm not fine, of course, but burying myself in manuscript edits and marketing plans is better than dwelling on my conversation with Ben.

Everything but the Truth

By late afternoon, my phone buzzes with a text. I expect it to be from Ben, but it's Xander.

"Hope your day got better. Offer still stands for that drink sometime."

I stare at the message, tempted by the simplicity of it. Xander is uncomplicated. Handsome. Available. Definitely interested. And yet…

"Everything okay?" Maci asks, appearing in my doorway. "You're staring at your phone like it might explode."

"The barista asked me out," I say, setting my phone down.

Maci's eyebrows shoot up. "Man-bun? The one Ben was jealous of?"

"He wasn't jealous," I correct automatically, then sigh at her knowing look. "Fine, maybe a little jealous. But it doesn't matter."

"Are you going to say yes to Barista Boy?"

I chew my lip, considering. "I don't know. Maybe I should. It might help me get my head straight."

"Or make things more complicated," Maci points out gently. "Look, I'm all for rebound dating, but not when you're still wearing another man's ring."

I glance down at the diamond still on my finger. "It's not real. The engagement, I mean."

"Keep telling yourself that," Maci says, leaning against my doorframe. "But I saw your face when you came back from that park bench conversation this morning."

"I don't know what you're talking about," I mutter, shuffling papers on my desk.

"Oh please." Maci rolls her eyes dramatically. "I've known you since college. You've been in a funk all day—sighing, staring into space, and aggressively highlighting things that don't need highlighting."

I glance down at the manuscript in front of me, now covered in fluorescent yellow streaks. "I'm being thorough."

"You're being avoidant." Maci pushes off the doorframe and plops into the chair across from me. "What did he say to you this morning?"

"Nothing important," I lie, capping my highlighter with perhaps more force than necessary. "Just more excuses about Vanessa."

Maci studies me for a moment, her expression softening. "You know what I think?"

"I'm sure you're about to tell me."

"I think you're scared," she says simply. "I think somewhere along the way, this stopped being fake for you, and that terrifies you more than any humiliation at some fancy party."

The accuracy of her assessment hits too close to home. "That's ridiculous," I say, but my voice lacks conviction.

"Is it?" Maci challenges. "Because from where I'm sitting, you're using this Vanessa thing as an excuse to push Ben away before he can hurt you for real."

"He already hurt me for real," I counter, my voice dropping to a whisper. "Or have you forgotten Saturday night?"

"I haven't forgotten," Maci says gently. "But I also haven't forgotten how you looked when you came back from dress shopping with him. Or how you blushed every time your phone buzzed last week. Or how you kept that ring on even after you stormed out of the gala."

I glance down at the diamond still sparkling on my finger. I should have taken it off. Why didn't I take it off?

"It doesn't matter," I say finally, looking away from both the ring and Maci's too-perceptive gaze. "In three months, this will all be over, and things will go back to normal."

"Will they, though?" Maci asks softly. "Or will you always wonder what might have happened if you'd been brave enough to admit how you really feel?"

Before I can respond, there's a knock at my office door. I look up, expecting an intern or maybe our receptionist, but instead find Eli standing there, looking uncharacteristically serious.

"Hey," he says, his eyes darting between Maci and me. "Got a minute?"

"For you? Always," Maci says, standing up and smoothing her skirt. "I was just leaving." She gives me a pointed look that clearly says our conversation isn't over before slipping past Eli with a warm smile.

Eli closes the door behind him and takes the seat Maci just vacated. "We need to talk about Ben," he says without preamble.

"There's nothing to talk about," I say, reaching for my highlighter again. "Everything's fine."

"Bullshit," Eli says bluntly, surprising me. He's usually so easygoing. "He's been a walking disaster since Saturday night."

Something tightens in my chest. "That's not my problem."

"Actually, it kind of is," Eli counters, leaning forward in his chair. "Look, I don't know exactly what happened between you two, but I do know he's been staring at your office door all day like a lost puppy. He's distracted, irritable, and just snapped at Angel so badly she actually cried."

Despite everything, I feel a small flicker of satisfaction at this last bit. "Angel cried? Really? I was unaware she was capable of emotions."

Eli rolls his eyes, but there's a hint of amusement there. "Don't change the subject. The point is, whatever's going on between you two is affecting more than just your fake relationship."

"I told him I'd maintain appearances at the office," I say defensively. "I'm wearing the ring, aren't I? I promised I would hold up my end of the bargain, and I will. But, he doesn't get to embarrass me and then expect me to just pick back up like everything is fine. I have the right to defend myself too, Eli."

He looks alarmed, like he wasn't expecting my impassioned response.

"Whoa, whoa," Eli holds up his hands in a placating gesture. "I'm not saying you should just roll over. Trust me, I get it. Ben can be… difficult."

"Difficult?" I laugh, the sound sharp even to my own ears. "That's one way to put it."

Eli studies me for a moment, his expression softening. "Can I tell you something about Ben? Something not many people know?"

My curiosity gets the better of me. "I'm listening."

"He's terrified of failure," Eli says simply. "Has been since I've known him. His father was this high-powered investment banker who never thought Ben was good enough. Nothing he did measured up."

"What does this have to do with me?" I ask, though I'm hanging on every word.

"Saturday night wasn't just a social event for Ben. It was his chance to prove himself—to show everyone, including his father, that he's worthy." Eli leans forward, his voice dropping. "And then there's you."

"Me?"

"You terrify him more than failure ever could."

I blink, caught off guard. "That's ridiculous. I'm just—"

"A woman who doesn't fit into his carefully ordered world," Eli interrupts. "Who challenges him, makes him laugh, makes him feel things he's spent years avoiding."

My heart is pounding in my chest. "I don't… that's not…"

"It is," Eli insists gently. "Look, I'm not saying you should forgive him right away if he hurt you. But maybe consider that he's navigating unfamiliar territory here. With the Murphy's, with his career stakes, and especially with you."

I stare at my hands, at the diamond ring that suddenly feels heavier than before. "He could have just told me how important the night was. Explained about Vanessa instead of letting me stand there feeling like an idiot."

"Ben's not great at explaining his feelings," Eli says with a wry smile. "In case you hadn't noticed."

"Understatement of the century," I mutter.

"Just… don't write him off completely yet, okay?" Eli stands, straightening his tie. "He's trying. In his emotionally stunted way."

After Eli leaves, I sit at my desk, his words replaying in my mind. Ben, terrified of failure. Ben, terrified of me. It seems impossible—arrogant, confident Ben Maddox, afraid of a woman who trips over her own feet and once got her hair stuck in a car window.

My phone buzzes with another text from Xander: "So about that drink…?"

I stare at it for a long moment before typing back: "I'm flattered, but I'm in a complicated situation right now. Rain check?"

His response comes quickly: "Standing offer. Let me know when uncomplicated sounds good."

I set my phone down, feeling oddly relieved. Dating Xander would be easier, simpler. But somehow, I'm not ready for simple yet.

By six o'clock, the office is nearly empty. I've made decent progress on my manuscript edits, though my highlighter may never recover from the abuse. As I'm packing up my things, there's a soft knock at my door.

Ben stands in the doorway, looking more disheveled than I've ever seen him. His tie is loosened, his hair mussed as if he's been running his hands through it all day, and there are shadows under his eyes that suggest he slept about as well as I did last night.

"Hey," he says, his voice uncharacteristically hesitant.

"Hey," I echo, continuing to gather my things, pretending my heart isn't doing gymnastics in my chest.

"Can we talk? Please?"

I glance at my watch, buying time while I try to calm my racing pulse. "I was just heading out."

"Five minutes," he says, and there's something in his voice—a vulnerability I've never heard before—that makes it impossible to refuse.

"Five minutes," I agree, setting my bag back down.

Ben steps into my office, closing the door behind him. He doesn't sit, just stands there looking at me with an intensity that makes me want to squirm in my chair. For once, he seems at a loss for words.

"I've been thinking about what you said this morning," he finally says, shoving his hands in his pockets. "About respect. And you're right."

I blink, surprised by the admission. "I am?"

"Yes." He takes a step closer, his eyes never leaving mine. "I should have handled the situation with Vanessa differently. I was so focused on maintaining professional relationships that I didn't consider how it would make you feel. That was... inexcusable."

"It was," I agree, but my voice lacks the anger from this morning. "I felt like an idiot, Ben. Standing there alone while everyone watched your ex hang all over you."

Pain flashes across his face. "I never meant to make you feel that way. The truth is, I was trying to get rid of her the entire time. I kept looking for you, but you'd disappeared."

"I was on the terrace," I admit. "With Eli, actually. Getting some air."

Ben nods, running a hand through his already disheveled hair. "I checked there eventually, but you were already gone."

An awkward silence falls between us. I fidget with a pen on my desk, avoiding his gaze.

"I'm sorry," he says again, his voice lower now. "For everything. For letting Vanessa corner me, for neglecting you at the gala, for not explaining how important the night was to me."

"Eli mentioned something about that," I say, glancing up at him. "About your father?"

Ben stiffens slightly, then relaxes with a sigh. "Of course he did. Eli has never understood the concept of privacy."

"He was trying to help," I defend, setting the pen down. "He said you've been… difficult today."

A rueful smile tugs at Ben's lips. "That's a diplomatic way of putting it."

"He said you made Angel cry."

"She deserved it," Ben mutters, then has the grace to look slightly ashamed. "But yes, I've been in a terrible mood. Because of…" He hesitates, his eyes meeting mine. "Because of us."

My heart skips a beat at the word 'us.' There shouldn't be an 'us' to speak of—this is all pretend, a business arrangement. And yet.

"There is no 'us,'" I remind him, though the words taste bitter on my tongue. "That's the whole point, remember? It's fake. I'll help you maintain appearances. I will even go to more events. Just, don't make me look like a fool anymore."

I hold his gaze, waiting for him to argue, to push back, to tell me I'm wrong.

Instead, his shoulders slump slightly, an uncharacteristic defeat in his posture. "I just want us to be good again." He says quietly.

"We're good, prefect even." I say wanting this conversation to be over like yesterday.

"Right." Ben nods, straightening his tie in a gesture so familiar it makes my chest ache. "Perfect."

We stand there in uncomfortable silence, neither of us knowing what to say next. I can feel the weight of unspoken words between us, heavy and suffocating.

"Well, I should go," I finally say, reaching for my bag again.

"Of course." Ben steps aside, clearing my path to the door. "Have a good evening, Lexie."

Something in his tone—a resigned sadness I've never heard before—makes me pause with my hand on the doorknob. I glance back at him, standing in the middle of my office looking lost.

"You too, Ben," I say softly, then escape before I can change my mind.

Sixteen

The Arrangement, Revisited

The week crawls by in a blur of awkward encounters and careful politeness. Ben and I maintain our professional facade—nodding hello in the hallway, exchanging pleasantries, when necessary, the perfect aloof couple. The diamond ring stays on my finger, a constant reminder of our arrangement.

But something has shifted between us. The easy banter, the lingering glances, the casual touches—all gone, replaced by a formality that feels wrong in every way.

By Friday afternoon, I'm exhausted from the emotional gymnastics of pretending everything is fine. I'm staring blankly at my computer screen, not really seeing the words, when Maci bursts into my office.

"Emergency meeting," she announces, dropping dramatically into the chair across from me. "We need to talk about the Halloween party."

"It's July 7th" I deadpan.

"I know it's July," Maci rolls her eyes. "But I'm talking about planning ahead. We're a big publishing house with clients now; we need to go big!"

I hate when she gets like this. It usually ends in large expenses. But, she's right. We need to make a name for ourselves, we need a Halloween party worthy of the industry. I begin daydreaming of places to rent out. My mind immediately goes to the small warehouse district a few blocks from our office. There's this one building with exposed brick and high ceilings that would be perfect.

"If you're thinking about the Redford Building, I'm already three steps ahead of you," Maci says, reading my mind as usual. "I've got a call with the property manager on Monday."

"How did you—"

"Because I know you," she says, waving away my surprise. "Plus, it's the only venue within our budget that's not completely tragic."

I lean back in my chair, grateful for the distraction from my Ben situation. "So what's the emergency then? Sounds like you've got everything under control."

"We need guest lists, caterers, a dj, publicity," she rambles off, deep in thought.

"Okay, you do that. I'm busy."

"Doing what? Avoiding your fake fiancé? The one you've been avoiding all week while pretending everything is fine?"

"I haven't been avoiding him," I protest weakly. "We've been… professionally distant."

"Uh-huh," Maci says skeptically. "That's why you've been taking the stairs instead of the elevator and timing your coffee runs for when you know he's in meetings."

I glare at her. "I've been getting my exercise and being

considerate of his schedule."

"Right," she drawls. "And I'm secretly a duchess."

"Your highness," I mock bow.

Maci throws a crumpled paper at me. "Look, all I'm saying is that this whole 'pretending we're not pretending' thing is exhausting to watch. You're miserable. He's miserable. Everyone in the building can feel the tension."

"There is no tension," I insist, smoothing out the paper ball. "We're fine."

"Fine is what people say when they're absolutely not fine," Maci says, leaning forward.

"There's nothing to talk about," I say, turning my attention back to my computer screen. "We had a business arrangement. There was a complication. We worked it out. End of story."

"God, you even sound like him now," Maci groans. "All business-speak and emotional repression."

Before I can defend myself, my office phone rings. I grab it gratefully, eager for any distraction.

"Lexie Phillips," I answer, using my professional voice.

"Ms. Phillips, there's a Mrs. Murphy here to see you," our new receptionist says, sounding slightly frazzled. "She doesn't have an appointment, but she's quite... insistent."

My eyes widen in panic. "Mrs. Murphy? As in Margaret Murphy?"

"Yes, ma'am. She says it's important."

I glance at Maci, who's looking at me with raised eyebrows. "Um, of course. Send her in."

I hang up and immediately start straightening my desk, smoothing my hair, checking my reflection in my computer screen.

"What's happening?" Maci asks, alarmed by my sudden flurry

of activity.

"Margaret Murphy is here," I hiss, frantically applying lip gloss. "Ben's client. The whole reason for this stupid charade."

Maci's eyes widen comically. "The Mrs. Murphy? As in fifty-million-dollar account Mrs. Murphy?"

"Yes," I whisper-hiss, frantically shoving papers into a drawer. "What do you think she wants? Oh god, has she found out we're faking it?"

"How would she—"

A gentle knock interrupts us, and there she is—Margaret Murphy in all her elegant glory, wearing a perfectly tailored cream suit and pearl earrings that probably cost more than everything I own.

"Lexie, darling!" she exclaims, sweeping into my office like she owns the place. "I hope you don't mind the impromptu visit. I was in the neighborhood for lunch at Margeaux and thought, 'I simply must stop by and see Ben's wonderful fiancé!'"

"Mrs. Murphy," I manage, rising to greet her with what I hope is a convincing smile. "What a lovely surprise."

"Please, I've told you to call me Margaret," she says, kissing both my cheeks in that European way that always makes me feel like I'm in a movie. Her eyes land on Maci, who's watching the scene with barely concealed fascination.

"This is Maci, my business partner and best friend," I introduce quickly. "Maci, this is Margaret Murphy."

"The famous Maci!" Margaret clasps Maci's hands in hers. "Lexie spoke so highly of you at dinner. Any friend of Lexie's is a friend of mine."

"Likewise," Maci says, clearly charmed despite herself. "Can I offer you something to drink? Coffee? Water? We might have some wine in the break room..."

"Oh, don't trouble yourself," Margaret waves her off. "I can't stay long. I just wanted to drop off these personally." She reaches into her designer handbag and pulls out two elegantly embossed envelopes. "Invitations to our summer garden party at our lake house. It's next weekend—I know it's short notice, but Richard and I would be absolutely crushed if you and Ben couldn't attend."

She hands me the envelopes with a warm smile. "We've invited several authors Richard admires. I thought it might be a networking opportunity for your publishing house as well."

"That's incredibly thoughtful," I say, genuinely touched despite my panic. "Thank you."

"Not at all, darling. Now, is that handsome fiancé of yours around? I thought I might pop in and say hello to him as well."

My stomach drops. Ben and I haven't been in the same room outside of necessary interactions all week. "I'm not sure if he's in a meeting, I haven't been over there yet this morning-"

"Very well, I'll let you tell him about the party," Margaret says, already heading for the door. "Richard is waiting in the car, so I really can't linger. I'll see you next weekend!"

Before I can say more, she's out the door as fast as she appeared leaving me stunned, confused, and dreading my trek over to Ben's office to tell him the "good" news.

As soon as Margaret disappears down the hall, Maci closes my office door and turns to me with wide eyes.

"Well, that was unexpected," she says, dropping back into the chair across from my desk. "A garden party at their lake house? That sounds…"

"Horrible," I finish for her. "Awful. Catastrophic."

"I was going to say 'fancy,' but your words work too." Maci eyes the invitation in my hand. "Are you going to tell Ben?"

I stare at the elegant cream envelope like it might bite me. "Do I have a choice? Margaret will expect us both there."

"You could claim a sudden case of bubonic plague," Maci suggests helpfully. "Or spontaneous combustion."

"Very realistic," I mutter, turning the envelope over in my hands. "I should just get this over with."

"Want me to come with you?" Maci offers, looking far too excited at the prospect of witnessing my discomfort.

"No, thank you," I say firmly, standing up and smoothing my skirt. "I'm a grown woman. I can deliver an invitation without backup."

"If you say so," Maci singsongs, not bothering to hide her doubt. "Text me if you need an emergency extraction. I'll call with a fake publishing crisis."

"You're a true friend," I say dryly, heading for the door with as much dignity as I can muster.

The walk to Ben's office feels like a death march. Each step brings me closer to the first real conversation we'll have had since our awkward office encounter on Monday. My palms are sweating by the time I reach his office, and I have to wipe them discreetly on my skirt.

Angel looks up from her desk as I approach, her perfectly plucked eyebrows rising in surprise. "Ms. Phillips," she says coolly. "Mr. Maddox is on a call."

"I'll wait," I reply, matching her tone as I settle into one of the visitor chairs. "It's important."

Angel's eyes narrow slightly, but she returns to her computer without further comment. I fidget with the envelope in my hands, rehearsing what I'll say. "Hey, Ben, funny story, Margaret Murphy just ambushed me and now we have to spend a weekend pretending to be in love at her lake house." No, too casual. "Mr. Maddox, we have a business matter to discuss regarding the Murphy account." No, too formal.

Before I can settle on an approach, Ben's office door opens. He's on his phone, wearing the charcoal gray suit that makes his eyes look like storm clouds, his hair perfectly styled as always. My heart does a stupid little flip at the sight of him, which I promptly ignore.

He freezes when he sees me, his professional mask slipping for just a second before sliding back into place. "I'll call you back," he says into the phone, disconnecting and pocketing his phone in one smooth motion. "Lexie," he says, his voice carefully neutral. "Is everything alright?"

"Fine," I say automatically, then wince at my choice of word. "I mean, there's something I need to discuss with you. Do you have a minute?"

His eyes flicker to the envelope in my hands, curiosity briefly overcoming his professional detachment. "Of course. Come in."

I follow him into his office, painfully aware of Angel's curious stare boring into my back. Ben closes the door behind us, then gestures to the chairs in front of his desk.

"No need for formality," I say, remaining standing. "This won't take long."

Ben nods, leaning against the edge of his desk rather than sitting behind it. "What can I do for you?"

The professional distance in his voice makes something twist painfully in my chest. It pisses me off too. I hold out the envelope like it bites. "I don't want to bother you so here, Margaret Murphy just stopped by my office and gave me these."

Ben reaches for the envelope, his fingers briefly brushing against mine. Even that fleeting contact sends an unwelcome spark up my arm.

"Invitations," I explain unnecessarily as he opens the envelope. "To their summer garden party at their lake house. Next weekend."

Ben's expression shifts almost imperceptibly as he reads the invitation. "I see."

"She ambushed me in my office," I continue, crossing my arms defensively. "Showed up unannounced after lunch at Margeaux. Said they'd be 'absolutely crushed' if we couldn't attend."

Ben looks up from the invitation, his gray eyes unreadable. "And what did you tell her?"

"What could I tell her? That we're in the middle of the world's most awkward fake engagement and can barely stand to be in the same room together?" I throw my hands up in frustration. "I thanked her for the invitation."

Ben's eyes scan the invitation again, his expression unreadable. "I see."

"Look," I say, crossing my arms defensively, "I know things have been… strained between us. But Margaret clearly expects us to keep playing happy couple, so we need to figure out how to handle this."

Ben sets the invitation on his desk, his gray eyes meeting mine once more. "You don't have to go if you don't want to. I can make your excuses."

I'm going to be mature about this. I count to ten to get my emotions under control before opening my mouth. "Yeah, that works for me. Hey, here's an idea, why don't you take Vanessa instead." So close.

Ben's jaw tightens, and for a moment I see a flash of real anger in his eyes. "That's uncalled for."

"Is it?" I challenge, my voice rising slightly. "Because it seems like she's just waiting in the wings for this charade to be over."

"You're being ridiculous," he says, pushing off from his desk to stand at his full height. "Vanessa has nothing to do with this."

"Doesn't she?" I take a step closer, my blood boiling now. "Because from where I'm standing, she's a much more logical choice for your perfect society wife. Same background, same connections, same world."

"That's not—" Ben runs a hand through his hair, messing it up in that way that makes him look unfairly attractive even when I'm furious with him. "I don't want Vanessa."

"No? Then why did you let her hang all over you at the gala? Why didn't you shut her down immediately instead of being 'polite'?"

"Because I was trying to be professional!" His voice rises to match mine. "Something you clearly know nothing about!"

The words land like a slap. We stare at each other, both breathing hard, the silence between us charged with anger and something else I refuse to name.

"Ah yes, professionals allow just anyone to hang all over them while their "fiancé" watches on the side lines." I take a step back, my voice eerily calm. "I'll remember my place next time Mr. Maddox." I say turning for the door.

"Lexie, wait." Ben's voice stops me, his tone softer now. "Please don't go. Not like this."

I pause with my hand on the doorknob, my back still to him. Part of me wants to walk out, to maintain the distance I've so carefully constructed this week. But another part—the part that made my heart skip when I saw him just minutes ago—keeps me rooted to the spot.

"I'm sorry," he says, the words barely audible. "That was completely out of line."

I turn slowly, studying his face. The professional mask has slipped, revealing something raw and vulnerable beneath. "Which part? The insinuation that I'm unprofessional, or the part where you let your ex make me look like a fool?"

Ben winces, running a hand through his hair again. "Both. All of it. I've handled this entire situation terribly."

"Yes, you have," I agree, but some of the fight has gone out of me. He looks genuinely remorseful, and despite everything, I find myself wanting to believe him.

"I don't want to take Vanessa to the garden party," he says quietly, taking a step toward me. "I want to take you."

My traitorous heart flutters at his words. "Why?"

"Because…" He hesitates, something shifting in his expression. "Because the Murphy's are expecting us both."

And just like that, the moment is broken. Of course it's about the clients. It's always about the clients with Ben.

"Right," I say flatly. "The Murphy's. The account. The business arrangement."

"That's not what I—" He stops, frustration evident in his expression. "Lexie, you know this is important for my career."

"I know," I say, suddenly exhausted by all of it. "And I told you I'd maintain appearances. So yes, I'll go to the garden party. I'll play the adoring fiancé. I'll charm the Murphy's and their friends. But let's be clear about what this is and isn't."

Ben's expression hardens slightly. "And what is it, exactly?"

"A business arrangement," I say firmly, ignoring the ache in my chest. "Nothing more, nothing less."

Ben looks like he wants to say something else, but instead he just nods, his professional mask sliding back into place. "Fine. I'll pick you up Saturday morning at 8 AM. The lake house is about a two-hour drive."

"I'll be ready," I say, opening the door. "And Ben? Next time, we should coordinate our stories better. So I don't get ambushed by your clients in my office."

I don't wait for his response, striding past Angel's curious gaze and back toward my office at the other end of the building.

My stride down the hallway falters as I hear Eli call my name. I consider pretending I didn't hear him, but that would be childish. With a sigh, I turn around to face him.

"Hey," he says, jogging to catch up with me. "Everything okay? You look like you're about to set something on fire with your mind."

"Everything's peachy," I reply with a brittle smile. "Just coordinating weekend plans with my loving fiancé."

Eli winces. "That bad, huh?"

"Worse." I start walking again, and he falls into step beside me. "Did you know we're attending the Murphy's garden party at their lake house next weekend? Because I sure didn't until Margaret ambushed me in my office twenty minutes ago."

"Ah," Eli says, understanding dawning on his face. "That explains why Ben just slammed his office door so hard the blinds fell down."

Despite everything, I feel a small flicker of satisfaction at this. "Good."

"You two are exhausting, you know that?" Eli shakes his head, but there's fondness in his voice. "Like watching a car crash in slow motion."

"Thanks for that flattering analogy," I mutter. "Don't you have financials to analyze or something?"

"Actually, I was coming to invite you and Maci to drinks tonight," he says. "A bunch of us are heading to Lakeview Tavern after work. Thought it might be good for everyone to blow off some steam before the weekend."

"Thanks, but I think I'll pass," I say, already imagining how awkward it would be with Ben there. "Rain check?"

"Ben won't be there," Eli says, reading my mind with annoying accuracy. "He's meeting with clients from New York tonight."

I hesitate. A night out might be exactly what I need to clear my head. And Lakeview Tavern makes those amazing spicy margaritas that always improve my mood.

"I'll think about it," I concede. "Text me the details?"

"Will do." Eli gives me a quick side hug before heading back toward the financial wing. "And Lexie? For what it's worth, I think you're both being idiots."

"Noted," I call after him, unable to suppress a small smile despite my irritation.

Back in my office, Maci is waiting with an expectant expression. "Well? How'd it go? Do I need to help you hide a body?"

"Not yet, but I'll keep you on standby," I drop into my chair with a groan. "We're going to the garden party. Two hours in a car together. A whole weekend of pretending we don't want to strangle each other. It's going to be magical."

"That bad, huh?" She closes her laptop, giving me her full attention.

"He called me unprofessional," I say, still stinging from the accusation. "Me! When he's the one who—" I stop, taking a deep breath. "You know what? It doesn't matter. This is just business. Two more months and we can stage our amicable breakup and be done with this whole ridiculous charade."

Maci studies me for a long moment. "Is that what you want? To be done with it?"

"Of course," I say too quickly. "Why wouldn't I?"

"No reason," she says innocently. "Just checking."

I narrow my eyes at her. "Don't start."

"I didn't say anything!" She holds up her hands defensively. "But since we're on the subject of the garden party, what are you planning to wear?"

The question catches me off guard. "I…haven't thought about it."

"Well, you should," Maci says, suddenly all business. "Garden party at a lake house? That's a specific dress code. Not quite cocktail, not quite casual. You'll need something summery but elegant."

The thought of another outfit crisis makes my head hurt. "I'll figure something out."

"Or," Maci says, her eyes lighting up with that dangerous gleam I know too well, "we could go shopping tomorrow. I need some retail therapy after this week, and you need something that will make Ben's eyes pop out of his head."

"I don't care what Ben thinks of my outfit," I lie.

"Sure you don't," Maci says with a knowing smirk. "But wouldn't it be satisfying to make him regret every stupid thing he's said this week? To remind him exactly what he's missing with his 'just business' attitude?"

I hate that she has a point. "Fine," I concede. "Shopping tomorrow. But I'm buying my own dress this time."

"Deal," Maci says, looking far too pleased with herself. "Now, let's get back to this Halloween party planning. I was thinking we could do a literary horror theme…"

The rest of the afternoon passes in a flurry of work and party planning, a welcome distraction from thoughts of Ben and the upcoming garden party. By six o'clock, I've almost convinced myself that I'm fine with everything—the fake engagement, the garden party, the professional distance between Ben and me.

Almost.

"Ready for drinks?" Maci asks, poking her head into my office. "Eli texted that they're heading over now."

I glance at the pile of manuscripts still waiting for my attention. "I don't know…"

"Oh no you don't," Maci says firmly, marching in and closing my laptop. "You need this. We both do. Spicy margaritas and no talk of fake fiancés or garden parties."

"That does sound appealing," I admit, reaching for my purse. "But only if you promise not to ditch me for that bartender you were flirting with last time."

"Scout's honor," Maci says, holding up her hand in what is definitely not the scout salute. "Though I make no promises if Mr. Tattoo Arms is working tonight."

"Fair enough," I laugh, feeling lighter than I have all week.

Seventeen

Tequila Confessions

Lakeview Tavern is already bustling when we arrive, the Friday evening crowd in full swing. Eli waves us over to a large booth where he's seated with Angel and a few other people from the financial wing whose names I can never remember.

"Ladies!" Eli greets us, sliding over to make room. "First round's on me. What are we drinking?"

"Spicy margaritas," Maci and I say in unison, earning a laugh from the table.

As promised, there's no talk of work or Ben. Instead, we swap stories about terrible first dates, debate the merits of various reality TV shows, and by my second margarita, I'm actually having fun. The tension that's been knotted between my shoulders all week begins to loosen, and I find myself laughing genuinely at Angel's surprisingly hilarious impression of one of their stuffier clients.

"See?" Maci whispers as she returns from the bar with our

third round. "Isn't this better than moping in your office?"

"I wasn't moping," I protest weakly. "I was being productive."

"Mmhmm," she hums skeptically, sliding a fresh margarita my way. "And I'm secretly a supermodel."

"Well, you could be," I say loyally, taking a sip of my drink. "You've got the cheekbones for it."

Maci laughs, bumping my shoulder affectionately. "This is why you're my best friend. Unwavering delusion."

The night continues pleasantly, the alcohol creating a warm buzz under my skin that makes everything seem a little funnier, a little lighter. After our 3rd margarita, Maci and I hit the dance floor, letting the alcohol coursing through our veins propel us.

I let the music take over, twirling and laughing with Maci like we're in college again. For a few blissful hours, I'm not thinking about Ben or fake engagements or garden parties—I'm just Lexie, having fun with friends on a Friday night.

It's nearly midnight when my phone buzzes in my pocket. I ignore it at first, too caught up in the song, but when it buzzes again insistently, I pull it out, squinting at the screen in the dim light.

Ben.

My stomach does a stupid little flip that has nothing to do with the margaritas. I hesitate, thumb hovering over the screen, before curiosity gets the better of me. "I'm really sorry for my careless words this afternoon. I hope you are having a good night."

I stare at the message for a long moment, my thumb hovering over the keyboard. The rational part of my brain—the part not swimming in tequila—tells me to ignore it. But three margaritas have significantly lowered my defenses, and before I can stop myself, I'm typing back.

"Apology accepted. Having fun with friends. Thought you had clients tonight?"

I hit send before I can overthink it, then immediately regret it. Why did I ask about his clients? Now he'll think I care about his whereabouts. Which I don't. Obviously.

My phone buzzes again almost immediately. "Meeting ended early. They wanted to see Chicago nightlife, so we're at Aviary."

The Aviary. Of course. Only Ben would take clients to a place where cocktails cost more than my electric bill. I'm about to pocket my phone when another text comes through.

"What are you doing tomorrow? Besides shopping with Maci."

I blink at the screen, wondering how he knows about our shopping plans. Then I remember—Eli. The traitor.

"How do you know I'm shopping with Maci?" I type back.

"Eli mentioned it. You need something for the garden party?"

I roll my eyes at the phone. "No, I was planning to go naked. Make it memorable."

Three dots appear, disappear, then reappear. I can practically see Ben trying to formulate a response that's both professional and not completely boring. Finally: "That would certainly make an impression. Though possibly not the one we're aiming for with the Murphy's."

Despite everything, I laugh. "Relax, Maddox. I'm just getting something appropriate for a garden party. No naked appearances planned."

"Disappointing, but understandable," he replies, and I almost drop my phone in shock. Did Ben Maddox just make a joke? A slightly suggestive one at that?

"Are you drunk?" I type back before I can stop myself.

"Slightly. Clients insisted on tequila shots. Bad idea."

The image of buttoned-up Ben Maddox doing tequila shots with clients is so absurd I have to stifle a giggle. "Tequila Ben. I'm intrigued."

"Don't be. I'm still boring. Just less coordinated."

"I don't think you're boring," I type, then immediately regret it. Damn margaritas making me honest.

There's a long pause before his reply comes through. "Thank you. That… means a lot."

The sincerity in those simple words makes my chest tighten. This is dangerous territory. I need to steer us back to safer ground.

"So what are YOU doing tomorrow besides nursing a tequila hangover?" I ask.

"Reviewing the Murphy portfolio. Preparing for the garden party. Possibly regretting life choices."

I snort at the last part. "Sounds thrilling."

"It would be more thrilling if you were there."

I stare at the message, reading it three times to make sure I'm not hallucinating. The alcohol must be affecting him more than he's letting on.

"Now I KNOW you're drunk," I type back.

"Maybe. Doesn't make it less true."

My heart is racing now, and I'm suddenly very aware of how hot the bar feels. "I'm drunk too," I type for no reason other than to prolong the conversation. "On cheap tequila though."

"Ah, the classic margarita drunk," Ben replies. "Very different from the high-end tequila drunk. Mine comes with regret AND a higher price tag."

I find myself smiling at my phone like an idiot. Who is this person and what has he done with uptight Ben Maddox?

"Tell me something I don't know about you," I type impulsively.

There's a long pause, and I wonder if I've crossed some invisible line. I'm about to pocket my phone when his reply finally comes.

"I wanted to be a musician when I was younger. Played guitar in a band in high school."

My jaw drops. "NO WAY. Ben Maddox, rock star? I need photographic evidence immediately."

"Absolutely not. Those photos are locked in a vault for national security reasons."

"Come on! I showed you my embarrassing author photo from my first book. The one with the turtleneck and serious expression."

"That was adorable, not embarrassing," he replies, and my cheeks warm. "My band photos involve eyeliner and a very regrettable attempt at spiky hair."

I burst out laughing, drawing curious looks from nearby dancers. "I will pay actual money to see these photos."

"Not enough money in the world, Phillips."

By the time we stumble into an Uber at 1 AM, I'm pleasantly drunk and exhausted in the best way. My phone buzzes once more as we pull away from the curb.

"Get home safe. Text me when you do."

Such a simple request, but it makes my heart do that stupid flip again. I blame the tequila.

"Will do," I type back.

True to my word, I text him when I'm safely inside my apartment, though my message is somewhat less coherent than I intend. "Home. Not dead. Tequila was a mistake. Shopping tomorrow still happening though."

Ben's response comes surprisingly quickly for someone who

should be either still out with clients or passed out from tequila: "Drink water. Take aspirin. Sweet dreams, Lexie."

I stare at those last two words, a warm feeling spreading through my chest that has nothing to do with alcohol. Sweet dreams. Such a simple phrase, yet it feels strangely intimate coming from Ben. I fall asleep with my phone still clutched in my hand, a small smile on my face.

Eighteen

Blue Lace and Bold Moves

Morning arrives with the subtlety of a jackhammer to my skull. I groan, burying my face in my pillow as memories from last night filter back through the fog of my hangover. Drinks with friends. Dancing. Texting Ben. Oh god, texting Ben. I grab my phone, squinting against the too-bright screen as I scroll through our conversation.

It's… not as bad as I feared. Flirty, yes. Revealing, definitely. But nothing I can't blame on the tequila if necessary. Still, there's an undeniable shift in our dynamic—a softening of the rigid boundaries we've maintained all week.

My phone buzzes with a text from Maci: "Still alive? Shopping in 2 hours. Bring sunglasses and ibuprofen."

I drag myself out of bed and into the shower, letting the hot water wash away some of the hangover fog. By the time I've dressed, downed two cups of coffee and half a bottle of water, I almost feel human again.

Maci looks just as rough when I meet her at the café near our favorite boutique strip. "I'm never drinking again," she moans, sliding large sunglasses up her nose.

"You say that every time," I remind her, sipping my third coffee of the morning.

"And I mean it every time," she insists. "For at least the next twelve hours."

We laugh, and for a moment it feels like any normal Saturday—just two friends nursing hangovers and planning a shopping trip. But as we finish our coffees and head toward the first boutique, I can't help checking my phone. No messages from Ben.

"So," Maci says as we browse through racks of summer dresses, "want to tell me why you spent half the night texting instead of dancing?"

I nearly drop the dress I'm holding. "I wasn't—"

"Save it," she interrupts with a knowing smile. "I saw you. Giant smile, furious typing. Very suspicious behavior."

"I was just… checking work emails," I lie weakly.

"You're a terrible liar," She says, throwing a sundress at me.

Maci holds up a flowy yellow sundress against herself. "Try this one on. And while you're in there, you can tell me all about your text conversation with Ben."

"It was nothing," I insist, taking the dress from her hands. "Just clearing the air about the garden party."

"At one in the morning? After multiple margaritas?" Maci raises an eyebrow so high it's visible above her sunglasses. "That's when people send regrettable nudes, not discuss social engagements."

"I did not send nudes!" I hiss, glancing around to make sure no one heard.

"Pity. Might have solved your problems faster," Maci quips, grabbing another dress from the rack. "This one too. It'll make your eyes pop."

We spend the next hour trying on dresses, with Maci vetoing most of my selections as "too corporate" or "not garden party enough." Finally, in the third boutique, I find it—a pale blue sundress with delicate floral embroidery around the hem. It's feminine without being frilly, sophisticated without being stuffy, and when I step out of the dressing room, Maci actually gasps.

"That's it," she declares, circling me like a fashion editor. "Perfect garden party vibes. Elegant but not trying too hard. And it makes your legs look amazing."

I turn to examine myself in the mirror. The dress fits perfectly, nipping in at the waist before flaring out in a flattering A-line. The color brings out the gold flecks in my hazel eyes, and the length is just right—showing enough leg to be interesting without veering into inappropriate territory.

"Ben won't be able to keep his eyes off you," Maci says with satisfaction.

"That's not the point," I protest, though I can't help imagining his reaction. "I just need to look appropriate for the Murphy's' party."

"Sure, sure," Maci says, clearly not believing me. "And the fact that it makes your ass look spectacular is just a happy coincidence."

I roll my eyes but can't suppress a smile. "Fine. I'll take it."

"Good," She says mildly, "because we have one more important stop to make."

My head snaps up at her tone, I hate when she has that look. Ten minutes later we are standing just inside of a lingerie store that showcases every kind of ass and tits you can imagine. "What," I sputter horrified, "Are we doing here?"

Maci gives me an innocent look that doesn't fool me for a second. "What? You need something under that dress."

"I have underwear at home," I hiss, trying to back away toward the entrance. "Perfectly functional, non-embarrassing underwear."

"Functional?" Maci looks horrified. "You're spending a weekend with your fake fiancé at a lake house party. Functional won't cut it."

"I'm not planning on him seeing my underwear!" My voice rises a bit too loud, causing a saleswoman to glance our way with interest.

"Plans change," Maci says with a shrug, already browsing through a rack of lacy things that barely qualify as clothing. "Besides, good lingerie isn't about who sees it. It's about how it makes you feel."

"And how will scratchy lace in uncomfortable places make me feel?" I ask, eyeing a particularly complicated-looking contraption with suspicion.

"Powerful. Confident. Sexy." Maci holds up a pale blue lace set that matches my new dress perfectly. "Like a woman who knows what she wants."

I stare at the delicate fabric, something shifting inside me. Maybe she has a point. The past week I've felt off-balance, defensive, reactive. Maybe a little confidence boost wouldn't be the worst thing.

"Fine," I sigh, snatching the hanger from her hand. "But nothing with weird straps or cutouts. I'm going for confidence, not contortionism."

Maci grins triumphantly. "That's my girl."

An hour and far too much money later, I'm the reluctant owner of three new lingerie sets that make my usual cotton briefs look like something from a nun's closet. The blue set to match my dress, a black lace number that Maci insisted was "a classic," and a deep emerald set that reminded me instantly of the gala dress—and the way Ben had looked at me in it. I also pick up a swimsuit that is as daring as it is sexy. I look like a swimsuit model in it with my breast lifted up high and a cheeky cut out to the bottoms.

"You're welcome," Maci says smugly as we leave the lingerie store. "Just wearing those under your clothes will make you walk differently. Trust me."

"I have no doubt," I say, remembering how the panties wedged so far up my ass.

The next week flies by, filed with edits, conference calls, and anticipation. Finally, the morning of our trip rolls around.

When my doorbell rings at precisely 8 AM, I've been awake for hours, alternating between outfit panic and rehearsing casual conversation starters. I take one final look in the mirror—sundress perfect, makeup subtle but flattering, hair in loose waves that look effortlessly chic but actually took forty-five minutes to achieve. Beneath it all, the pale blue lingerie set sits against my skin, a secret confidence boost that no one needs to know about.

I open the door to find Ben in a casual outfit that still somehow looks expensive—khaki shorts, a light blue button-down with the sleeves rolled up, and brown leather boat shoes that probably cost more than my monthly utilities. He looks annoyingly handsome and well-rested.

"Good morning," he says, his eyes doing a quick scan of my outfit. Something flickers in his expression—appreciation, maybe—before his professional mask slides back into place. "You look nice."

"Thanks," I reply, aiming for casual. "So do you. Very lake house appropriate."

An awkward silence falls between us, the easy banter from our late-night texts nowhere to be found. I grab my overnight bag from beside the door, but Ben reaches for it before I can pick it up.

"Let me," he says, our fingers brushing briefly. Even that small contact sends that ridiculous tingle up my arm.

"Thanks," I mutter, locking my door behind us. I follow him out onto the street where his car sits. As he loads the luggage into the trunk, a gust of Chicago wind blows my skirt up just enough to reveal my tiny lingerie underneath. Kill me now. Hopefully I was quick enough and he didn't get an impromptu show.

Ben's eyes widen slightly, and a blush creeps up his neck. So much for him not seeing. I quickly push my dress down, praying for the ground to swallow me whole.

"All set?" I ask with forced cheerfulness, desperate to move past the moment.

"Yes," Ben says, his voice slightly strained. He clears his throat and opens the passenger door for me. "It's about a two-hour drive to the lake house, depending on traffic."

I slide into the car, hyper-aware of the lace against my skin and the fact that Ben just got a preview of what I'm wearing underneath my carefully chosen dress. Perfect start to what's sure to be a totally not awkward weekend.

Ben gets in and starts the car, the silence between us thick with unspoken tension. He fiddles with the radio, finally settling on a classic rock station playing softly in the background.

"So," I say, desperate to break the awkward silence. "The Murphy's' lake house. Is it actually on a lake, or is it one of those rich people things where they call it a 'lake house' but it's really just a mansion with a decorative pond?"

Ben's lips twitch with the hint of a smile. "It's actually on Lake Geneva. About twelve thousand square feet, if I remember correctly. Eight bedrooms, private dock, boat house."

"Twelve thousand—" I sputter, trying to wrap my head around the number. "My entire apartment could fit in their bathroom."

"Probably," Ben agrees, relaxing slightly as we fall into easier conversation. "The Murphy's come from old money. Very old money."

"And here I was, planning to impress them with my ability to identify the salad fork," I mutter, suddenly feeling out of my depth.

"You'll be fine," Ben says, his voice gentler than I expect. "They already adore you."

"They adore the version of me that doesn't spill wine or say inappropriate things," I point out. "A whole weekend is a lot of time to maintain that illusion."

Ben glances over at me, his gray eyes surprisingly warm. "I think they like the real you more than you realize. I know I—" He stops abruptly, returning his attention to the road.

"You what?" I press, curious despite myself.

"Nothing," he says quickly. "Just… don't worry about impressing them. Just be yourself."

The conversation drifts to safer topics after that—work projects, the upcoming publishing season, Maci's ambitious Halloween party plans. It's almost normal, this back-and-forth between us, like the tension of the past week never happened.

As we leave the city behind, the landscape opens up, highways giving way to tree-lined country roads. The morning sun filters through the windshield, warming my skin and making me drowsy despite my earlier nerves.

"You can nap if you want," Ben says, noticing my stifled yawn. "I'm fine," I say waving off his concern. "So, I'm assuming we are sharing a room, what else will be expected of us?"

Ben's hands tighten slightly on the steering wheel. "Yes, we'll be sharing a room," he confirms, his voice carefully neutral. "As for expectations… the usual couple behavior, I suppose. Hand-holding, occasional displays of affection. The Murphy's will expect us to be comfortable with each other."

"Right," I say, fiddling with the diamond ring on my finger. "Comfortable. Got it."

"We don't have to do anything you're not comfortable with," Ben adds quickly, glancing over at me. "If at any point things feel… too much, just give me a signal."

"A signal?" I raise an eyebrow. "Like a safe word?"

Ben coughs, a flush creeping up his neck. "I was thinking more along the lines of a discreet tap on the arm or something."

I laugh, giving him a break from my teasing.

"I'll pinch your butt twice if things get too intense," I offer with a straight face. "That should be discreet enough."

Ben nearly swerves the car, his eyes widening. "That's not—I don't think—"

"Relax, Maddox," I laugh, enjoying his discomfort far too much. "I'm kidding. How about I just say I need to use the restroom if I need an escape?"

He exhales, regaining his composure. "That works."

We fall into comfortable silence, the countryside rolling past our windows. I steal glances at Ben's profile when I think he won't notice—the strong line of his jaw, the way his hair curls slightly at the nape of his neck, the elegant hands gripping the steering wheel. It's infuriating how attractive he is, even when I'm trying to maintain emotional distance.

"What?" he asks suddenly, catching me mid-stare.

"Nothing," I say quickly, turning to look out the window. "Just… thinking about the party."

"Nervous?" His voice is gentle, surprising me.

I consider lying, but what's the point? "A little. I'm not exactly from lake house society."

As we approach Lake Geneva, the houses grow steadily larger and more impressive, until Ben turns down a long private drive lined with ancient oak trees. At the end sits what can only be described as a mansion—a sprawling structure of weathered stone and gleaming windows, perched on a bluff overlooking the sparkling blue lake.

"Holy shit," I breathe, taking in the scene. "That's not a lake house. That's Downton Abbey with a boat dock."

Ben chuckles, pulling up to a circular driveway where several expensive cars are already parked. "Remember, just be yourself.

The real Lexie is much more interesting than any society persona you could put on."

The sincerity in his voice catches me off guard. I glance over at him, but he's already focused on parking the car perfectly between a Bentley and what appears to be a vintage Jaguar.

"Ready?" he asks, turning off the engine.

"As I'll ever be," I reply, taking a deep breath to steady my nerves.

Ben comes around to open my door, offering his hand to help me out. As I step from the car, his hand slides naturally to the small of my back—a gesture that's becoming alarmingly familiar. The warmth of his palm through the thin fabric of my dress sends a shiver up my spine.

Before we can even reach for our bags, the massive front door swings open, and Margaret Murphy emerges, resplendent in a flowing caftan that probably costs more than my monthly rent.

"You made it!" she exclaims, gliding down the steps with her arms outstretched. "Welcome, welcome!"

"Margaret," Ben greets her warmly, accepting her air kisses. "Thank you for having us. Your home is spectacular."

"Oh, this old place," she says with a dismissive wave that makes me want to laugh. "It's been in Richard's family for generations. Lexie, darling, that dress is absolutely perfect! The color brings out your eyes beautifully."

"Thank you," I say, genuinely flattered. "And thank you for inviting us. Your home is… breathtaking." That's an understatement—the place looks like it should be featured in Architectural Digest.

"Come, come," Margaret urges, linking her arm through mine. "Richard is out on the boat with some of the guests, but he'll be back for lunch. Let me show you to your room so you can freshen up before joining the others on the terrace."

Ben grabs our bags from the trunk while I'm whisked into the house. The interior is just as impressive as the exterior— soaring ceilings, gleaming hardwood floors, and what appears to be actual museum-quality art on the walls.

"This is the east wing," Margaret explains as we climb a grand staircase. "You'll have a lovely view of the sunrise, though I suspect young people like yourselves might sleep right through it." She gives me a conspiratorial wink that makes me blush.

The "room" she leads us to is actually a suite larger than my entire apartment. A king-sized four-poster bed dominates one side, while a sitting area with plush couches occupies the other.

French doors open onto a private balcony overlooking the lake.

"The bathroom is through there," Margaret points to a door on the right. "Towels for the pool and lake are in the cabinet. Lunch will be served on the main terrace at one, but please feel free to explore the grounds before then."

"This is too generous," I say, suddenly feeling overwhelmed by the luxury surrounding us. "We're honored to be included."

"Nonsense! Any friends of Ben's are friends of ours," Margaret says warmly. "Besides, I've been dying to introduce you to some of our author friends. Richard is quite the literature enthusiast."

With one final smile, she leaves us alone in the suite, closing the heavy door behind her with a soft click. The silence that follows is deafening. Ben sets our bags down carefully, his eyes scanning the room before finally landing on the enormous bed we'll apparently be sharing.

"I can sleep on the couch," he offers immediately, nodding toward the sitting area.

"Don't be ridiculous," I say, aiming for casual while my heart hammers in my chest. "That thing is bigger than my entire bedroom. We can share without even knowing the other person is there."

Ben nods, though he doesn't look entirely convinced. "If you're sure."

"I'm sure," I say, moving to the French doors to admire the view. "We're adults. We can handle sleeping in the same bed for two nights."

The lake stretches out before us, sunlight dancing on its surface. In the distance, I can see a sleek boat cutting through the water, leaving a white trail in its wake.

"It really is beautiful here," I murmur, more to myself than to

Ben.

"Yes," he agrees, and when I glance over my shoulder, I find him watching me rather than the view. He quickly looks away, clearing his throat. "Should we unpack before heading downstairs?"

I nod, grateful for the mundane task to focus on. We move around each other awkwardly, trying to establish some sort of routine in this unfamiliar space. I claim the left side of the closet and the bathroom first, carefully hanging up my dress for tonight's dinner and arranging my toiletries on the marble countertop.

When I emerge, Ben is standing by the balcony again, his back to me, phone in hand. He's changed into a different shirt—a pale green that makes his shoulders look even broader than usual.

"Everything okay?" I ask, noticing the tense set of his shoulders.

"Just checking in with the office," he says, pocketing his phone. "Ready to face the socialites?"

"Absolutely," I reply with a nervous laugh. "Lead the way, Mr. Maddox."

He hesitates, then steps closer, his eyes serious. "Remember what I said in the car. Just be yourself. That's who they want to meet."

Before I can respond, he offers his hand, the perfect gentleman. I take it, trying to ignore the warmth that spreads through me at his touch.

The main terrace is already bustling with guests when we arrive—about twenty people in various summer outfits, all looking effortlessly wealthy in that way only old money can achieve. Waiters in crisp white uniforms circulate with trays of champagne and elegant hors d'oeuvres.

Ben's hand finds the small of my back again, guiding me through the crowd. I feel several curious glances as we make our entrance, and I resist the urge to check if my dress is straight or if there's lipstick on my teeth.

"Ben!" A distinguished older gentleman waves us over. He's tall and trim, with silver hair and the kind of tan that comes from sailing rather than tanning beds. "And this must be the famous Lexie we've heard so much about."

"Mark," Ben shakes his hand warmly. "Yes, this is my fiancé, Lexie Phillips. Lexie, this is Mark Mayhew, one of my clients."

"It's wonderful to meet you," I say, offering my hand, as Richard, fresh off of his boat makes his way towards us.

"Richard," Ben says in a deep, professional voice that does weird things to my body, "Your home is magnificent."

"Thank you, Benjamin," Richard says, his eyes twinkling. "Though I can't take any credit. The place has been in the family for generations, and Margaret is the one with the decorating eye."

"Don't believe a word he says," Margaret appears at his side, linking her arm through his. "Richard personally selected every piece of art in the east wing. He has quite the eye."

"Only for beautiful things," Richard says, giving his wife a fond smile that makes my heart twist unexpectedly. They're genuinely in love, these two wealthy, powerful people. It's oddly touching.

"Now," Margaret claps her hands lightly, "let me introduce you to everyone. We have quite the literary crowd today— I mentioned to a few friends that we had an exciting young publisher joining us, and suddenly everyone wanted to attend!"

Before I can process this statement, I'm being whisked from

group to group, Ben at my side. I meet a Pulitzer Prize-winning novelist, a literary agent whose client list reads like my college syllabus, and the editor-in-chief of a prestigious publishing house that's been on my dream collaboration list for years.

"And this," Margaret says, bringing us to a distinguished-looking man with kind eyes, "is James Porter, the author of—"

"'The Silent Hour,'" I finish, unable to contain my excitement. "I'm a huge fan. Your exploration of grief through magical realism was revolutionary."

James Porter looks delighted. "A reader who actually understood what I was going for! Most people just focus on the ghost."

"The ghost is a metaphor," I say earnestly. "For the way memory haunts us long after loss."

"Precisely!" James beams at me. "Margaret, where have you been hiding this delightful young woman?"

"She's Ben's fiancé," Margaret explains proudly, as if taking credit for our match. "And a publisher in herown right."

"You run a publishing house?" James looks even more interested now. "Tell me more."

I launch into an explanation of our small but growing company, the types of authors we represent, and our philosophy about championing unique voices. As I speak, I can feel Ben's gaze on me, warm and… proud? I glance over to find him watching me with an expression I've never seen before—something soft and admiring that makes my cheeks flush.

"You've found yourself quite the partner," James tells Ben with a knowing smile. "Smart, passionate, and she actually understands the Oxford comma. Hold onto this one."

"I intend to," Ben says, his arm holding me tighter, as he places a kiss to my head. When I glance up at him, the warmth in his eyes makes my breath catch. He's a very good actor—almost too good.

The afternoon unfolds in a pleasant blur of introductions, conversations, and surprisingly good champagne. I find myself genuinely enjoying the company of these people who, despite their wealth and status, seem genuinely interested in my work and opinions. Ben stays close to my side, his hand occasionally brushing mine or resting lightly on my back—small touches that feel increasingly natural.

By the time lunch is served—an elegant spread of seafood and summer salads—I've almost forgotten again that this is all pretend. Ben pulls out my chair, his fingers grazing my bare shoulders as I sit. He leans in close to whisper, "You're amazing, you know that?" His breath tickles my ear, sending goosebumps down my neck.

"Just playing my part," I whisper back, though something in me protests the lie.

"It's not playing if it's real," he murmurs, taking his seat beside me. "They're enchanted by you. Especially James Porter—I think he's ready to dump his publisher for you."

I laugh, the sound light and genuine. "That would be quite the coup."

"You deserve it," Ben says, his eyes meeting mine with unexpected intensity. "You're brilliant at what you do."

There's a moment—just a heartbeat really—where the rest of the party fades away, and it's just us, looking at each other with something unspoken hanging in the air between us.

"Ah, young love," Richard's voice breaks the spell as he takes his seat at the head of the table. "Margaret and I were just like you two once—couldn't take our eyes off each other, even in a crowded room."

"Still can't," Margaret says with a wink, taking her place beside him. "Now, let's enjoy this beautiful meal before the afternoon activities begin."

"Activities?" I ask, reaching for my water glass to hide my sudden nervousness.

"Nothing too strenuous," Margaret assures me. "Boating for those who want it, a wine tasting in the garden, and the pool is always available. This evening we'll have cocktails followed by a slightly more formal dinner."

"Sounds lovely," I say, relieved that there's no mandatory croquet tournament or whatever rich people do at lake houses.

Lunch is a leisurely affair, full of witty conversation and subtle name-dropping. I find myself seated between Ben and James Porter, who peppers me with questions about my publishing philosophy and the authors I admire. Ben watches our exchange with that same warm expression, occasionally joining in but mostly letting me take center stage.

"Your fiancé is quite the literary mind," James tells Ben as dessert is served—some kind of deconstructed strawberry shortcake that looks too pretty to eat.

"I'm well aware," Ben replies, his eyes meeting mine with genuine warmth. "It's one of the many things I love about her."

The word 'love' sends a jolt through me, even though I know it's part of our act. He says it so convincingly, with such soft sincerity, that for a moment I almost believe it myself.

After lunch, the party disperses for the afternoon activities. Some guests head for the boats, others to the pool, while a small group follows Richard to the wine cellar for a tasting.

"What would you like to do?" Ben asks as we linger on the terrace, his voice low and private.

I glance toward the sparkling lake, then back at Ben. "I packed a swimsuit, but." I say trailing off, afraid to reveal the super daring two-piece Maci made me buy.

"But what?" Ben's eyes are curious, a hint of playfulness in them I've rarely seen.

"But it might be a bit… daring for a garden party," I confess, thinking of the cheeky cut and plunging neckline Maci had insisted was "totally lake-appropriate."

Something flashes in Ben's eyes. "Now I'm intrigued."

"Don't be," I say quickly, feeling heat rise to my cheeks. "It's just—Maci convinced me to get something a little outside my comfort zone."

"Ah," Ben nods, his lips quirking up at the corners. "The infamous Maci influence. Well, if it helps, most of the guests will be at the wine tasting for at least an hour. The pool would be relatively private."

I consider this, glancing at the crystal blue pool visible from the terrace. It does look inviting, and the afternoon sun is warm on my skin. "Alright," I decide. "Swimming it is."

Back in our room, I grab my swimsuit and head to the bathroom to change, suddenly self-conscious. The black swimsuit is far more revealing than anything I'd normally wear—high-cut bottoms that make my legs look endless and a top that showcases more cleavage than I'm used to displaying in public.

"You can do this," I mutter to my reflection, adjusting the straps one last time. "It's just a swimsuit."

I wrap a fluffy white towel around myself before stepping back into the bedroom. Ben has already changed into navy swim trunks that sit low on his hips, revealing a body that makes my mouth go dry. He's all lean muscle and smooth skin, and I have to force myself not to stare at his chest or the defined

V disappearing into his waistband.

"Ready?" he asks, and I realize I've been standing frozen for several seconds.

"Let's go!" I reply, maybe a bit too enthusiastically clutching my towel a little tighter.

We make our way down to the pool area, which is mercifully empty except for a young staff member arranging fresh towels on the lounge chairs.

"Can I get you anything to drink?" he asks politely. "Perhaps some iced tea or lemonade?"

"Lemonade would be wonderful," I reply, still holding my towel like a shield.

"Two, please," Ben adds, settling into one of the lounge chairs. The attendant nods and disappears, leaving us alone by the shimmering water.

"Are you planning to swim in the towel?" Ben asks, amusement dancing in his eyes.

I narrow my eyes at him. "I'm working up to it."

"I could close my eyes if that would help," he offers, though he makes no move to do so.

"That won't be necessary," I say with more confidence than I feel. With a deep breath, I drop the towel onto a nearby chair.

Ben's reaction is immediate and visceral. His eyes widen, his lips part slightly, and a flush creeps up his neck. For a moment, he seems completely speechless.

"You look…" he starts, then clears his throat. "That's definitely not what I was expecting."

I shift uncomfortably under his gaze. "Too much?"

"No," he says quickly, his voice rougher than usual. "Not at all. You look incredible."

The sincerity in his voice makes my stomach flip. I dive into the pool before he can see the blush spreading across my cheeks, the cool water a welcome relief against my heated skin.

"Are you coming in?" I call, pushing wet hair from my face. "Or are you just going to stare?"

That seems to snap him out of his daze. With a small smile, he slides into the water in one smooth motion, barely making a splash. Show-off.

The pool is perfect—just cool enough to be refreshing without being cold. We swim lazy laps for a while, keeping a careful distance from each other. I'm hyperaware of Ben's presence, of the way water droplets cling to his shoulders when he pauses at the edge of the pool, of how his wet hair falls across his forehead in a way that makes him look younger, less guarded.

"Hey, are you okay?" I ask, noticing his far-off look.

He blinks, seeming to come back to himself. "Yeah, I'm fine. Just thinking."

"About?"

He hesitates, then swims closer until we're both treading water in the deep end, face to face. "About how I've always hated these things. I've been coming for some time to these at my father's insistence," He practically spits the word father. "But, with you, it's a lot of fun."

The sincerity in his voice catches me off guard. I've never heard Ben speak so candidly about his father before.

"Your father made you come to these parties?" I ask gently, moving a bit closer in the water.

Ben's expression darkens slightly. "Not explicitly. But there was always an expectation that I would… network. Make connections. Prove my worth." The bitterness in his voice is unmistakable.

"That sounds exhausting," I say, resisting the urge to reach out and touch him.

"It was." His eyes meet mine, vulnerability evident in their gray depths. "Is. But having you here… it changes things. Makes it feel less like an obligation and more like…"

"Like what?" I prompt when he trails off.

"Like something I might actually enjoy," he finishes, a small smile playing at his lips.

"Your father," I begin hesitantly. "Eli mentioned he's… difficult."

Ben's expression clouds slightly. "That's one word for it. 'Impossible' would be another. 'Perpetually disappointed' would be the most accurate."

"I'm sorry," I say, genuinely meaning it. "That must be hard."

"It is what it is," he says with a shrug that doesn't quite achieve the casualness he's aiming for. "He'd parade me around like a show pony at these kind of events, then criticize everything I said or did on the drive home."

"He sounds charming," I say dryly, trying to lighten the mood.

Ben's lips quirk up slightly. "A real delight. The kind of man who points out your failures over breakfast so you have all day to think about them."

My heart twists at the image of a younger Ben, trying desperately to please an impossible father. "Is he… still in the picture?"

"Technically," Ben says, pushing wet hair from his forehead. "He's semi-retired in Florida. We speak on holidays and when he wants to critique my investment strategies."

"Hence the Murphy account pressure," I say, understanding dawning. "You want to prove him wrong."

Ben looks surprised, as if he hadn't expected me to make the connection. "I guess I do." He looks so defeated speaking about his father, I have the sudden urge to comfort him. I reach my arms around his neck, drawing him in for a tight hug.

For a moment, Ben stiffens in surprise. Then his arms wrap around my waist, pulling me closer in the water. We stay like that for several heartbeats, my cheek against his bare shoulder, his hands warm on my back despite the cool water.

"I'm sorry," I whisper against his skin. "Your father sounds like an ass."

Ben chuckles, the sound rumbling through his chest where it's pressed against mine. "He is." He pulls back slightly to look at me, his eyes softer than I've ever seen them. "Thank you."

"For what?" I ask, suddenly aware of how close we are, of his hands still resting on my waist beneath the water.

"For listening," he says simply. "For understanding. For not being impressed by any of this." He gestures vaguely at our surroundings with one hand before returning it to my waist.

"Well, the house is pretty impressive," I admit with a small smile. "But I get what you mean."

His eyes search mine, something unspoken passing between us. For a moment, I think he might kiss me—right here in this borrowed pool, surrounded by borrowed luxury. His gaze drops to my lips, and I feel myself leaning in almost involuntarily.

"Lemonade for the happy couple!" The cheerful voice of the attendant shatters the moment. We spring apart like guilty teenagers, both of us turning to see the young man setting two tall glasses on a nearby table.

"Thank you," Ben says, his voice slightly hoarse. He clears his throat. "We'll be right there."

The attendant nods and retreats, leaving us alone again but with the spell decidedly broken. I swim to the edge of the pool and pull myself out, hyperaware of Ben's eyes on me as water streams from my body.

"We should probably get ready for dinner soon," I say, wrapping a towel around my waist. "I imagine these things require extensive preparation."

"Not for another couple of hours," Ben says, following me out of the pool. Water droplets cling to his chest and shoulders, making him look like something from a cologne advertisement. "But we could head back to the room if you want to rest before tonight."

The thought of being alone with Ben in our suite, with that massive bed between us, sends a flutter through my stomach. "Sure," I say, trying to sound casual. "A nap sounds good."

We gather our things and head back to the east wing, passing a few guests returning from the wine tasting on our way. They nod politely, though I catch a few curious glances at our wet hair and swimwear.

Nineteen

The Fiction Falls Apart

Once back in our suite, an awkward silence falls between us. The intimacy of the pool seems both very close and very far away.

"You can shower first," Ben offers, gesturing toward the bathroom.

"Thanks," I mutter, grabbing my toiletry bag and a change of clothes. The bathroom is as luxurious as the rest of the house—marble countertops, a rainfall shower big enough for four people, and fluffy towels that feel like clouds. I take my time, letting the hot water wash away chlorine and nervous energy alike. When I finally emerge, wrapped in a plush robe with my hair in a towel, I find Ben on the balcony, still in his swim trunks, phone in hand.

"All yours," I say, gesturing toward the bathroom.

He turns, his eyes lingering on me for a moment longer than necessary. "Thanks," he says, setting his phone aside. As he passes me, our shoulders brush, sending an electric current through my body despite the layers of terry cloth between us.

While Ben showers, I blow-dry my hair and apply a light layer of makeup. The formal dinner tonight calls for something more polished than my daytime look, but I'm careful not to overdo it. I want to look like I belong here without seeming like I'm trying too hard.

Still in my little robe, with lingerie the only thing on underneath, I freeze as the door to the bathroom opens and out comes Ben dressed in dark blue jeans, and a tight gray tee.

His hair is still damp, curling slightly at the ends in a way I've never seen before. The t-shirt clings to his chest, revealing the muscles I'd been admiring in the pool. I suddenly feel very exposed in just my robe.

"I thought you might want to nap," he says, his voice soft as his eyes meet mine. "Since we have a couple hours before dinner."

"Right," I say, clutching my robe tighter. "A nap."

But neither of us moves toward the bed. Instead, we stand there, the air between us charged with something I'm afraid to name. He hesitates for a moment, then gently grabs my hand, pulling me towards him.

I hold my breath as his fingers trace up my arm, leaving goosebumps in their wake. His eyes are dark, questioning, giving me every opportunity to pull away. But I don't want to. For the first time since this fake engagement began, I let myself admit how much I want this to be real.

"Lexie," he whispers, his voice rough with something that sounds like desire. "I need to tell you something."

My heart hammers against my ribs. "What is it?"

"This weekend... I don't want to pretend anymore."

I freeze, unsure what he means. "You want to call it off?

Now?"

"No," he says quickly, his hand moving to cup my cheek. "I mean I don't want to pretend that I don't feel something for you. Something real."

For a heartbeat, I'm completely still, as if stunned by his boldness. Then I come alive, my arms wrap around his shoulders to pull me flush against him. His lips are soft but insistent as our lips meet passionately, the kiss deepening as his tongue traces the seam of my mouth, asking for permission I gladly give.

I melt into him, my hands sliding up his chest to tangle in his damp hair. He makes a sound low in his throat—half groan, half sigh—that sends heat pooling in my belly. The world narrows to just this: his mouth on mine, his hands spanning my waist, the solid warmth of his body against me.

"Tell me to stop," He says, clearly struggling to compose himself.

"Hell no, you better not stop Mr. Maddox."

He groans, pulling me even closer, his hands sliding down to cup my ass through the thin material of the robe. I gasp against his mouth as he lifts me effortlessly, my legs wrapping around his waist as he carries me toward the bed.

"Are you sure?" he asks, his breathing ragged as he lowers me onto the mattress. "We can stop—"

"If you stop now, I might actually kill you," I warn, reaching for the hem of his t-shirt.

Ben laughs, a warm, genuine sound that makes my heart flutter. He pulls the shirt over his head in one smooth motion, revealing the full expanse of his chest that I'd been admiring at the pool. I reach up to trace my fingers along his collarbone, down to the defined muscles of his abdomen. His hand finds the tie of my robe, hesitating. "May I?"

I nod, my breath catching as he slowly undoes the knot, pushing the sides of the robe open with agonizing deliberation. His sharp intake of breath when he sees the lacy lingerie underneath sends a thrill through me.

"Christ, Lexie," he breathes, his eyes roaming over me with undisguised hunger. "You're going to be the death of me."

"That was the plan," I say, trying for humor even as desire makes my voice shake. "Maci's idea, actually."

"Remind me to send her a thank you card," he says, tracing the edge of the lace with one finger. The touch is featherlight but sends electricity coursing through my veins.

"Less talking," I demand, pulling him back down to me. "More kissing."

He obliges, his mouth hot and demanding against mine. His hand skims up my side, thumb brushing the underside of my breast in a way that makes me arch into his touch. When his lips leave mine to trail down my neck, I moan softly, my fingers digging into his shoulders.

"I've wanted this," he confesses against my skin, "for so long."

"Me too," I admit, the truth finally spilling out. "Even when I was furious with you."

"Especially then," he agrees with a low chuckle. "You're magnificent when you're angry."

"I'm about to get very angry if you don't—" My words dissolve into a gasp as his mouth finds my breast through the lace, teeth grazing my nipple just enough to send sparks shooting through me.

His hands are everywhere—tracing the curve of my waist, gripping my thigh, sliding beneath the lace to find the heat between my legs. I'm lost in sensation, in the feel of his weight above me, in the taste of his skin as I explore his chest with eager hands.

"Ben," I gasp as his fingers find exactly the right spot, teasing through damp lace. "Please…"

He understands immediately, shifting to rid himself of his jeans while I wiggle out of my lingerie. There's a moment of perfect stillness as we take each other in, completely bare for the first time. His eyes darken as they roam over me, making me feel more beautiful, more desired than I've ever felt before.

"You're incredible," he murmurs, lowering himself back to me. The feel of his skin against mine, nothing between us, is intoxicating.

His kisses turn deeper, more urgent as his hand slips between my thighs again, fingers teasing and stroking until I'm writhing beneath him, desperate for more. When he finally positions himself between my legs, he pauses, his eyes finding mine.

"Are you sure?" he asks one last time, his voice strained with the effort of holding back.

"I've never been more sure of anything," I tell him, and it's the truth.

The feeling of him pushing inside me draws a moan from both of us. He moves slowly at first, giving me time to adjust, his forehead pressed against mine. But as the tension builds, our movements become more frantic, more desperate. His hands grip my hips, angling me to take him deeper, and I wrap my legs around him, urging him on.

"Lexie," he groans against my neck, the sound of my name on his lips pushing me closer to the edge. "God, you feel amazing."

I can't form coherent words, just broken gasps and moans as he drives me higher. When his hand slides between us to circle my most sensitive spot, the combination of sensations sends me spiraling over the edge. I cry out his name as waves of pleasure crash through me, my body clenching around him.

He follows moments later, his rhythm faltering as he buries his face in my neck, a hoarse groan escaping him as he finds his release.

For several minutes afterward, we lie tangled together, breathing hard, neither willing to break the spell. His weight on me feels right, anchoring me to this perfect moment. Eventually, he shifts to his side, pulling me against his chest, his arm wrapped securely around my waist.

"Well," I say when I finally find my voice, "that wasn't in the contract."

Ben laughs, the sound vibrating through his chest against my back. "I think we've moved well beyond the terms of our original agreement."

I turn in his arms to face him, suddenly serious. "What does this mean? For us?"

He brushes a strand of hair from my face, his eyes soft. "It means I don't want to pretend anymore. Not with you."

"So what do you want?" I ask, my heart racing.

"You," he says simply. "Not just for sex. Not for the Murphy's. Not for pretend." His thumb traces my lower lip, his expression earnest. "I want all of you, Lexie. The real you. The one who trips over her own feet and makes inappropriate jokes and challenges me at every turn."

My heart feels like it might burst. "Even when I drive you crazy?"

"Especially then," he says with a smile that makes my toes curl. "I think I've been falling for you since that first day by the elevator when you took a wrecking ball to my corporate world."

I laugh, remembering the outrage on his face. "You looked so offended."

"I was," he admits, pulling me closer. "No one had ever spoken to me like that before. It was… refreshing. Terrifying, but refreshing."

"So what now?" I ask, tracing patterns on his chest with my fingertip. "We just… date for real? While pretending to be engaged?"

"Why not?" He asks. "At least we won't be pretending about our feelings."

"That's actually… perfect," I say, the idea growing on me. "We get to figure this out without any pressure."

Ben's fingers trace lazy patterns on my bare shoulder. "Well, maybe a little pressure. We're still technically here to convince the Murphy's."

"I think we're doing a pretty convincing job," I murmur, pressing a kiss to his chest.

"Mmm, very convincing," he agrees, his hand sliding down my back. "Though we might need more practice."

I laugh, swatting his chest playfully. "We have dinner in—" I glance at the bedside clock and gasp, "—an hour! I need to get ready!"

Ben groans but releases me, watching appreciatively as I scramble naked from the bed. "Fine, but we're continuing this conversation later."

"Is that what we're calling it? A conversation?" I tease, gathering my clothes.

"Among other things," he says with a wicked grin that sends heat flooding through me all over again.

Getting ready for dinner becomes a delightful challenge with Ben constantly finding excuses to touch me—a kiss on my shoulder as I apply makeup, his hands on my waist as I zip my dress, his fingers threading through mine as we make final adjustments in the mirror.

"We're going to be late," I warn, though I make no effort to move away from his embrace.

"Worth it," he murmurs against my neck. "You look stunning, by the way."

I smooth down the front of my navy cocktail dress, a simple but elegant design that Maci insisted was "dinner party perfect." "You clean up pretty well yourself," I tell him, admiring his crisp white shirt and tailored slacks.

"Ready to dazzle the literary elite?" Ben asks, offering his arm with exaggerated formality.

"Yes, sir, I am," I reply, linking my arm through his.

The evening passes in a blur of exquisite food, flowing wine, and surprisingly engaging conversation. With the weight of pretense lifted from my shoulders, I find myself genuinely enjoying the company of the Murphy's and their guests. Ben stays close to my side, his hand often finding mine under the table, his eyes meeting mine with secret smiles that make my heart race.

"So tell me," James Porter asks over dessert, "how did you two meet? I'm always collecting stories for my characters."

Ben and I exchange glances, a silent communication passing between us.

"We work in the same building," I begin, deciding to stick close to the truth. "I own the publishing company on the third floor."

"And I thought she was the most infuriating woman I'd ever met," Ben adds with a fond smile.

"The feeling was mutual," I assure everyone, earning a round of laughter.

"Love and hate," James nods sagely. "Such close emotions, really. The best romances often start that way."

The Calm After The Storm

After returning from a romantic weekend getaway, something shifts between Ben and me. Where before we were pretending to show affection, now, we can't stay away from each other stealing kisses in the elevator, having impromptu sex sessions in his office.

One Tuesday afternoon, I'm sitting at my desk reviewing a manuscript when my office door flies open. Angel marches in, her usual cool demeanor replaced with something that looks suspiciously like panic.

"You need to fix him," she announces without preamble.

I blink up at her, momentarily confused. "Fix who?"

"Ben," she says, as if it should be obvious. "He's been impossible all morning. He made an intern want to quit, snapped at a client, and just threw his coffee mug against the wall."

"And this concerns me because…?" I ask, though my heart

rate picks up at the thought of Ben in distress.

Angel gives me a look that could wither plants. "Because you're the only one who can calm him down when he gets like this. Something about his father calling this morning."

My stomach drops. Ben has mentioned his father exactly twice since our weekend at the lake house three weeks ago—both times with a tension in his voice that made me change the subject.

"Where is he now?" I ask, already standing and smoothing my skirt.

"His office. Door locked. Blinds closed." Angel's perfect posture slumps slightly. "Please help. The entire office is walking on eggshells."

I nod, grabbing my phone. "I'll see what I can do."

The walk to Ben's office feels longer than usual. When I arrive, his office is eerily quiet, with staff members hunched over their desks, speaking in hushed tones. Eli spots me from the conference room and hurries over.

"Thank god you're here," he says, relief evident in his voice. "It's bad, Lexie."

"What happened?" I ask, keeping my voice low.

"His father called. Something about the Murphy account. I didn't hear everything, but there was a lot of shouting from Ben's end, which never happens." Eli runs a hand through his hair. "Then the coffee mug incident, and he's been locked in there ever since."

I take a deep breath, steeling myself. "I'll handle it."

Eli squeezes my arm gratefully. "Good luck."

I approach Ben's office door and knock softly. "Ben? It's me."

No response.

"Ben, please open the door."

Silence stretches for so long I think he's going to ignore me. Then I hear movement, and the lock clicks. The door opens just enough for me to slip inside before Ben closes and locks it again.

His office looks like a tornado hit it—papers scattered across the floor, a dark coffee stain dripping down one wall, his normally immaculate desk in disarray. But it's Ben himself who makes my heart clench. He looks wrecked—tie loosened, hair standing up in all directions from where he's clearly been running his hands through it, a wildness in his eyes I've never seen before.

"Hey," I say softly, approaching him like I might a wounded animal. "What happened?"

He turns away, moving to the window though the blinds are drawn. "Nothing that concerns you."

Nothing that concerns me? Boy is tripping. "Excuse me," I say irritated and a little hurt by his tone.

For a moment, I consider turning around and walking right back out the door. But something in the tense line of his shoulders stops me.

"Bullshit," I say, crossing my arms. "I'm your fiancé, remember? Even if it's fake, I'm still your—" I hesitate, not sure what to call myself. Girlfriend feels too casual, lover too intimate. "I'm still someone who cares about you."

Ben's shoulders slump, the anger seeming to drain from him. "It's my father," he admits, still not turning to face me. "He heard about the Murphy account. Said I was 'lucky' to land it."

I move closer, stopping just behind him. "Lucky? You've been working on that account for months."

"Exactly." His voice is tight with suppressed emotion. "According to him, there's no way I could have secured it on my own merits. Must have been my 'connections' or 'dumb luck.'"

"That's ridiculous," I say, anger flaring on his behalf. "You're brilliant at what you do."

He laughs, the sound harsh and empty. "Not according to William Maddox. In his world, I'm still the disappointing son who'll never measure up."

I place a hand on his back, feeling the tension in his muscles. "Ben, look at me."

He turns slowly, his gray eyes stormy with emotion. The vulnerability there makes my chest ache.

"Your father is wrong," I say firmly. "Dead wrong. And I'm not just saying that because we're sleeping together."

A ghost of a smile touches his lips. "No?"

"No. I'm saying it because it's true." I take his face in my hands, forcing him to meet my eyes. "You're smart, dedicated, and damn good at your job. The Murphy's chose you because you're the best, not because of luck."

Something in his expression softens, the storm in his eyes receding slightly. "How do you always know exactly what to say?"

"It's a gift," I shrug, offering a small smile. "Also, I just tell the truth."

He pulls me against him then, burying his face in my hair. I wrap my arms around his waist, holding him tight as he takes deep, shuddering breaths.

"I'm sorry," he murmurs after a long moment. "For the mess. For snapping at you."

"You'll make it up to me," I assure him, pulling back to look at his face. "Starting with apologizing to that poor intern you traumatized."

He winces. "Was it that bad?"

"Angel says you made them want to quit."Ben groans, running a hand down his face. "I'll apologize. And send them flowers or something."

"And coffee for Angel," I add. "She's the one who came to get me, you know."

His eyebrows shoot up in surprise. "Angel? Ice Queen Angel actually sought you out?"

"Turns out she does have feelings," I say with a small smile. "Mainly terror, but still."

Ben laughs, the sound more genuine this time. He pulls me closer, his forehead resting against mine. "Thank you," he whispers. "For coming. For knowing what to say."

"Always," I reply, the word carrying more weight than I intended.

His eyes search mine, something vulnerable still lingering there. "I've never told anyone how much my father gets to me. Not even Eli. It's... embarrassing."

"There's nothing embarrassing about being hurt by someone who's supposed to love you unconditionally," I say, running my fingers through his disheveled hair, trying to smooth it down. "Parents have a special power to wound us."

"Voice of experience?" he asks gently.

I nod, thinking of my own complicated relationship with my mother. "My mom had very specific ideas about what success looked like. Let's just say becoming a writer wasn't on her approved career list."

"What did she want you to be?" Ben asks, his thumb tracing circles on my lower back.

"A lawyer, like her." I shrug. "We didn't speak for almost a year after I dropped out of college to pursue writing."

"I didn't know you went to college," Ben says, looking

genuinely surprised.

"For exactly one semester," I confirm. "Long enough to know I'd be miserable doing it for the rest of my life."

"And now?" he asks. "Are you and your mother…?"

"Better," I say. "Not perfect, but better. She came around when my first book was published. Even bragged to her friends about her 'author daughter.'" I smile at the memory. "Parents are complicated."

"That's an understatement," Ben mutters, but some of the tension has left his body. He glances around at the chaos of his office and sighs. "I should clean this up."

"We should clean this up," I correct him, already bending to gather papers from the floor. "And then you're going to apologize to your staff and take the rest of the day off."

"I can't just leave," he protests. "I have meetings—"

"That Eli can handle," I interrupt. "Trust me, everyone will be relieved to see you go. You're kind of terrifying when you're angry."

"I'm not—" he begins, then stops at my raised eyebrow. "Fine. Maybe a little terrifying."

We spend the next fifteen minutes restoring order to his office, working in comfortable silence. When we finish, Ben looks more like himself—still tired. "Come on, let's get out of here. We can have a sleep over at my place." I say, hoping to inspire a better mood. It does the trick if the devilish smirk that crosses his face is any indication.

We spend the rest of the night holed up in my apartment with takeout, wine, and movies. I can't think of a better way to spend my evening.

Twenty-One

The Breaking Point

July turns into August, and before we know it, it's almost Labor Day. Ben and I have fallen into a routine centered around each other. One Friday afternoon, Zephyr stops by the office to go over edits for his upcoming release. We do our normal routine including smoking his version of "inspiration." Once we are finished, he bids me goodbye and his on his way out the door.

I rush out not long after. As I take the down elevator, I already have my phone out ordering an Uber to get me to the fancy yacht party Ben wants me to attend. As I settle into the backseat, scrolling aimlessly on my phone, I see Ben, my Ben tagged in a photo. No, I did not know Vanessa would be there or that they would be smiling in a picture together. Sure, there are other people in the picture, but seeing her anywhere near him sends me into a bit of a tailspin. It feels as though I've been punched in the gut, the world around me starts to spin and I don't know if it's from the pot or the revelation that Ben is hanging with

Vanessa. I try to remain mature about this, obviously she's a daughter of a big client and he has to remain friendly. Once we arrive at the marina, I have all but pushed the doubts out of my mind, putting on a smile, I get out of the car and set off to find Ben.

I spot him standing off to the side, Vanessa close beside him, her laughter bubbling up like champagne. The two are absorbed in conversation with one another. I maneuver through the bustling crowd, weaving my way past clusters of people engaged in their own animated discussions. My heart races with anticipation as I edge closer, careful to appear casual and not like an eavesdropper. The murmur of their voices mingles with the surrounding chatter, and I strain to catch snippets of their exchange without drawing attention to myself.

"You know, Benji. You could do so much better than a little writer. What does your dad think about this arrangement anyway? I can't imagine he is thrilled with you stooping so low." Vanessa leers goading him intentionally. I wait a beat, then two, hoping he will defend me, but the moment doesn't come. I feel my eyes well up as I turn and dart away before anyone notices me, jumping into the first cab I see.

I barely recall the drive back to the office, my mind swirling with a relentless storm of painful thoughts, each one taunting me for my foolishness. The cityscape outside blurred into a haze, a backdrop for the turmoil within.

Nearly twenty minutes later, I stagger into the office, my senses dulled and unfocused. I clumsily bump into Maci, Eli, and Angel, who are gathered near the entrance of our cozy workspace. Their presence, unexpected and solid, jolts me back to the present, a stark contrast to the chaotic whirlpool in my head.

"Lexie? Are you okay?" Maci asks, her brow furrowing as she takes in my unsteady stance.

"What are you three doing together?" I ask, my words slurring slightly. I narrow my eyes at Angel, who looks decidedly uncomfortable. "And why are you in my office?"

"We were discussing the Halloween party," Maci explains, exchanging a concerned glance with Eli. "Angel's helping with the guest list since Ben's clients will be invited."

"Ben," I repeat, the name feeling strange on my tongue. I hold up my phone, showing them the photo that's currently ripping my heart out. "Look at this."

Maci takes my phone, the three of them huddling around it. Eli's eyebrows shoot up, and Angel's lips press into a thin line.

"It's just a client event, Lexie," Eli says carefully. "Those photos are for social media promotion."

"Yes, that's what I told myself too," I say fighting to keep my tone light. "However, when I got there, Ben and Vanessa were over to the side talking shit about me."

"You smell like weed," Angel observes, wrinkling her nose. "Have you been smoking?"

"Zephyr was here," Maci explains quickly. "Author meeting."

Eli looks horrified on Ben's behalf. "Lex, I don't know what happened, but I know he cares-"

"-Save it Eli," I say on the verge of tears 2.0. "I can't do this anymore."

Maci's arms are around me in an instant, guiding me toward my office. "Come on, let's get you some water and talk about this."

I let her lead me, my legs feeling disconnected from my body. Everything feels surreal—the fluorescent lights too bright, the sounds too sharp. Between the lingering effects of Zephyr's "inspiration" and the emotional whiplash, I'm barely holding it together.

"I'll go find Ben," Eli says, already backing toward the elevator.

"Don't you dare," I warn, my voice brittle. "I mean it, Eli. Stay out of this."

Eli hesitates, clearly torn between loyalties. "Lexie, there has to be—"

"There isn't," I snap. "I heard what I heard."

Angel, who's been uncharacteristically quiet, clears her throat. "I'll go back to the office. Tell Ben you weren't feeling well if he asks."

"Angel, I will be bringing over a letter for Ben, will you make sure he gets it?" I ask, already coming up with how I'm going to handle it. "Then, I'm taking the week off, getting out of town. I need to clear my hear-I need. I just need to go for a few days."

Maci nods her head in understanding. She knows when things get tough, I like to isolate myself. I need to take care of me.

Angel nods, a flicker of what might be sympathy crossing her normally impassive face. "Of course."

Once they've gone, Maci closes my office door and guides me to the couch. "Okay, talk to me. What exactly did you hear?"

I sink into the cushions, kicking off my heels and pulling my knees to my chest. "She called me 'a little writer' and asked what his dad would think of our 'arrangement.' And he just… stood there. Didn't say anything."

"I'm sorry, Lex." She says, sympathy coloring her tone. "I know you really care for him. Some men don't know what they've got until it's going."

I nod, unable to say more as I pull out a pen and paper and begin to write. -

Ben,

While I have enjoyed the fancy dinners, the weekend getaways, and the general excitement of your lavish lifestyle, your life is not one where I belong. I cannot do this anymore; this is taking too much of a toll on my life, my emotions, my wellbeing. Tell your clients whatever you need to, but I am done. I wish you the best in your business and future endeavors, but our arrangement ends now.

Best,

Alexandria Phillips

I wrap up the ring carefully in tissue paper and fold the note closed. After delivering it to Angel who assures me Ben will get it.

"Where are you going?" Angel asks, thrown off her game by my sudden personality change.

"Don't know." I say, shrugging my shoulders. "I'll see what plane is going where when I get there. That will be a problem for airport Lexie."

I have a tendency to run and retreat into myself when things get tough. This is one of those times. Maci knows I need this, to get away and hide, so she doesn't push back though the look of concern on her face speaks volumes.

"Lexie, wait," Eli steps forward, his expression serious. "Think about this. Ben will be worried sick."

"Will he?" I ask, my voice sounding distant even to my own ears. "Or will he be too busy with Vanessa to notice I'm gone?"

"Of course he'll notice," Maci says firmly. "But if you need space, I understand." She squeezes my arm. "Just… don't do any irrational, okay?"

"When have you known me to be irrational?" I ask, slightly offended.

The three of them stare at me blankly.

"The burning man festival? The time you jumped off that cliff in Mexico? The time you slept with the Elvis impersonator?" Maci lists, counting on her fingers.

"That involved tequila," I wave dismissively. "And the cliff wasn't that high."

"It was forty feet!" Maci exclaims.

"Details," I mutter, grabbing my purse from my office. "I'll text you when I land somewhere. Don't tell Ben where I am."

"Lexie—" Eli starts, but I'm already heading for the elevator.

"Don't worry," I call over my shoulder. "I'll be back before anyone even notices I'm gone."

Two hours later, I'm at O'Hare with a small carry-on I hastily packed from the emergency clothes I keep at the office- don't ask why I have those. I'm still slightly high, but the panic has been replaced by a strange, detached calm. This is what I do when emotions get too intense—I run. I've always run. It's easier than facing the possibility that I might have misread things with Ben, that what felt real to me might be another performance for him.

I stare at the departure board, letting fate decide my destination. My eyes land on a flight to Vegas leaving in an hour with seats still available. Perfect. Sunshine, debauchery, and enough distance to clear my head.

Twenty-Two

The Fallout

Ben's POV

"What does your father think about this arrangement anyway? I can't imagine he is thrilled with you stooping so low." Vanessa's voice drips with disdain, her eyes narrowing like a predator sizing up its prey. I stare at her, a surge of incredulity washing over me as I wonder how I ever got entangled with someone so venomous. Her words hang in the air, sharp and cutting, leaving me momentarily speechless. This girl just doesn't get it. Finally, I muster a response, my voice steady and resolute. "My personal life is none of your business, but I will let you in on a little secret anyway. Lexie is the most incredible woman I have ever met. She is brilliant, sweet, funny, beautiful; everything that you are not. I thank God every day that I have her in my life instead of a vicious viper like you." My words linger, a stark contrast to the toxic atmosphere she tries to create.

I step back, needing distance from her toxicity. "And for the record, my father's opinion stopped mattering to me the day I met Lexie. She showed me what it means to be valued for who I am, not what I can accomplish."

Vanessa's face contorts with rage. "You can't be serious. She's nobody—"

"She's everything," I cut her off, my voice firm but controlled. "Now if you'll excuse me, I need to find my fiancé."

I scan the crowd, expecting to see Lexie's familiar figure making her way toward us. The yacht is filling with guests, but there's no sign of her. I check my watch—she should be here by now.

Pulling out my phone, I dial her number. It rings several times before going to voicemail. "Hey, it's me. Just wondering where you are. Call me when you get this."

Something doesn't feel right. Lexie is usually punctual, especially for events she knows are important to me. I send a quick text, then make my way to the entrance of the marina, hoping to spot her arrival.

After twenty minutes of waiting and three more unanswered calls, worry gnaws at me. This isn't like her. I flag down the event coordinator.

"I need to step out for a bit. Family emergency," I explain, already heading toward my car.

The drive to the office feels interminable. Traffic crawls, and each red light seems deliberately positioned to delay me. When I finally arrive, the main office is quiet, but I spot Maci at her desk, typing furiously with a thunderous expression.

"Have you seen Lexie?" I ask, loosening my tie. "She was supposed to meet me at the marina."

Maci looks up, her eyes narrowing. "No idea."

Her tone is cold, setting off alarm bells. "Did something happen?"

"You tell me," she says cryptically, returning to her typing with unnecessary force.

A knot forms in my stomach as I head back to my own office. Angel won't even look at me while Eli gives me a look that could freeze the sun. "You have a package on your desk that requires you immediate attention." Angel tosses over her shoulder flatly as she walks to the door, Eli just shakes his head, walking back to his own office shutting the door a bit firmer than usual. I'm left dumfounded.

When I walk into my office, my eyes immediately land on a small package on my desk. The knot in my stomach tightens as I approach it cautiously, as if it might explode. With trembling fingers, I unwrap the tissue paper to find Lexie's engagement ring nestled inside, along with a folded note.

My heart plummets as I read her words. Each sentence feels like a physical blow, knocking the air from my lungs. I have to read it three times before the reality sinks in—she's gone. She's ended our arrangement. And based on Maci and Eli's reactions, I'm at fault.

"No," I whisper, grabbing my phone to call her again. Straight to voicemail. "Dammit, Lexie!"

I burst out of my office, startling Angel who's gathering her things to leave. "Where is she?" I demand, my voice harsher than intended.

Angel's expression remains carefully neutral. "I don't know, Mr. Maddox."

"Bullshit," I snap, running a hand through my hair. "Something happened. What was it?"

For a moment, I think she won't answer. Then her professional mask slips slightly. "It turns out you can't have your cake and eat it too." She explains with cold detachment.

"I don't know what that means, Angel."

"It means, that you should not be taking cutesy pictures with your ex. You should not be talking over in the corner away from everyone with your ex. You should not treat my best friend as a disposable accessory you can remove whenever you itch needs to be scratched." Maci says coming up behind me, vitriol in her words.

The color drains from my face as I realize what she's saying. "Lexie was at the marina? She saw me with Vanessa?"

"Bingo, got it in one" Maci snaps, crossing her arms. "And she heard enough to know exactly where she stands with you."

"No, no, no," I say, panic rising in my chest. "She misunderstood. Vanessa approached me. I was telling her to back off."

"Well, Lexie didn't hear that part," Maci says coldly. "All she heard was Vanessa insulting her and you saying nothing in her defense."

My mind races, trying to piece together what happened. "I did defend her! I told Vanessa my personal life was none of her business and that I'm happier with Lexie than I've ever been."

"Too little, too late," Maci says coldly. "Even if you did defend her, you should have never been even close to Vanessa. Much less letting her take pictures with you and post it all over the internet."

"That picture was for the company's social media page," I explain, my voice rising with frustration. "All the financial advisors were asked to pose with guests. It wasn't personal!"

"Tell that to Lexie," Maci says, unmoved. "She's gone, Ben. And honestly? I don't blame her."

The reality of the situation hits me like a physical blow. Lexie is gone. She thinks I've betrayed her. And I have no idea where she is.

"Where did she go?" I ask, my voice softer now, almost pleading.

"GONE, Ben." Maci says as if I were slow. "She doesn't want to see you; she wants to be left alone. So, respect her at least one time, and let her put herself first."

"She's a grown woman who can make her own decisions," I say, hating how defensive I sound even to my own ears. "If she wants to run away without giving me a chance to explain, that's her choice."

Maci's eyes narrow dangerously. "And there it is. The real Ben Maddox, ladies and gentlemen. When things get tough, blame Lexie."

Her words hit like a slap. Am I really doing that? Blaming Lexie instead of taking responsibility?

"I didn't mean—" I start, but Maci cuts me off.

"Save it. I have work to do." She turns to leave, then pauses. "You know what your problem is, Ben? You think you're entitled to people sticking around no matter how you treat them."

I watch as Maci storms off, leaving me standing in the middle of the office, completely stunned. The engagement ring feels heavy in my palm, the metal already cooling without Lexie's warmth. How did everything fall apart so quickly?

"You really screwed up," Eli says, appearing at my side. His usual easygoing demeanor is replaced with something harder, more judgmental.

"I need to find her," I say, already pulling out my phone. "I need to explain."

Eli places a hand on my arm, stopping me. "Ben, listen to me. Give her space. She saw something that hurt her deeply, and right now she needs time. Maybe it was a misunderstanding, but she was hurt none the less."

"Time for what?" I demand, frustration making my voice sharper than intended. "Time to convince herself that I don't care about her? Time to disappear completely?"

"You think it's just about the conversation between you and Vanessa. No mention of the cozy picture of the two of you." Angel says, sneer still in place. "If I were Lexie, I would have thrown the damn ring at your head."

I glare at Angel, but I can't deny she has a point. The photo looks bad. If I saw Lexie in a picture like that with another man, I'd be livid.

"I need to fix this," I say, more to myself than to them.

"And how do you plan to do that when you don't even know where she is?" Eli asks, his tone gentler now.

I run a hand through my hair, thinking frantically. "Her apartment. She must have gone home first to pack."

"She didn't," Angel says, examining her perfect manicure. "She went straight to the airport. Apparently, she is prone to running."

"The airport?" My heart sinks further. "So, she could be anywhere."

"That's the point," Eli says, patting my shoulder. "Listen, man. I know you care about her. It's obvious to everyone except maybe her. But Lexie needs space right now."

I pace the length of the hallway, the ring still clutched in my palm. "This is insane. We're adults. We should be able to talk about this."

"Says the man who threw a coffee mug at the wall last month," Angel mutters.

I ignore the jab, pulling out my phone to try Lexie again.

Straight to voicemail, as expected. After the beep, I take a deep breath.

"Lexie, it's me. Please call me back. Whatever you think you heard or saw today, it's not what you think. I—" I hesitate, aware of Eli and Angel watching me. "I need to talk to you. Please."

I hang up, feeling utterly helpless. "I can't just sit here and do nothing."

"Maybe that's exactly what you need to do," Eli suggests. "Give her the weekend. She left hours ago, meaning her plane is somewhere in the air by now and you'll never find her. She'll cool off."

"And if she doesn't?" I ask, hating the vulnerability in my voice.

Neither of them answers, which is answer enough.

Back in my office, I stare at the ring in my palm, the diamond catching the late afternoon sunlight streaming through my window. How did everything fall apart so quickly? Just this morning, Lexie was curled against me in bed, her hair tickling my chin as she mumbled something about needing five more minutes.

"Mr. Maddox?" Angel's voice interrupts my thoughts. She stands in the doorway, her expression softening slightly. "I'm leaving for the day."

I nod absently, still turning the ring over in my fingers.

"For what it's worth," she says, hesitating, "I've never seen you look at anyone the way you look at her."

The comment surprises me enough to look up. "What?"

"Lexie," Angel clarifies. "You're different with her. Better." She shrugs, already retreating. "Just an observation."

After she leaves, I sink back into my chair, Angel's words echoing in my mind. She's right. I am different with Lexie—

more relaxed, more honest, more myself. The thought of losing her permanently makes my chest physically ache.

I try her phone again. Voicemail.

"Lexie, please," I say after the beep, not caring how desperate I sound. "Just tell me where you are. We need to talk about this."

I hang up, knowing it's futile. If Lexie doesn't want to be found, she won't be. Her stubborn streak is a mile wide—it's one of the things I love about her.

Love.

The realization hits me like a physical blow. I love her. Not just care for her, not just want her, but love her—completely, irrationally, inconveniently love her. And I never told her.

The weekend passes in a torturous marathon of unanswered calls, restless sleep, and growing anxiety. By Monday morning, I've left seventeen voicemails, sent twenty-three texts, and shown up at her apartment twice, only to find it empty. I've even resorted to calling Maci, who answered just long enough to tell me to "give Lexie the space she asked for" before hanging up.

I'm a wreck when I arrive at the office, having barely slept or eaten. Eli takes one look at me and whistles low.

"You look like hell," he observes, following me into my office.

"Thanks for the update," I mutter, dropping into my chair. "Any word from her?"

Eli shakes his head. "I did receive a text. She's safe."

"That's something at least," I say, relief mingling with frustration. "Where is she?"

"Don't know," Eli shrugs. "She just said she's safe and taking some time to clear her head."

I press the heels of my hands against my eyes, trying to stave off the headache that's been building since Friday. "This is ridiculous. Instead of talking about it, she just runs off like an immature child."

"Says the man who's been dodging emotional conversations his entire life," Eli points out, settling into the chair across from my desk.

"That's not fair," I protest, though I know he's right. "This is different."

"Because you love her," Eli states simply.

I look up sharply. "How did you—"

"Please," Eli scoffs. "I've known you forever. I've never seen you like this over anyone. Not even Vanessa at your most serious."

I slump back in my chair, exhausted. "It doesn't matter how I feel if she won't even talk to me."

"So what are you going to do about it?" Eli asks, leaning forward. "And don't say 'leave more voicemails,' because that's clearly not working."

I run a hand through my hair, thinking. "I don't know. I've tried everything I can think of."

"Have you?" Eli raises an eyebrow. "Because from where I'm sitting, you've tried the same approach seventeen times. Maybe it's time for something different."

Before I can respond, Angel appears in the doorway. "Mr. Maddox, Mrs. Murphy is on line one. She says it's important."

Perfect. Just what I need right now—to pretend everything's fine for our biggest client.

"I'll take it," I say, reaching for the phone.

Eli stands to leave, but pauses at the door. "Think about what I said. Different approach."

I nod distractedly as I pick up the phone. "Margaret, good

morning. What can I do for you?"

"Ben, darling," Margaret's voice comes through, warm as ever. "I hope I'm not interrupting anything important."

"Not at all," I lie, pinching the bridge of my nose. "What can I help you with?"

"Well, it's about the charity gala next weekend," she says. "Richard and I were so looking forward to seeing you and Lexie there. She's such a delight, and several of our author friends have been asking about her publishing house."

My stomach drops. The charity gala. With everything that's happened, I'd completely forgotten about it.

"Of course," I say smoothly, my mind racing. "We're both looking forward to it."

"Wonderful! And I must tell you, that publishing contact you introduced Lexie to at our lake house? James Porter? He's been singing her praises to everyone who'll listen. Such a talented young woman you've found."

Each compliment feels like a knife twisting in my gut. "Yes, she is."

"Well, I won't keep you. Just wanted to confirm you'll both be attending. Table seven, as usual."

"We wouldn't miss it," I lie, wondering how I'm going to explain Lexie's absence—or worse, how I'm going to admit that my perfect fiancé has left me.

After hanging up, I stare at the phone, Margaret's words echoing in my head. Lexie's success with James Porter, the connections she was making, the doors that were opening for her publishing house—all potentially jeopardized because of my carelessness.

I've screwed up everything.

A knock on my door pulls me from my spiraling thoughts.

Angel stands there with a stack of folders.

"Your ten o'clock canceled," she says, setting the folders on my desk. "And these need your signature by end of day."

I nod absently, still distracted. Angel turns to leave, then hesitates.

"Mr. Maddox? If I may…"

"What is it, Angel?" I ask, not bothering to hide my exhaustion.

"When you care about someone, sometimes you have to show them, not just tell them." She shifts uncomfortably, clearly unused to giving personal advice. "Actions over words."

I blink at her, surprised by both the insight and the fact that it's coming from Angel, of all people.

"Thank you," I say finally. "I'll keep that in mind."

Twenty-Three

The Runaway Fiancé

Lexie's POV

Las Vegas is just what I was looking for—vibrant, noisy, and entirely separate from my everyday life. On the first day, I stroll along the Strip in a daze, trying my luck at penny slots and sipping on complimentary cocktails, steering clear of any thoughts that resemble reality.

By day two, I've settled into a routine – pool in the morning, shopping in the afternoon, and roaming the strip at night. I've made friends with a bachelorette party from Milwaukee who've adopted me as their "honorary bridesmaid." They don't ask why I'm alone or why I sometimes stare at my phone with a wistful expression. They just hand me another cocktail and drag me to another dance floor.

On day three I find myself lounging by the pool when an older gentleman with a British accent takes the seat to my right.

"My dear, are you okay?" He asks, giving me a fatherly look of concern.

"I'm just dandy, thank you." I say giving him my brightest smile before freezing. This is Jerome Bastille, one of the most famous lead singers of one of the most popular 80s bands on the planet.

"Jerome Bastille? From The Fallen Kings?" I sputter, trying not to fangirl too obviously.

He chuckles, the sound warm and rich. "The very same, though I'm surprised someone your age recognizes me without the eyeliner and leather pants."

"My mom was obsessed with your music," I explain, then wince. "Sorry, that probably makes you feel ancient."

"Darling, I am ancient," he says with a self-deprecating smile. "Now, you didn't answer my question. Are you really okay? Because you've been staring at that same page in your book for twenty minutes without turning it."

I glance down at the novel in my lap, realizing he's right. "That obvious, huh?"

"I've spent forty years reading people in crowds. You're running from something." He signals a pool attendant. "Mojito for the lady, scotch neat for me."

"I don't need—"

"Humor an old rock star," he interrupts gently. "Consider it research for my memoir."

I can't help but smile. "Fine. But only if you tell me if Keith Richards is actually immortal."

"Classified information," he says with a wink. "Now, what brings a beautiful young woman to Vegas alone?"

"Oh, I'm just here for work." I lie smoothly. "I'm an author and publisher and am currently looking for inspiration."

Jerome peers at me from over his sunglasses, clearly skeptical of my story. "Oh, inspiration, you say? And does this so-called 'inspiration' have anything to do with whoever has you looking so sad and gloomy?"

"It's complicated," I admit finally.

"Matters of the heart usually are," Jerome says as our drinks arrive. He raises his scotch in a toast. "To complicated love affairs and the magnificent stories they inspire."

I clink my glass against his. "I'm not sure this one has a happy ending."

"The best ones never seem to, right in the middle," he says cryptically. "Tell me about him."

And somehow, sitting by a Vegas pool with a rock legend, I find myself spilling the whole ridiculous story—the fake engagement, the real feelings, the photo with Vanessa. Jerome listens without interrupting, occasionally nodding or raising an eyebrow.

"So you ran," he concludes when I finish.

"I needed space," I correct, though it sounds weak even to my ears. I was scared, anxious, and prone to running after all.

"Space," Jerome repeats thoughtfully. "You know, I once ran from the love of my life. Toured Japan for three months instead of facing what I felt."

"What happened?"

"She married someone else," he says simply. "Biggest regret of my life, and I've snorted cocaine off the Eiffel Tower."

I nearly choke on my mojito. "That's... specific."

"The point is," Jerome continues, patting my hand, "running feels good in the moment. Protective. But feelings follow you, darling. Trust me on that."

"I just don't know if I can trust him," I confess. "Or myself, for that matter."

"Has he tried to contact you?"

"Yes, but I need space." I say feeling the truth in my words.

He nods his understanding. "I get it. I do." He says standing up. "How about you join us tonight at our show? You're about my daughters age and she's in town with me, I believe you two will hit it off well. Then, afterwards we can discuss the memoir of mine."

Whoa. My eyes bug out as I take in his words.

"A memoir? With you?" I stammer, star-struck all over again.

"Don't look so shocked, darling. I've been watching you all afternoon. You have a writer's eyes—observant, questioning. I need someone who can capture my voice, not just the facts." He hands me a VIP pass. "The show starts at nine. My daughter Imogen will meet you at the entrance."

I stare at the laminated badge in my hand, momentarily forgetting all about Ben and Vanessa and my escape from Chicago. "I… this is… thank you."

"Don't thank me yet," Jerome says with a mischievous grin. "Wait until you've heard some of my stories. They'll make your fake engagement drama seem positively tame."

That night, I find myself backstage at one of Vegas's premier venues, sipping champagne with Imogen Bastille, a stunning woman in her early thirties with her father's charismatic presence and none of his weathered edges.

"So you're the runaway fiancé," she says after introductions, eyeing me with amused interest. "Dad told me about your situation. Very rom-com."

I wince. "It sounds ridiculous when you put it that way."

"Most love stories do, from the outside," she shrugs, handing me another flute of champagne. "For what it's worth, I think you're being smart. Take the time you need."

"You don't think I'm overreacting?" I ask, surprised by her support.

"About seeing your man with his ex? Hell no." Imogen leans against the wall, studying me. "But the question isn't whether you're justified in being upset. It's whether he's worth fighting for when you're done being upset."

Her words stick with me through the show—an intimate acoustic set that has the audience hanging on every note. Jerome dedicates a song to "new friends and second chances," looking pointedly in my direction.

After the show, Jerome invites me to a late dinner with the band and a few close friends. The conversation flows easily, and for a few hours, I'm not Lexie-running-from-her-problems. I'm just Lexie, hanging out with rock legends, laughing at outrageous stories, and feeling like perhaps the world isn't ending after all.

It's nearly 2 AM Monday when I pull out my phone and post a picture of myself with the band, and Imogen on Instagram with the caption "When life gives you lemons…:)"

Almost instantly, my phone starts blowing up with notifications. It seems the world is very interested in why I'm hanging out with Jerome Bastille at 2 AM in Vegas. I silence my phone and slip it back into my purse, determined to enjoy the rest of the evening without real-world intrusions.

"So," Jerome says, leaning toward me across the table, "about that memoir. I'm serious, you know. My agent's been after me for years."

"I'd be honored," I say, still not quite believing this is happening. "But I should warn you, I typically publish fiction."

"Perfect," Imogen interjects with a laugh. "Half of Dad's

stories are made up anyway."

"They most certainly are not," Jerome protests, though his eyes twinkle with mischief. "Slightly embellished, perhaps."

The conversation shifts to book details—timeline, structure, approach—and for the first time in days, I feel like myself again. This is what I love—talking about stories, shaping narratives, finding the heart of an experience. By the time we part ways, we've sketched out a rough plan for the memoir and scheduled a proper meeting for Wednesday.

Back in my hotel room, I finally check my phone. Twenty-seven text messages, fourteen missed calls, and an explosion of social media notifications. Most are from Maci, who's clearly seen my Instagram post:

OMG ARE YOU WITH JEROME BASTILLE?? THE Jerome Bastille??? LEXIE ANSWER ME RIGHT NOW How are you casually hanging with rock royalty while I'm stress-eating donuts over our Q3 projections??

I smile, typing back a quick response: Long story. Might have landed us a huge book deal. Will explain when I'm back.

There are also messages from Eli, checking if I'm okay, and even one from Angel that simply says: He's a mess without you.

I ignore that one.

But it's the missed calls from Ben that make my heart clench. Eight since I posted the photo. I hover my thumb over his name, tempted to call back, but Imogen's words echo in my mind: Take the time you need.

Instead, I send a text to Maci: Still need space, but I'm okay. Will be back Friday.

As I'm about to set my phone down, it buzzes with an incoming call—Ben again. My finger hovers over the decline button, but something makes me hesitate. Maybe it's the late hour, or the lingering buzz from champagne, or just the exhaustion of maintaining my anger, but I find myself answering.

"Hello?" My voice comes out smaller than I intended.

There's a pause, as if he's surprised I actually picked up. "Lexie," he breathes, my name sounding like a prayer on his lips. "You're okay."

"Yes," I say, trying to keep my voice steady. "I'm in Vegas."

Another pause. I can almost picture him running a hand through his hair, the way he does when he's stressed. "With Jerome Bastille," he says finally, a question in his tone.

"It's a long story," I reply, suddenly tired. "Why are you calling, Ben?"

"I've been calling for days," he says, and I can hear the frustration in his voice. "You just disappeared, Lexie. No explanation, no chance to talk."

"I left you a note," I remind him.

"A note," he repeats incredulously. "A cold, formal note ending everything we had with no discussion. After everything, I deserved more than that."

"Oh, that's rich considering how much more I deserved than you hanging in secret corners with your ex, posting pics with her on social media. Give me a break." I say, pissed with his tone.

"That's not what happened," Ben says, his voice strained. "The photo was for the company's social media. It meant nothing. And I defended you to Vanessa. You just didn't stay long enough to hear it."

"Convenient," I mutter, though a small seed of doubt plants itself in my mind. "So I'm just supposed to believe you were defending me while cozied up in a corner with her?"

"I wasn't 'cozied up' with anyone!" Ben's frustration is palpable even through the phone. "She cornered me, made that comment about you, and I told her my personal life was none of her business and that I'm happier with you than I've ever been in my life."

"Yeah, well too little too late." I say furious that he thinks he can get off that easy. "You told me that there would be no more embarrassments involving Vanessa, yet here we are. Since it was just a simple photo, next time I'm around one of my exes, I'll just climb in his lap and hold on for dear life. Let me know how that makes you feel."

I hear Ben exhale sharply. "That's not fair and you know it."

"Isn't it?" I snap. "Tell me what's fair about me having to see you with her plastered all over social media. Do you have any idea how humiliating that was?"

"I didn't post that picture, Lexie. The company did." His voice softens slightly. "And I hate that it hurt you. I hate that you felt humiliated. That's the last thing I ever wanted."

"So, you're telling me," I ask, completely baffled by his line of thinking. "That it would have been okay if the picture wasn't posted. Not, because the picture exists at all. This, is why I don't fit into your world. I'm not some trophy that you can show off when you need something, but put back on the shelf when you have an itch apparently I can't scratch. Vanessa is much more your type, the Murphey's will adore her."

There's a long silence on the other end of the line, and for a moment I think he's hung up.

"Is that what you think?" Ben finally says, his voice so quiet I can barely hear him. "That you're just some… trophy I'm using?"

"What else am I supposed to think?" I ask, pacing my hotel

room. "You parade me around at parties, you introduce me to all the right people, but when it comes down to it, you'll still stand there and let Vanessa talk about me like I'm nothing."

"For fuck's sake, Lexie!" Ben explodes, his voice sharp enough to make me pull the phone away from my ear. "Will you just listen to me for one minute? This isn't about Vanessa or types or the Murphy's. This is about you and me."

I stay silent, my heart hammering against my ribs.

"I love you," he says, the words landing like a thunderclap in the quiet of my hotel room. "I am completely, stupidly in love with you. Not Vanessa. Not some imaginary society wife. You."

"I love you," he repeats, softer now. "The real you. The woman who challenged me from the very first time we met. Who drinks cheap tequila and publishes books she believes in and makes me laugh more in a day than I did in a year before I met you."

I sink onto the edge of the bed, my legs suddenly unable to support me.

"I should have told you sooner," he continues, his voice raw with emotion. "I should have told you at the lake house, or after the gala, or any of the hundred moments when I felt it but was too afraid to say it. And I definitely should have told Vanessa to back off more forcefully."

"The charity gala," Ben says suddenly. "It's this Saturday. The Murphy's are expecting both of us."

Of course. Always back to the Murphy's. Always back to business.

"I'm sure you'll think of something," I say coldly. "Tell them I had a work emergency. Or better yet, take Vanessa. She's clearly eager for the opportunity."

"Damn it, Lexie, that's not fair!" Ben's frustration explodes through the phone. "I don't want Vanessa. I never did. I want you. Just you."

"Well, sometimes we don't get what we want," I say, my own anger flaring. "You made your choices, Ben. I'm making mine."

"So that's it?" he asks, his voice suddenly quiet. "You're just… done with us?"

"What do you want me to say Ben?" I ask genuinely confused. "I played the part, I did everything right, and I still got my heart broken. In one breath, you tell me you love me. In the next, you're cuddling up with her or worrying about appearances at galas because at the end of the day, that's all you really care about."

"I'm not—" Ben stops, and I can almost see him pinching the bridge of his nose in frustration. "This isn't about a gala, Lexie. This is about us. I mentioned the gala because I can't bear the thought of being there without you. Not because of the Murphy's or appearances or business. Because it won't feel right without you by my side."

His sincerity catches me off guard, making my carefully constructed walls wobble. "Ben…"

"I know I've messed up," he continues, his voice softening. "And I know you need space. I'll respect that. But please, don't make any final decisions until we can talk face to face. That's all I'm asking."

I close my eyes, torn between the hurt that drove me to Vegas and the undeniable pull I still feel toward him. "I don't know if that's a good idea."

"Just think about it," he says. "I'll be here when you're ready. Whether that's tomorrow or next week or…" He trails off, as if unable to contemplate a longer separation.

"I should go," I say, suddenly exhausted by the emotional whiplash of the conversation. "It's late."

"Lexie, wait—" Ben's voice is urgent. "I meant what I said. I love you. Not as part of some arrangement. Not for show. For real."

My throat tightens with unshed tears. "I want to believe you, I do. But actions speak louder than words and so far, your actions demonstrate that no matter what, you will be there for Vanessa, even at my expense."

There's a long silence on the other end of the line. When Ben finally speaks, his voice sounds hollow. "I understand how it looks, Lexie. I do. But that's not the reality. I need you to know that."

"Goodnight, Ben," I say softly, unable to continue this conversation that's tearing me apart.

"Goodnight, Lexie," he replies, resignation in his tone. "Be safe."

I end the call and toss my phone onto the bed beside me, burying my face in my hands. The tears I've been holding back all trip finally break free, streaming down my cheeks in hot trails. I hate that I still care this much. I hate that his "I love you" made my heart soar, even as my brain screamed warnings.

Damn him.

Damn him for making me feel like this—raw and conflicted and longing for something I'm not sure I can trust.

I'd come to Vegas to escape, to clear my head, and somehow I feel more tangled up than before. Ben loves me. The words echo in my mind, setting off little explosions of hope that I quickly try to extinguish.

Twenty-Four

The Letter and the Lemon

Brunch with Jerome and Imogen is both wonderful and bitter-sweet. We discuss the memoir project—a legitimate, exciting opportunity that could put our small publishing house on the map—but there's an undercurrent of "real life is waiting" that I can't quite shake.

"You've been good for my dad," Imogen says as we sip mimosas on the restaurant's patio overlooking the Strip. "I haven't seen him this excited about a project in years."

"He's been incredible," I admit. "I came to Vegas to escape my problems, and somehow found a dream opportunity instead."

"Sometimes running away leads you exactly where you need to be," Jerome says, joining our conversation. "Though eventually, we all have to go home."

His words hit me harder than intended. Home. Ben. Reality.

"Speaking of which," I say, forcing brightness into my voice, "I should probably head back to my hotel soon to pack."

Jerome reaches across the table to pat my hand. "Before you go, I want you to have this." He slides a small velvet box toward me.

I open it to find a delicate silver bracelet with a single charm—a tiny lemon. I laugh despite the sudden lump in my throat.

"When life gives you lemons," Jerome says with a wink. "A reminder that sometimes the sourest moments lead to the sweetest opportunities."

"I don't know what to say," I murmur, fastening the bracelet around my wrist.

"Say you'll call me when you land," Imogen instructs, pulling me into a hug as we say our goodbyes. "And that you'll let me know how things go with Mr. Financial Advisor."

"I will," I promise, hugging Jerome next. "Thank you both. For everything."

Back at my hotel, I pack my few belongings and the ridiculous number of shopping bags I've accumulated. As I fold my new clothes—my thoughts return to the drama awaiting me at home.

With a deep breath, I pull out my phone and finally listen to Ben's voicemails. The first few are what I expected—confusion, concern, questions about where I am.

I'm not ready to forgive him yet or even talk to him for that matter. But, I'm ready to go home. Baby steps.

The flight back to Chicago is long and filled with dread. I spend most of it staring out the window, absentmindedly twisting Jerome's bracelet around my wrist, rehearsing what I'll say to Ben when I see him. By the time we land, I still haven't come up with anything that doesn't sound either pathetically desperate or childishly petulant.

It's late when I unlock my apartment door, the familiar scent of home wrapping around me like a blanket. Everything looks exactly as I left it five days ago, though it feels like a lifetime has passed. I drop my bags by the door and collapse onto my couch, too exhausted to even make it to my bedroom.

My phone buzzes with a text from Maci: "Landed safely?"

"Home sweet home," I reply. "See you tomorrow."

————————————————————————————————

Morning comes too quickly. I wake to sunlight streaming through my blinds and the insistent beeping of my alarm. Back to reality. I shower, dress in my favorite outfit, the pre-Ben Lexie who dresses casual in leggings and off the shoulder sweatshirts. I'm not trying to impress Ben's corporate world anymore.

The familiar routine feels strange after my Vegas adventure. Just a week ago, I was excited to get to work, knowing I'd see Ben at some point during the day. Now, the thought of running into him makes my stomach churn with anxiety.

"You can do this," I mutter to myself in the elevator, clutching my coffee cup like a shield. "It's just another day at the office."

But it's not, and I know it. Everything has changed.

When the elevator doors open on our floor, I hesitate for just a moment before stepping out. The publishing side is to the left, the financial advisors to the right. For months, I've been bouncing between both worlds. Now, I need to stay firmly in mine.

"Lexie!" Maci squeals, launching herself at me the moment I walk through our office doors. She wraps me in a hug so tight I nearly spill my coffee. "You're back! And you look… different."

"Good different or bad different?" I ask, extracting myself from her embrace.

She studies me, head tilted. "Just different. Less… polished? More you."

"That's the point," I say, heading toward my office. "I'm done pretending to be someone I'm not."

Maci follows, closing my office door behind us. "So, are we going to talk about the fact that you were partying with Jerome Bastille in Vegas while the rest of us were stuck in rainy Chicago? Or about the fact that Ben has been walking around like someone shot his puppy? Or about—"

"The memoir deal," I interrupt, setting my coffee down and pulling out my laptop. "That's what we're going to talk about. Jerome wants us to publish his memoir."

Maci's eyes widen. "Holy. Shit."

"Exactly," I say, grateful for the distraction. "It could be huge for us. Career-changing."

"Okay, we're definitely circling back to the Ben situation," Maci warns, "but first, tell me everything about this deal."

For the next hour, I brief her on the memoir project—Jerome's vision, the timeline, the marketing potential. It feels good to focus on work, on something concrete and exciting that has nothing to do with Ben or fake engagements or broken hearts.

"This is incredible," Maci says when I finish. "Like, legitimately life-changing for the company."

"I know," I say, allowing myself a genuine smile. "Something good came out of my impulsive Vegas escape after all."

Maci leans forward, her expression turning serious. "Speaking of which…"

I groan. "I knew you wouldn't let it go."

"Of course not! You disappeared to Vegas for five days after leaving your fake fiancé a Dear John letter. That's not exactly normal behavior, even for you."

"I needed space," I say defensively. "And clarity."

"And did you find it?" Maci asks, her voice gentler now.

"Clarity?"

I twist Jerome's bracelet around my wrist, considering the question. "I'm not sure. I know I can't go back to pretending. And I know that whatever was happening between Ben and me—real or not—is over."

Even as I say the words, something inside me protests. Is it really over? Can I just walk away from someone who claimed to love me? But then I remember the photo, the hurt, the feeling of being second-best.

"Have you talked to him?" Maci asks, studying my face carefully.

"Briefly. He called last night." I fiddle with my coffee cup, avoiding her eyes. "He said he loves me."

Maci's eyebrows shoot up. "Wow. That's… big."

"Is it?" I challenge. "Or is it just something he said to get me to come back? To salvage his precious Murphy account?"

"Do you really believe that?" Maci asks, her voice unusually serious. "Because from where I'm sitting, that man has been completely wrecked without you. Eli says he's been impossible to work with—distracted, irritable, barely sleeping."

"Good," I say, though the pettiness feels hollow. "He should feel bad."

"Lexie," Maci sighs, "I love you, but you're being ridiculous. You're both miserable without each other."

"I'm not miserable," I protest. "I'm… processing."

Maci gives me a look that says she's not buying it. "Well, process faster. We have the Halloween party next month, and half the guest list is from your fake ex-fiancé's company."

I roll my eyes dramatically. "I'll be professional. It's fine."

"Professional," Maci repeats skeptically. "Like you were when you fled the state after seeing a photo?"

"That was different," I mutter, though I know she has a point. "Look, I'll be civil. Adult. Mature. All those boring adjectives."

"Mmhmm," Maci hums, clearly unconvinced. "And what about the charity gala this weekend? The one Ben mentioned?"

My stomach drops. I'd managed to push that conversation out of my mind. "What about it?"

"Are you going? The Murphy's are expecting both of you."

"That's Ben's problem," I say, more harshly than intended. "I'm sure he'll figure something out."

Maci studies me for a long moment. "You know, for someone who claims to hate pretending, you're doing a pretty good job of pretending you don't care."

I shoot her a withering look. "Stop psychoanalyzing me. I have work to do."

"Fine," Maci says, throwing her hands up in surrender. "But just so you know, James Porter called again. He specifically asked if you'd be at the gala. Apparently, he wants to introduce you to his editor."

My heart sinks. James Porter – the Pulitzer Prize winner who'd been so impressed with me at the lake house. The connection that could change everything for our publishing house.

"I'll…figure something out," I mutter, turning to my computer in dismissal.

Maci leaves with one final pointed look, and I spend the next few hours buried in work, responding to emails that piled up during my absence and reviewing manuscripts with forced concentration. By noon, I've almost convinced myself that I can handle this – being in the same building as Ben, pretending our paths never crossed beyond a professional capacity.

Then my office door flies open without warning.

"You're back," Eli says, slightly out of breath as if he's rushed over. His eyes scan my face with obvious concern. "Are you okay? When did you get in?"

"Last night," I say, surprised by his appearance. "I'm fine, Eli. Really."

He drops into the chair across from my desk, studying me intently. "You don't look fine. You look like you haven't slept in days."

"Thanks," I mutter dryly. "Just what every girl wants to hear."

"Have you talked to Ben?" he asks, cutting straight to the chase in typical Eli fashion.

I sigh, pushing away from my desk. "Briefly. On the phone. It didn't go well."

"He's a mess, Lexie," Eli says quietly. "I've never seen him like this."

"That's not my problem," I say, though the words sound hollow even to my own ears.

Eli's expression turns uncharacteristically serious. "Isn't it, though? You care about him. I know you do."

"Caring isn't always enough," I counter, twisting Jerome's bracelet nervously. "Sometimes people just… don't fit."

"Bullshit," Eli says bluntly. "You two fit perfectly. You're just both too stubborn to admit when you're wrong."

I bristle at his assessment. "I'm not wrong for being upset about seeing him with his ex!"

"No, you're not," Eli agrees, surprising me. "You're wrong for running away instead of talking it out. And he's wrong for not making it absolutely clear to everyone – including Vanessa – how much you mean to him."

His words hit uncomfortably close to home. I stare down at my desk, unable to meet his eyes.

"Look," Eli says, his voice gentler now. "I'm not here to tell you what to do. I just… I care about both of you. And it sucks watching you both fall apart without each other. Here, before I forget. He wanted you to have this."

I slide my finger under the seal, carefully opening the envelope. Inside is a thick stack of papers, neatly bound with a paper clip. The top sheet bears a formal letterhead: BENJAMIN MADDOX, FINANCIAL ADVISOR.

A contract, maybe?

But as I scan the first page, I realize it's not a contract at all. It's a letter.

"Dear Lexie," I read aloud, my voice catching slightly. *"Since you won't take my calls, and since words seem to fail me whenever I'm around you anyway, I thought perhaps putting everything in writing might help."*

I stare at the opening lines, my heart hammering in my chest. Eli watches me silently, giving me space to process.

"I'll leave you to it," he says gently, rising from his chair. "Just… read it, okay? Before you make any final decisions."

After he leaves, I take a deep breath and continue reading.

"I've never been good at expressing how I feel. My father taught me early that emotions were weakness, that vulnerability was failure. For most of my life, I believed him. It made me efficient in business but utterly inept at relationships. Then I met you.

From that first day outside of the elevator, you challenged everything I thought I knew. You were infuriating, brilliant, beautiful, and completely unimpressed by the carefully constructed version of Ben Maddox I presented to the world.

Our arrangement was supposed to be simple. Professional. But nothing about you has ever been simple, Lexie.

When you left, I realized how completely I'd failed to show you what you mean to me. So here it is, in black and white—the truth I should have told you long before now."

I flip to the next page, my hands trembling slightly.

"*I love your laugh. The real one, not the polite society chuckle you perfected for the Murphy's. The one that bursts out of you when something genuinely amuses you, loud and unrestrained.*

I love how passionate you are about books. The way your eyes light up when you talk about a manuscript you believe in. How you fight for stories that might otherwise go untold.

I love your honesty. How you called me out on my bullshit from day one and never stopped, even when it would have been easier to play along.

I love watching you sleep. The way you curl toward me in the night, your hand always finding mine even in unconsciousness."

Tears blur my vision as I continue reading. Page after page of specific, detailed things Ben loves about me—from the freckle behind my left ear to the way I unconsciously hum when concentrating on work. It's not generic flattery; these are intimate observations that could only come from someone who's been paying close attention.

On the final page, his handwriting shifts from the neat, professional script to something more hurried, as if he couldn't contain the words anymore:

"*I know I've made mistakes. I know I hurt you. And if you truly want to end this—us—I'll respect your decision. But before you decide, I need you to know one thing: You were never pretend for me, Lexie. Not for a single moment.*

Whatever you choose, I'll be at the charity gala on Saturday. Table seven. Hoping against hope that you'll be there too, but I understand that if you don't show.

Always yours (whether you want me or not), Ben"

I sit back in my chair, the letter trembling in my hands. My chest feels tight, like I can't get enough air.

I set the letter down on my desk, my thoughts swirling. Part of me wants to run straight to Ben's office, while another part—the wounded, cautious part—holds me back. Can words on paper, no matter how beautiful, erase what happened?

My phone buzzes with a text from Maci: "You alive in there? You've been staring at those papers for an hour."

Has it really been that long? I glance at the clock—she's right.

"I'm fine," I text back. "Just thinking."

"About a certain financial advisor's love letter?" she replies immediately, adding an eyebrow-raising emoji.

I roll my eyes. "How did you know about that?"

"Eli told me. Obviously."

Of course he did. The publishing company and financial firm gossip network remains undefeated.

I tuck the letter into my desk drawer, needing to focus on something—anything—else. The memoir project. That's something concrete, positive, unrelated to my romantic disaster. I throw myself into drafting a formal proposal for Jerome, outlining our vision for his book.

By late afternoon, I've successfully avoided leaving my office and potentially running into Ben. But my bladder has other ideas. Cursing biology, I peek out my door, scanning for any sign of expensive suits or slicked-back dark hair before darting toward the restroom.

I'm washing my hands when the door swings open and Angel walks in. We lock eyes in the mirror, both freezing momentarily.

"You're back," she says, her usual cool demeanor firmly in place.

"Observant as always," I reply, reaching for a paper towel.

Angel studies me, her head tilting slightly. "You look terrible."

"Thanks. The Vegas aesthetic didn't quite travel well."

A ghost of a smile touches her lips. "Vegas suits you better than corporate Chicago ever did."

Coming from Angel, this feels like high praise. I find myself smiling back. "I'm beginning to think so too."

She steps closer, lowering her voice. "He hasn't slept in days, you know. Canceled three client meetings. Nearly bit my head off when I suggested rescheduling the Murphy's."

I swallow hard. "Angel, I—"

"I'm not taking sides," she interrupts, raising a perfectly manicured hand. "Just stating facts. What you do with them is your business."

With that, she turns to the mirror, efficiently touching up her already flawless lipstick. I'm about to leave when she speaks again.

"The charity gala is black tie, by the way. In case you were wondering."

"I wasn't," I lie, my hand on the door.

Angel meets my eyes in the mirror. "Whatever you say, Lexie."

I slip out before she can see the confusion on my face. Even Angel seems to be pushing me toward reconciliation. Is everyone in on this?

Back in my office, I stare at the letter some more. My mind at war with itself as I contemplate what to do. Finally, before I can talk myself out of it, I pull out my phone and text Ben. "I will be at the gala Saturday. I'm not forgiving you, but I don't want your business to suffer on my account."

His response comes almost immediately: "Thank you. I appreciate it more than you know."

No declarations of love this time. No pleading. Just a simple acknowledgment that makes my heart twist in my chest. I toss my phone onto my desk and drop my head into my hands. What am I doing?

The rest of the week passes in a blur of work and anxiety. I throw myself into the memoir project, finalizing details with Jerome via video calls that leave Maci starstruck every time she walks by my office. The distraction is welcome, but the gala looms like a storm on the horizon.

Twenty-Five

Back Where We Belong

By Saturday evening, I'm a bundle of nerves as I stand in front of my closet, staring at the row of dresses I've accumulated during my time with Ben. Each one holds memories—the emerald gown from our first public appearance, the blue sundress from the lake house, the red cocktail dress from a client dinner where Ben couldn't keep his eyes off me all night.

None of them feel right anymore. They belong to a different Lexie—the polished, society-ready version I created for our arrangement.

My phone buzzes with a text from Maci: "What are you wearing tonight? Need me to bring over options?"

"I've got it handled," I reply, though I'm far from certain.

After another ten minutes of deliberation, I pull out a dress I bought online—a floor-length fire engine red gown with a plunging neckline and an open back. It's elegant but bold, nothing like the safe, appropriate choices I've made for Ben's events before. Perfect.

I hired a hair and makeup team, who have become my fairy godmothers for the evening.

The team transforms me into a woman I barely recognize in the mirror—my eyes smoky and dramatic, my hair swept up in an elegant updo with a few strategic tendrils framing my face. The effect is sophisticated but with an edge of danger. I look like someone who makes her own rules.

"You look incredible," my makeup artist says, putting the finishing touches on my lips. "Whoever he is, he won't know what hit him."

I smile enigmatically, slipping her an extra tip. "That's the plan."

Maci comes over to help me with the finishing touches.

An hour later, I'm standing in the shimmering red gown that hugs every curve before flowing to the floor in a silky waterfall. The neckline dips into a low v, showcasing my ample chest in a daring vision, and the back features an intricate lattice of delicate straps that make my shoulders look elegant and strong.

"Holy shit," Maci breathes when I emerge from the dressing room. "You look like a goddess. An angry, vengeful goddess who's about to ruin a man's life in the best possible way."

"It's too much," I protest weakly, though I can't stop staring at my reflection. I look... powerful. Beautiful. Like someone who knows exactly what she wants.

"It's perfect. And just in time, he will be here any minute." She says, taking out her phone to glance at the time.

My doorbell rings, and I feel my heart hammering against my ribs. Maci gives me a reassuring squeeze on my shoulder before rushing to answer it.

"Showtime," she whispers with a wink.

I hear Ben's voice in the hallway, the deep timbre sending an involuntary shiver down my spine. I take a deep breath and step into the living room.

The conversation between Maci and Ben stops abruptly. He stands frozen in the doorway, his eyes widening as they take me in from head to toe. He looks devastatingly handsome in his tuxedo, the perfect cut emphasizing his broad shoulders and trim waist. His hair is styled less severely than usual, a few strands falling across his forehead in a way that makes him look younger, more vulnerable.

For a moment, neither of us speaks. The air between us feels charged, electric with unspoken words.

"You look…" Ben finally says, his voice hoarse. "Lexie, you're breathtaking."

"Thank you," I reply, pleased that my voice sounds steadier than I feel. "You don't look so bad yourself."

Maci glances between us, smirking. "Well, I'll leave you two to your awkward sexual tension. Have fun at the gala!" She grabs her purse and slips past Ben.

The door closes behind her with a decisive click, leaving Ben and me alone.

"I wasn't sure you'd actually come," Ben admits, still standing by the door as if afraid to move closer.

"I said I would," I reply, gathering my clutch and wrap. "I keep my promises."

A shadow crosses his face. "I deserved that."

"Probably," I agree, softening slightly. "But tonight isn't about us. It's about the Murphy's and your business. And apparently James Porter wants to introduce me to his editor."

Ben nods, holding the door open for me. "Right. Professional."

The ride to the gala is silent and tense. Ben keeps stealing glances at me when he thinks I'm not looking, his knuckles white on the steering wheel. I stare out the window, determined not to be the first to break.

The charity gala is being held at the Art Institute, its grand staircase illuminated with thousands of tiny lights that make the whole building glow against the night sky. Couples in formal wear stream up the steps, a parade of wealth and privilege that once would have intimidated me.

Tonight, though, I feel different. My time in Vegas, the memoir deal with Jerome, even the heartbreak with Ben—it's all shifted something fundamental in me. I belong here as much as anyone, not because I'm Ben Maddox's fiancé, but because I've earned my place.

Ben hands the car keys to the valet and comes around to open my door. As I step out, Ben offers his arm. I hesitate for just a moment before taking it, acutely aware of how natural it feels despite everything.

"Ready?" he asks, his voice low and intimate.

I can only give a small nod as I straighten my shoulders.

We ascend the steps together, the picture of elegance and harmony. If anyone saw us now, they'd never guess the chaos swirling beneath the surface—the hurt, the longing, the unresolved tension.

The main hall has been transformed into a glittering wonderland. Crystal chandeliers cast a warm glow over tables draped in white silk, each centered with elaborate floral arrangements that must have cost a small fortune. A string quartet plays softly in one corner while waiters circulate with champagne and hors d'oeuvres.

"Ben! Lexie!" Margaret Murphy's voice cuts through the

ambient noise. She glides toward us, resplendent in a midnight blue gown, arms outstretched. "You're here at last!"

"Margaret," Ben greets her warmly, accepting her air kisses. "The event looks spectacular."

"Doesn't it?" she beams, taking my hands in hers. "Lexie, my dear, you look absolutely ravishing. That dress is a triumph."

"Thank you," I say, genuinely warmed by her enthusiasm. "It's wonderful to see you again."

"Richard will be thrilled you both made it," she continues, looping her arm through mine and guiding us deeper into the hall. "He's been cornered by the mayor, poor thing, but he'll find us soon enough. And James Porter has been asking after you all evening, Lexie."

My pulse quickens at the mention of James. "I'd love to speak with him."

"I'll make sure of it," Margaret promises. "Now, let me show you to your table. We've seated you with the Porters and the Handleys—all literary people, just as you'd prefer."

As she leads us through the crowd, I'm hyperaware of Ben's hand at the small of my back, a gesture so familiar it aches. His touch is gentle but firm, guiding me through the sea of people with the practiced ease of a man who's done this countless times before.

We reach table seven, where several couples are already seated. James Porter rises immediately, his face lighting up when he sees me.

"Lexie Phillips," he says warmly, taking my hands. "The literary world's newest powerhouse. I was beginning to think you were avoiding me."

I laugh, genuinely pleased to see him again. "Never. I've been out of town on a project."

"So I heard," he says with a knowing smile. "A little bird told me you're working with Jerome Bastille on his memoir."

News travels fast in publishing circles. "Word gets around," I acknowledge.

"Only good words in your case," James assures me. "Ben, good to see you again," he adds, shaking Ben's hand. "Margaret tells me you've been working wonders with their portfolio."

"Just doing my job," Ben replies modestly, though I notice a flash of pride in his eyes.

James turns back to me. "I promised to introduce you to my editor, didn't I? She's just over there—Caroline Hayes. Brilliant woman. Terrifying, but brilliant."

"I'd love to meet her," I say eagerly.

James glances between Ben and me, a knowing twinkle in his eye. "Perhaps I could borrow your fiancé for a few minutes, Ben? Shop talk, I'm afraid—dreadfully boring for non-literary types."

Ben's hand tightens almost imperceptibly at my waist before dropping away. "Of course," he says smoothly. "I should check in with Richard anyway."

As James leads me toward a striking woman in a silver gown, I glance back over my shoulder. Ben stands watching us, an unreadable expression on his face. Our eyes meet for a brief moment before he turns and disappears into the crowd.

Caroline Hayes is everything James promised—brilliant, intimidating, and unexpectedly funny. Within minutes, we're deep in conversation about Jerome's memoir and the changing landscape of publishing. She seems genuinely interested in our small company, asking thoughtful questions about our approach and vision.

"You've got a good eye," she says after I explain our focus

on diverse voices. "And clearly some impressive connections. Jerome Bastille is notoriously selective about who tells his story."

"We connected in Vegas," I explain. "Sometimes the best professional relationships start in unexpected places."

"Indeed," Caroline agrees, her eyes drifting past me. "Speaking of unexpected connections, your fiancé has been watching you like a hawk for the past fifteen minutes."

I resist the urge to turn around. "Has he?"

"Mmm," she hums, sipping her champagne. "That level of intensity is either concerning or wildly romantic, depending on one's perspective."

I laugh despite myself. "Which perspective do you take?"

"Oh, romantic, definitely," Caroline says with a wicked smile. "Though I'm a sucker for grand gestures and dramatic declarations. Hazard of the job—too many romance novels crossing my desk."

Before I can respond, the string quartet stops playing, replaced by the gentle tapping of silver against crystal. Richard Murphy stands at a small podium, calling for attention.

"Ladies and gentlemen," he begins, his voice warm and commanding. "Thank you all for joining us tonight. Your generosity will help fund art education programs for underserved communities across Chicago…"

I make my way back to table seven as Richard continues his speech, slipping into my seat beside Ben. He leans close, his breath warm against my ear.

"How did it go with Caroline?" he whispers.

"Well," I murmur back. "She's interested in potential collaborations."

"Good," Ben says, a genuine smile lighting his face. "You

deserve these connections."

I study him in the dim lighting, noticing the shadows under his eyes that hadn't been there before. Has he really been sleeping as poorly as Eli claimed?

Richard's speech continues, highlighting the charity's achievements and thanking key donors. I should be paying attention, but all I can focus on is the warmth of Ben beside me, the familiar scent of his cologne, the way his hand rests on the table inches from mine.

When the applause finally dies down, dinner is served—an elegant five-course meal that I barely taste. Ben and I maintain polite conversation with the others at our table, acting the part of the happy couple whenever anyone looks our way. It's painfully familiar, this performance we've perfected over months.

Except it doesn't feel like a performance anymore. Not for me.

As dessert is cleared away, the string quartet transitions to a full band, and couples begin moving to the dance floor. James and his wife join them, along with several others from our table.

"Would you like to dance?" Ben asks quietly, his eyes searching mine.

I hesitate, weighing the wisdom of putting myself in his arms. "I'm not sure that's a good idea."

"Just one dance," he says. "Please, Lexie."

Against my better judgment, I nod. Ben takes my hand, leading me to the edge of the dance floor where the crowd is thinner. His arm slips around my waist, drawing me close but not too close—respectful of the boundaries I've established. I rest my hand on his shoulder, acutely aware of the space between us, so different from how we used to dance.

"Thank you for coming tonight," Ben says as we sway to the music. "It means a lot."

We go quiet as I let the music guide us. Being in his arms again is like coming home. As the music comes to an end and we begin to leave the dance floor panic sets in as my mouth appears to have taken over my brain, I lean close to his ear and whisper, "I love you, too." Afraid to hear his response, I turn ready to do what I do best, run.

Ben's hand catches my wrist before I can escape, his grip gentle but firm. His eyes lock with mine, a storm of emotions swimming in their gray depths.

"Did you just—" he starts, his voice barely audible over the music.

"I shouldn't have said that," I whisper, heart hammering against my ribs. "Forget it."

"Not a chance," Ben says, pulling me closer. "Say it again."

I shake my head, suddenly terrified of the vulnerability I've exposed. But Ben isn't letting me retreat this time. He guides me swiftly through the crowd, his hand never leaving mine, until we reach a secluded alcove away from prying eyes.

"Lexie," he says, his voice rough with emotion. "Please. I need to hear it again."

I take a shaky breath, looking anywhere but his face. "This doesn't change anything. What happened with Vanessa—"

"Look at me," Ben interrupts, his fingers gently tilting my chin up. "Really look at me."

When I finally meet his gaze, the raw honesty there steals my breath.

"I love you," he says simply. "Not Vanessa. Not anyone else. Just you. The real you—messy, stubborn, brilliant you. And if you love me too, then everything else is just… details we can work through."

"It's not that simple," I protest weakly.

"It can be," he insists. "I know I messed up. I should have made it crystal clear to Vanessa and everyone else that you're the only woman who matters to me. But Lexie, running away doesn't solve anything. We need to face problems together, not apart."

The truth of his words hits me hard. I have been running—from conflict, from vulnerability, from the possibility that what we have might actually be real.

"I'm scared," I admit finally. "This wasn't supposed to be real. I wasn't supposed to fall in love with you. And then when I saw that picture…"

"It hurt," Ben finishes for me. "I understand that. And I'm so sorry I put you in that position."

He takes my hands in his, his thumbs tracing gentle circles on my skin.

"The day you left," he continues, "I realized something. All these months, I've been so focused on what our relationship could do for my career, for the Murphy account. But when you were gone, none of that mattered. I couldn't sleep. Couldn't eat. All I could think about was you."

My heart clenches at the pain in his voice.

"I read your letter," I say softly. "Every word."

A flicker of hope crosses his face. "And?"

"And it was beautiful," I admit. "But words are easy, Ben."

"You're right," he agrees, surprising me. Without another word, he laces his fingers through mine and begins leading me through the crowd. We weave between dancing couples and chatting guests, past the curious glances of the Murphy's, straight toward the exit.

"Ben, where are we—"

"Somewhere we can talk," he says over his shoulder, not slowing his pace. "Really talk."

The cool night air hits my bare shoulders as we step outside. Ben hands the valet his ticket, then turns to me, shrugging off his jacket and draping it over my shoulders in one smooth motion.

"You didn't have to do that," I say, though I'm grateful for the warmth.

"I know." His eyes are intense, focused entirely on me. "But I wanted to."

The valet brings Ben's car around, and before I know it, we're driving through the Chicago streets, the city lights blurring past my window. Neither of us speaks. The silence is heavy with everything unsaid, with the weight of my confession and whatever comes next.

Finally, Ben pulls into a familiar parking lot—the one beneath our office building.

"Why are we here?" I ask, confused.

"You'll see," is all he says, coming around to open my door.

We ride the elevator in silence, but instead of stopping at our normal floor, Ben presses the button for the roof. I raise an eyebrow but don't question him.

When the doors slide open, I gasp. The rooftop has been transformed. String lights create a canopy of stars overhead, illuminating a small table set with champagne and strawberries. Beyond, the Chicago skyline glitters against the night sky.

"Ben," I breathe, stepping out of the elevator. "What is all this?"

"Plan B," he says with a small smile. "In case you actually showed up tonight."

"You did this?" I turn to him, stunned. "When?"

"This afternoon." He runs a hand through his hair, suddenly nervous. "I had Angel help. Turns out she's quite the romantic when properly motivated."

I laugh, picturing Angel stringing lights with her perfect manicure. "I find that hard to believe."

"She said, and I quote, 'If this doesn't work, nothing will,'" Ben continues, a hint of laughter in his voice. "She's surprisingly invested in our relationship."

"I'm beginning to think everyone is," I admit, taking in the beautiful scene before me. "This is… incredible."

Ben steps closer, his eyes never leaving mine. "I wanted to show you, not just tell you. Words are easy, like you said. So this is me, showing you that what we have is real. That I'll do whatever it takes to make this work."

My heart feels too big for my chest, swelling with emotion I can barely contain. I reach out, my fingers brushing his cheek. "Ben…"

"Let me finish," he says softly, catching my hand and pressing a kiss to my palm. "When you left, I realized something. All those society events, client meetings, business dinners—none of it means anything without you beside me. Not because you play the part well, but because you make everything better just by being you."

He leads me to the edge of the roof where the city stretches out before us, a tapestry of lights against the darkness.

"I love you, Lexie Phillips," he says, turning to face me fully. "Your stubbornness, your passion, your ridiculous habit of running away when things get tough." He smiles, the expression tender and teasing at once. "I love how you fight for stories that matter, how you call me out when I'm being an ass, how you dance around your kitchen when you think no one's watching."

I laugh through the tears gathering in my eyes. "How do you know about that?"

"You're not as sneaky as you think," he says, his own eyes suspiciously bright. "And I've been paying attention, even when you thought I wasn't."

He takes a deep breath, reaching into his pocket. My heart stutters when he pulls out the engagement ring—my engagement ring—the one I'd returned with my goodbye note.

"This started as pretend," he says, holding the ring between us. "But nothing about how I feel for you is fake. I want this to be real, Lexie. All of it."

"Are you proposing?" I ask, my voice barely a whisper.

"Do you want me to propose?" He asks cryptically.

I stare at him, my heart pounding so hard I swear he must hear it. The city lights reflect in his eyes as he waits for my answer, vulnerable and hopeful.

"I want…" My voice falters. "I want this to be real too. But I'm scared, Ben. What if we mess this up? What if I run again or you shut down when things get tough?"

Ben takes my hand, his thumb brushing over where the ring used to sit. "Then we'll figure it out. Together. That's what real couples do—they don't give up when it gets hard."

"And Vanessa?" I can't help asking, needing to clear the air completely.

"I've already handled it," he says firmly. "I told her explicitly that her comments about you were unacceptable and that if she can't respect my relationship, she can find another financial advisor."

"You did that?" I ask, surprised. "But the Murphy connection—"

"Isn't worth losing you," he finishes simply. "Nothing is."

The sincerity in his voice melts the last of my resistance. I step closer, eliminating the space between us. "Ask me," I whisper.

Ben's eyes widen slightly. "Are you sure?"

"Ask me," I repeat, more firmly this time.

He takes a deep breath, then slowly lowers to one knee, still holding my hand. The sight of him there, looking up at me with such raw emotion, steals my breath away.

"Alexandria Phillips," he says, his voice steady despite the vulnerability in his eyes, "will you marry me? For real this time?"

Tears spill down my cheeks as I nod, unable to speak for a moment. "Yes," I finally manage. "Yes, I'll marry you."

Ben's face breaks into the most beautiful smile I've ever seen as he slides the ring back onto my finger where it belongs. Then he's standing, lifting me off my feet in a spinning embrace that makes me laugh through my tears.

When he sets me down, his hands frame my face, thumbs gently wiping away the moisture on my cheeks. "I love you," he says, his forehead touching mine.

"I love you too," I reply, the words feeling right, natural, true. "Even when you drive me crazy."

"Especially then," he murmurs, and then his lips are on mine, soft at first, then increasingly urgent. I melt into him, my arms winding around his neck as the kiss deepens, months of tension and longing pouring into this one perfect moment.

When we finally break apart, both breathless, Ben smiles against my lips. "So, what now, future Mrs. Maddox?"

I raise an eyebrow, pretending to consider the question seriously. "Now? Well, I think we should finish that champagne before it gets warm. Then maybe you can take me home and show me how much you missed me."

Ben's eyes darken at my suggestion, his hands tightening at my waist. "I like the way you think." He leads me to the small table, pouring two glasses of champagne with a steadiness that belies the heat in his gaze.

"To us," he says, raising his glass. "No more pretending."

"No more running," I add, clinking my flute against his.

The champagne is perfectly chilled, bubbles dancing on my tongue as I sip. Ben watches me over the rim of his glass, his expression so full of love it makes my heart stutter.

"I can't believe this is real," I admit, turning the ring on my finger. "A few hours ago I was convinced we were over."

"I was never going to let that happen," Ben says, setting down his glass and pulling me closer. "Not without a fight."

"My stubborn, determined man," I murmur, trailing my fingers along his jaw.

"Always," he promises, capturing my hand and pressing a kiss to my palm. "Though I should warn you—I've already texted Eli that Plan B worked."

I groan, dropping my head to his shoulder. "Which means by now, Maci knows, and probably half the office."

"Almost certainly," Ben agrees, not sounding the least bit sorry. "Angel's been updating them in real-time. Apparently, there was a betting pool."

"Of course there was," I laugh, shaking my head. "Who won?"

"Eli, naturally. He had 'grand gesture at charity gala' on his card."

"Did I tell you that I one $5,000 in Blackjack. Never played before but I kicked its ass."

Ben's eyes widen. "Seriously? Five grand on your first try?"

"Beginner's luck," I shrug, though I can't keep the pride from my voice. "The dealer thought I was counting cards."

"My fiancé, the secret card shark," Ben says with an admiring shake of his head. "Any other hidden talents I should know about?"

"Several," I say with a wink that makes his eyes darken. "But those are better demonstrated in private."

Ben groans, pulling me tighter against him. "You're killing me, Lexie."

"Patience," I murmur, though my own is rapidly waning. The feel of his body against mine, the lingering taste of champagne on my lips, the night air cool on my skin—it's all heightening my senses, making me acutely aware of how much I've missed him.

"I've been patient," Ben counters, his lips finding the sensitive spot just below my ear. "For five excruciating days while you were living it up in Vegas with rock stars."

I laugh, tilting my head to give him better access. "Jealous?"

"Terrified," he admits against my skin. "That you'd realize you're too good for me and never come back."

The vulnerability in his voice makes my heart clench. I pull back to look at him, framing his face with my hands. "Hey. I'm not too good for you. We're good for each other. The real versions of us, not the polished society people we've been pretending to be."

Ben's eyes soften. "I like the real versions better anyway."

"Even the part where I occasionally flee the state when emotionally overwhelmed?"

"Even that," he says with a small smile. "Though maybe next time you could flee to somewhere less exciting than Vegas. Nebraska, perhaps."

"No promises," I say, returning his smile. "But I'll try to work on the whole 'staying and talking things through' concept."

"That's all I ask." He brushes a strand of hair from my face. "That, and maybe we could go home now? As romantic as this rooftop is, I'd really like to continue our reunion somewhere more private."

The heat in his gaze sends a shiver of anticipation down my spine. "I think that could be arranged."

We gather our things, Ben's hand never leaving mine as we make our way back to the elevator. The ride down is charged with tension, our bodies deliberately not touching though we stand close enough to feel the heat between us.

The drive to his apartment is charged with anticipation. Ben's hand rests on my thigh, his thumb tracing small circles that send shivers up my spine. I lean over at a red light to press a kiss to his jaw, enjoying the sharp intake of breath my action elicits.

"You're making it very difficult to drive safely," he murmurs, his grip tightening slightly on the steering wheel.

"That sounds like a you problem," I tease, trailing my fingers along his arm.

He shoots me a look that's half exasperation, half hunger. "Five more minutes. Then it becomes an us problem."

True to his word, we arrive at his building in record time. The elevator ride to his penthouse is a test in restraint. Ben keeps me close, his arm around my waist, but maintains a gentlemanly distance that drives me crazy. When the doors finally open, he leads me inside with a deliberate calm that I know is hanging by a thread.

The moment the door closes behind us, everything changes. Ben's hands are in my hair, cradling my face as his mouth claims mine in a kiss that steals my breath. I respond with equal fervor, my fingers working at his bow tie, desperate to feel his skin against mine.

"I've missed you so much," he says against my neck, leaving a trail of kisses that make me gasp. "Every night without you was torture."

"Show me," I challenge, my voice husky with desire.

Ben's eyes lock with mine, a smile spreading across

his face that makes my heart race. In one swift motion, he lifts me into his arms, my legs wrapping around his waist as he carries me toward the bedroom.

"Gladly," he murmurs against my lips.

The bedroom is bathed in moonlight streaming through the floor-to-ceiling windows. Ben sets me down gently beside the bed, his hands moving to the zipper of my dress.

"You have no idea what this dress has been doing to me all night," he says, slowly lowering the zipper. "Every man in that ballroom was staring at you."

"I only cared about one man's attention," I admit, shivering as the dress falls to pool at my feet, leaving me in just a strapless bra and lace panties.

Ben's eyes darken as they roam over me. "You have it. Always."

I reach for him, undoing the buttons of his shirt with trembling fingers. "Too many clothes," I complain, pushing the fabric from his shoulders.

He chuckles, the sound vibrating through his chest under my hands. "Impatient."

"Five days is a long time," I remind him, working at his belt next.

"The longest of my life," he agrees, capturing my hands and bringing them to his lips. "But we have all night. I want to savor every moment."

His words send heat pooling low in my belly. I watch,

transfixed, as he finishes undressing, revealing the body I've dreamed about every night we've been apart. When he's down to just his boxer briefs, he steps close again, his hands skimming down my sides to rest at my hips.

"You're so beautiful," he whispers, lowering his head to press a kiss to my collarbone. "I still can't believe you're here. That you're mine."

"I am," I assure him, threading my fingers through his hair. "All yours."

His lips trace a path down my chest, between my breasts, to my stomach. My breath hitches as he kneels before me, looking up with a question in his eyes. I nod, unable to speak as he hooks his fingers in my panties and slowly draws them down my legs.

"I've thought about this every night," he confesses, his hands warm on my thighs. "About how you taste, how you sound when you come apart for me."

My knees weaken at his words. "Ben, please…"

He smiles wickedly as our bodies come together with the familiarity of lovers who know each other well, yet with the wonder of a connection.

Later that night, I fall asleep content in his arms.

Twenty-Six

Cleopatra Gets High

It's October 31st, the night of the Halloween party and I'm freaking out. My crowd will be there including Zephyr and Jerome, but so will Ben's financial clients and crew. To say that we are from different worlds would be an understatement. I have a rockstar and a stoner author. They have old money, refined taste, and a measured lifestyle. We are not the same.

I take a deep breath, staring at myself in the mirror. I've gone with a Cleopatra costume—elegant but with enough edge to feel like me. The gold headdress sits perfectly on my styled hair, and the form-fitting white dress with intricate gold detailing makes me look like Egyptian royalty while still being appropriate for both crowds.

"You look amazing," Ben says, appearing behind me in the mirror. He's dressed as Mark Antony, his costume a perfect complement to mine. The Roman general's attire suits him—authoritative but somehow less stuffy than his usual suits.

"You don't think it's too much?" I ask, fidgeting with my costume jewelry. "Your clients are going to think I'm ridiculous."

Ben's hands settle on my shoulders, his eyes meeting mine in the reflection. "My clients are going to think I'm the luckiest man alive. Besides, it's Halloween. Everyone's supposed to be a little ridiculous."

I turn to face him, smoothing my hands over his chest. "You're just saying that because you want to get lucky later."

"That's just a bonus," he grins, pulling me close. "Seriously, stop worrying. Your worlds colliding isn't a disaster—it's exactly what makes us work."

"Is it, though?" I can't help voicing my deepest fear. "We're so different, Ben. Your idea of a wild night is having two glasses of scotch. Mine is… well, you've met Zephyr."

Ben laughs, the sound warming me from the inside. "And yet, here we are. Making it work. Besides, I've been known to have three glasses of scotch on occasion."

"Such a rebel," I tease, feeling some of my anxiety melt away.

"For you? Always." He kisses me softly, careful not to smudge my makeup. "Now come on, Queen of the Nile. We have a party to host."

We decided to hold the party at a trendy loft space downtown—neutral territory that doesn't feel too corporate or too publishing-world bohemian. When we arrive, Maci is already there, directing the final setup in her Wonder Woman costume.

"There you are!" she calls, rushing over. "The bar is ready, the DJ is set up, and the caterers are just putting out the first round of food. Oh, and Eli's already started a drinking game with some of the finance guys. Something about taking a shot whenever someone asks if you two have set a date yet."

"He'll be unconscious before nine," Ben predicts dryly.

"That's the plan," Maci winks. "Angel's running the betting pool on how long he lasts."

"Of course she is," I laugh. "Where is our resident ice queen tonight?"

"Over by the bar, dressed as—I kid you not—the White Witch from Narnia. It's terrifyingly perfect."

I nod, very accurate indeed.

As the party gets into full swing, I'm amazed at how seamlessly our two worlds blend. Jerome holds court near the windows, regaling a mixed group of literary types and financial advisors with tales from his rock star days. Zephyr, surprisingly, is deep in conversation with one of Ben's most conservative clients about investment opportunities in the cannabis industry.

"See?" Ben whispers in my ear, his hand warm on the small of my back. "Not so different after all."

I lean into him, watching as Maci challenges Eli to a arm-wrestling match while Angel coolly collects bets from the gathering crowd. "I guess you're right."

"Mark my words," he says, nodding toward Jerome. "By the end of the night, he'll have convinced half my clients to invest in his next album."

"And Zephyr will have the other half funding his 'herbal wellness retreat' in Colorado," I laugh.

Ben's arm tightens around my waist as he presses a kiss to my temple. "I love seeing you like this."

"Like what?" I ask, turning to face him.

"Happy. Relaxed. Not running away to Vegas at the first sign of trouble."

I playfully swat his chest. "Too soon, Maddox. Way too soon."

His laugh rumbles through me as he pulls me closer. "You know what's not too soon? Setting a date."

My heart skips a beat. "For the wedding?"

"No, for our deep-sea fishing expedition," he teases. "Yes, for the wedding. Unless you're getting cold feet already?"

"Not a chance," I assure him, twining my arms around his neck. "I was thinking spring. April, maybe?"

The smile that spreads across his face is worth all the anxiety I felt earlier. "April sounds perfect. That gives us, what, six months to plan?"

"Five months, three weeks, and two days," I specify, earning another laugh.

"Someone's been counting."

"Someone's been planning Pinterest boards," I admit. "But if you tell Maci, I'll deny everything."

Ben's eyes soften as he looks down at me. "I can't wait to marry you, Lexie Phillips."

"Even though I come with a rockstar memoir deal and a stoner poet who thinks shirts are 'tools of capitalist oppression'?"

"Especially because of that," he says firmly. "Though I draw the line at Zephyr officiating the ceremony."

"Damn, there goes my dream wedding," I pout playfully.

Our moment is interrupted by Maci's triumphant whoop as she defeats Eli in their arm-wrestling match. Angel coolly collects her winnings while Eli demands a rematch.

"Should we go rescue your best friend?" I ask, watching Eli flex dramatically for round two.

"Nah," Ben says, his eyes never leaving mine. "I think he's exactly where he needs to be."

As the night wears on, I find myself whisked outside on the balcony with Jerome, Zephyr, Imogen, and Angel of all people.

"All right people, now the real party starts." Zephyr says pulling out a bong.

I panic for a moment and then relax. This my party, not the rich people galas. I am who I am and I can do what I want. Hopefully Ben doesn't see.

Jerome chuckles, taking the bong from Zephyr. "Now, the real fun begins." He expertly lights it and takes a long hit, passing it to Imogen who rolls her eyes but accepts it anyway.

"Dad, really? You promised no embarrassing rockstar moments tonight."

"Darling, this is tame compared to the stories in the memoir," Jerome says with a wink in my direction.

Angel, to my absolute shock, takes the bong next with practiced ease. She catches my wide-eyed stare and shrugs. "What? I wasn't born an executive assistant, Phillips."

The door to the balcony slides open and I nearly jump out of my skin, but it's just Maci joining our little circle.

"There you guys are! I've been looking—oh." She spots the bong and grins. "Starting the real party without me?"

I relax, leaning against the railing. "Just a little publishing industry team building."

"Move over," Maci says, nudging Zephyr. "Wonder Woman needs to unwind after defeating the forces of finance."

We pass the bong around, sharing stories and laughs.

Twenty minutes later, we're all lounging on the balcony furniture, passing around the bong and sharing increasingly ridiculous stories. I'm pleasantly buzzed, relaxed in a way I haven't been since Vegas.

"So then," Jerome is saying, gesturing wildly, "the goat just walks into the recording studio like he owns the place!"

We dissolve into laughter, Zephyr nearly spilling his drink as he doubles over.

I glance back inside where I catch sight of Ben through the glass doors. He's laughing with Eli, completely at ease. Guests are mingling about; everyone seems to be having a good time. Once the bong is out, we go back inside to enjoy the rest of the party. I'm higher than I've ever been but I'm doing my best to hide its effects. One glance at my fellow stoners shows similar situations. Angel is by the buffet table trying to get her munchies under control. Maci is staring off into space, deep in some ridiculous thought now doubt.

Jerome is on the dance floor doing some sort of disco move that hasn't been relevant since 1978, and Zephyr is deeply engaged with a potted plant, apparently explaining his latest poetry collection to it. I catch Ben's eye across the room, and he raises an eyebrow questioningly. I give him what I hope is a casual smile and make my way toward him, focusing intently on walking in a straight line.

I make my way to Ben, trying my absolute best to appear completely sober. My movements feel exaggerated, like I'm walking through water, but surely no one can tell, right?

"Having fun?" he asks when I reach him, his arm slipping around my waist.

"Mmhmm," I hum, leaning into him perhaps a bit too heavily. "Your clients seem to be enjoying themselves."

Ben studies my face for a moment, his lips twitching with barely suppressed amusement. "Lexie Phillips, are you high right now?"

I widen my eyes in what I hope is innocent surprise. "What? No! That's… ridiculous."

"Your eyes are redder than your lipstick," he points out, pulling me closer so we're not overheard. "And you've been staring at that bowl of mini sliders for the last five minutes like they hold the secrets of the universe."

"They might," I whisper conspiratorially, then giggle. "Okay, fine. We had a little… team building exercise on the balcony."

To my surprise, Ben laughs, the sound warm and genuine. "Let me guess—Zephyr's contribution to the party?"

"With an assist from Jerome," I admit.

Ben looks around the room, taking in the scene—Angel now openly demolishing the dessert table, Maci teaching some financial analysts a complicated dance move, Jerome holding court with a mixture of literary and finance types hanging on his every word. "What the hell is going on with Angel?" Ben asks finally, brows scrunching up in question.

"Your perfect, ice queen executive assistant has the munchies," I whisper, trying not to laugh too loudly. "I'm pretty sure she's eaten her body weight in chocolate-covered strawberries."

Ben watches Angel with newfound fascination. "I've never seen her eat more than a salad in five years of working together."

"Cannabis changes people," I say sagely, nodding with exaggerated wisdom. "Oh! Speaking of food…" I trail off, my attention captured by a passing waiter with a tray of appetizers.

Ben chuckles, guiding me toward the food. "Let's get you something to eat before you start examining the philosophical implications of cheese puffs."

"Too late," I mumble around a mouthful of hors d'oeuvres. "Did you know that the puffiness represents the transient nature of happiness? Here one moment, gone the next."

"Very profound," Ben says, his eyes crinkling with amusement. "And the spinach dip? Any existential insights there?"

I consider this seriously for a moment. "It's green like money but messy like life. A perfect metaphor for your profession."

Ben throws his head back and laughs, drawing curious glances from nearby guests. "God, I love you," he says, pressing a kiss to my temple.

The simple declaration warms me more than the high. "Even when I'm stoned at our company party?"

"Especially then," he assures me. "Though maybe we should get you some water before you start analyzing the cosmic significance of the chocolate fountain."

"Too late for that too," I admit. "Maci and I already decided it represents the flow of creative energy in the universe."

Ben leads me to a quiet corner, handing me a glass of water. "Drink this. All of it."

I obey, suddenly realizing how thirsty I am. "You're not mad?" I ask between gulps.

"Why would I be mad?"

"Because I'm high at a professional event? Because half your clients are probably wondering why your fiancé keeps giggling at the wallpaper?"

Ben takes the empty glass, setting it aside before cupping my face in his hands. "Lexie, this is who you are—spontaneous, authentic, a little wild sometimes. It's why I fell in love with you. I don't want you to change or hide parts of yourself, even around my clients."

"Really?" I ask, my high making me more emotional than usual. "Because I was worried our worlds wouldn't mix well."

"Look around," he says, turning me gently to survey the room. "What do you see?"

I follow his gaze. Jerome is now leading an impromptu sing-along with several of Ben's normally buttoned-up colleagues enthusiastically joining in. Eli and Maci are attempting to teach Angel some dance move that has her actually smiling. Zephyr has somehow acquired a small audience of investment bankers. I glance back at Ben, pride and satisfaction coursing through me.

"I love you Ben Maddox."

"I love you too," Ben replies, his eyes soft with an emotion that makes my heart flutter despite my altered state. "More than I ever thought possible."

The DJ transitions to a slow song, and Ben extends his hand with a slight bow. "May I have this dance, my queen?"

"You may," I giggle, allowing him to lead me to the dance floor.

As we sway together, my head resting against his chest, I feel a sense of contentment wash over me. The high is still there, but underneath it is something more solid—a certainty that this is exactly where I'm meant to be.

"Ben?" I murmur against his shoulder.

"Hmm?"

"I think I want a spring wedding. With wildflowers everywhere and maybe some of Jerome's band playing during the ceremony."

Ben's arms tighten around me. "Whatever makes you happy, love."

"You make me happy," I say, looking up at him. "Even when you're being all stuffy and financial advisor-y."

He laughs, the sound vibrating through his chest. "And you make me happy, even when you're analyzing cheese puffs and getting high with rockstars."

"We're quite the pair, aren't we?" I muse, watching Angel attempt to discretely stuff another chocolate strawberry into her mouth.

"The best kind," Ben affirms, dipping me dramatically as the song ends.

I squeal in surprise, clinging to his shoulders. When he pulls me back up, his lips find mine in a kiss that makes my already spinning head whirl even more.

"Get a room!" Eli calls from somewhere nearby, earning laughter from the surrounding guests.

"Don't tempt me," Ben calls back, not taking his eyes off me.

Epilogue

11 months later, I'm standing in a small room at the Chicago Botanical Gardens, staring at my reflection in a full-length mirror. My wedding dress is simple but elegant—a fitted silk gown with delicate lace detailing that makes me feel like the best version of myself.

"Stop fidgeting," Maci scolds, adjusting my veil for the hundredth time. "You're going to wrinkle the silk."

"I can't help it," I admit, smoothing my hands over the fabric. "I'm nervous."

"You? Nervous?" Maci raises an eyebrow. "The woman who once jumped off a cliff in Mexico because someone dared her?"

"That was different," I protest. "This is… forever."

Maci's expression softens as she takes my hands in hers. "And you're ready for it. You and Ben—it's right, Lex. Everyone can see it."

A knock at the door interrupts us. Imogen pokes her head in, resplendent in her bridesmaid dress. "Five minutes, ladies. The garden is packed, Dad is charming the pants off everyone, and Ben looks like he might pass out from anticipation."

"Is he okay?" I ask, fingers fidgeting with my bouquet.

"He's perfect," Imogen assures me with a grin. "Nervous as hell, but perfect. Angel's keeping him from hyperventilating."

I laugh, picturing Angel's no-nonsense approach to pre-wedding jitters. "I bet she threatened to staple his boutonniere to his chest if he doesn't calm down."

"Something like that," Imogen confirms. "Oh, and Zephyr is… well, being Zephyr. He's wearing an actual suit, though, which is a minor miracle."

"With shoes?" I ask skeptically.

"Let's not push our luck," Maci interjects, handing me a glass of champagne. "One last toast before you become Mrs. Maddox?"

I accept the glass, my hand trembling slightly. "To new beginnings."

"And happy endings," Imogen adds, raising her own glass.

We clink glasses just as another knock sounds at the door. My father peers in, looking handsome and slightly overwhelmed in his tuxedo.

"Ready, pumpkin?" he asks, his eyes suspiciously bright. "It's time."

I take a deep breath, setting down my glass and giving my reflection one final check. "I'm ready."

The garden is transformed into something from a fairy tale. White chairs line either side of a flower-strewn aisle that leads to an arch dripping with wildflowers and fairy lights. Soft music plays as I take my father's arm, my heart pounding so loudly I'm sure everyone can hear it.

As we begin our walk down the aisle, my eyes find Ben waiting for me beneath the arch. He looks devastatingly handsome in his tuxedo, his normally slicked-back hair slightly tousled in the way I love. But it's his expression that steals my breath—a mixture of awe, joy, and such profound love that tears spring to my eyes.

My father squeezes my arm as we approach the altar. "He's a good man," he whispers.

"The best," I agree, not taking my eyes off Ben.

When we reach the altar, my father places my hand in Ben's, the gesture centuries old yet freshly meaningful. Ben's fingers are warm and steady around mine, anchoring me in this perfect moment.

"Hi," I whisper, suddenly shy.

"Hi yourself," he whispers back, his eyes drinking me in. "You're breathtaking."

The ceremony passes in a blur of emotion. We've written our own vows, and when it's Ben's turn to speak, his voice is clear and steady, reaching every corner of the garden.

"Lexie Phillips," he begins, holding both my hands in his. "From the moment you told me my tie made me look like a stuffy accountant, I was done for. I just didn't know it yet."

"You challenged everything I thought I knew about myself, about love, about what really matters in life. You showed me that a life filled with spreadsheets and client meetings isn't really living at all. You taught me to laugh more, worry less, and occasionally break the rules."

A tear escapes down my cheek, and Ben gently wipes it away with his thumb.

"I promise to love all of you—the professional publisher and the woman who dances in the kitchen when she thinks no one's watching. The brilliant businesswoman and the impulsive spirit who occasionally flees to Vegas." There's a ripple of laughter through the guests. "I promise to be your partner in every sense of the word—to support your dreams, challenge you when you need it, and always, always fight for us, even when it's hard. Especially when it's hard."

My hands tremble in his as I begin my own vows, my voice wavering with emotion.

"Ben Maddox, when I first met you, I thought you were the most irritating man I'd ever encountered." More laughter from our guests. "But somewhere between fake engagement rings and real arguments, between charity galas and rooftop confessions, I fell completely, irrevocably in love with you."

Ben's eyes shine as I continue.

"I love your determination, your loyalty, the way you hold me like I'm the most precious thing in your world. I love how you've embraced every chaotic part of my life without trying to change me. I promise to be your safe harbor and your greatest adventure. To support your ambitions while reminding you to pause and enjoy the moment. To always come home to you, no matter how far I might run."

I take a deep breath, steadying my voice for the last part.

"Most of all, I promise that this—us—will always be real. No more pretending, no more hiding. Just you and me, building a life that's better than anything either of us could have imagined alone."

As we exchange rings, Jerome's band plays softly in the background—a special arrangement of a song he wrote just for us. When the officiant finally pronounces us husband and wife, Ben pulls me into a kiss that makes our guests cheer and Eli wolf-whistle from his place as best man.

"Ladies and gentlemen," the officiant announces as we turn to face our loved ones, "I present to you Mr. and Mrs. Maddox!"

The reception is everything I dreamed—elegant but relaxed, with Jerome's band playing during dinner and a DJ taking over afterward. Ben and I move from table to table, greeting guests and accepting congratulations. The Murphy's are there, of course, Margaret dabbing at her eyes and telling anyone who'll listen that she "knew from the start they were perfect for each other."

The lights dim for our first dance. Ben leads me to the center of the dance floor, one hand on my waist, the other holding mine as we begin to sway to the music.

"Happy?" he murmurs against my ear.

"Deliriously," I reply, leaning back to look at his face. "I still can't believe this is real sometimes."

"Better than anything we could have pretended," Ben says, his eyes crinkling at the corners. "Though I have to admit, I was terrified you might run off to Vegas again this morning."

I laugh, letting him spin me in a graceful twirl. "The thought crossed my mind, but only for about three seconds."

"Progress," he teases, pulling me back into his arms.

As we dance, I catch glimpses of our guests—Maci dabbing tears while trying to maintain her tough-girl image, Eli raising a glass in our direction, Angel actually smiling as she chats with Jerome. Zephyr, miraculously, has kept his shoes on for the entire ceremony and is now deep in conversation with one of Ben's oldest clients.

"Our worlds didn't just collide," I observe, nodding toward the unlikely pairing. "They merged."

"Like us," Ben agrees, his hand warm against the small of my back.

When the dance ends, Jerome's band strikes up a livelier tune, and soon the dance floor is packed. I find myself whisked from partner to partner—my father, Eli, even Richard Murphy who surprises me with his nimble footwork.

"You've been good for him," Richard says as we dance, nodding toward where Ben stands laughing with Maci. "I've known that boy since he was in college, and I've never seen him this happy."

"He's been good for me too," I admit, warmth spreading through my chest at the sight of my husband. My husband. The words still feel new and wonderful.

"Margaret and I expect front row seats at the christening," Richard adds with a wink.

I nearly miss a step. "Let's get through the honeymoon first," I laugh, deflecting the comment.

Speaking of which, Ben has been mysteriously tight-lipped about our destination. All I know is to pack for warm weather and that we leave tomorrow morning. The mystery is driving me crazy in the best possible way.

As the night progresses, traditional wedding activities give way to more… unconventional ones. Jerome insists on performing his newest song, which turns out to be about Ben and me—thankfully more romantic than scandalous. Zephyr, several glasses of champagne in, delivers an impromptu poetry reading that has half the guests in tears and the other half in confused silence.

"Did he just compare our love to 'the sacred dance of celestial jellyfish'?" Ben whispers as we applaud politely.

"Be grateful," I whisper back. "The first draft mentioned your 'financial phallus.'"

He laughs and shakes his head. "Well, Mrs. Maddox, we did it."

We did indeed.

Thanks for Reading!

If you made it to the end of *Professionally Unprofessional*, you officially survived the emotional whiplash of fake dating, workplace chaos, and one very confused finance bro. You deserve a trophy. Or at least a cocktail.

This book was an absolute blast to write (read: equal parts caffeine, emotional damage, and late-night "what if" texts to my editor), and I'm ridiculously grateful you came along for the ride.

If you're into exclusive bonus content, behind-the-scenes drama, and monthly giveaways where I 100% bribe you with gift cards and chaos, then come hang out with me on my mailing list.

☞ **Mailing List**
Come for the freebies. Stay for the sarcasm.

And if you're already wondering what happens next (hint: Maci is not done stirring the pot), don't worry—Book 2 is coming. And it's got wine, weddings, and a best man who doesn't know what's about to hit him.

With love, mischief, and way too many tabs open,

Eliza Nevius

About the Author

While for her fictional tales she goes by her pen name, Eliza Nevius, you may know her by her real name, Erin Egnatz. When she isn't chasing ghosts, wrangling college students, or decoding ancient ruins, she's spinning tales that blend romance, fiction, and sometimes a touch of the paranormal. A published author, seasoned ghost hunter, and professor of history, archaeology, and English, she is also the creator of *Hauntings Around America*—a platform dedicated to all things eerie and unexplained. Armed with a BA from Central State University and an MEd from the American College of Education, she has been featured in *Newsweek*, Fox Chicago, WAVE TV, Fox Cincinnati, NBC Seattle, and beyond. She lives somewhere between chaos and caffeine with her husband, three kids, two dogs, four cats, and one incredibly judgmental bearded dragon.

You can connect with me on:

- 🌐 https://www.phantompublishing.com
- 🐦 https://x.com/PhantomPubllc
- 📘 https://www.facebook.com/alexa.phillips.16503
- 🔗 https://www.elizanevius.com

Subscribe to my newsletter:

- ✉️ https://phantompublishing.com/newsletter

Also by Eliza Nevius

Professionally Unraveled

The other side of the chaos, control, and completely unplanned love story.

Benjamin Maddox has everything under control—his firm, his future, and his finely tailored life. As the youngest partner at one of Chicago's most prestigious financial firms, Ben lives by one rule: feelings complicate the bottom line. But all that control unravels the moment Lexie Phillips stumbles into his office building with a chaotic energy and a mouth that doesn't know when to quit.

Their fake engagement was supposed to be strategic. A polished illusion to help land a multimillion-dollar client. But the longer Ben plays the role of Lexie's fiancé, the more the lines blur— and the harder it becomes to remember where the performance ends and the truth begins.

From awkward elevator run-ins to tequila-fueled confessions, Ben is forced to confront the emotions he's spent a lifetime avoiding. Lexie challenges his every instinct—and makes him want more than just professional success. She makes him want her.

But when secrets, exes, and Lexie's fear of vulnerability collide with Ben's own emotional blind spots, their carefully built façade comes crashing down. To win her back, Ben will have to risk the one thing he's never risked before—his heart.

Told entirely from Ben's perspective as it dives into the mind of the man behind the suit, exposing the insecurities, passion, and quiet longing beneath his polished surface. Get ready to fall in love with Ben Maddox all over again.

Note: This is a companion novella to Professionally Unprofessional from Ben's Point of View.

Strategically Inappropriate

Maci has a plan for everything—except maybe her own love life. As the co-founder of Bound Books Publishing, she's used to controlling chaos, not starring in it. But after an alcohol fueled one-night stand with her friend Eli occurs, that chaos she has been trying to avoid hits her head on. Now, everything is messy. Crossing that line has made things awkward. Add to that the emotional crisis that is her best friend, Lexie, and Maci's life has turned into one big ball of drama.

Eli doesn't do relationships, emotions, or spontaneous anything, but Maci seems to be the exception to his rules. He thought they could keep things casual—until his ex resurfaces, his family starts pushing for a reconciliation, and Maci starts dodging him like he's contagious. Suddenly, he's not so sure detachment is working out.

When Lexie and Ben rope them into helping plan their wedding, the romantic tension between Maci and Eli goes from simmer to full-on inferno. Between rogue glitter explosions, cake disasters, and tipsy grandmas, the line between friends and lovers is not just blurred—it's basically a smoldering crater.

Now Maci has to decide: is she brave enough to break her own rules for a chance at something real?

And can Eli finally open his carefully guarded heart—before he loses the one person who makes him want to?

Because love? It's never part of the plan... but sometimes it's exactly what you need.

The Jaded Knight Book 1 In The Lux Bellator Series

In a world where magic simmers just beneath the surface, one witch is about to shake the foundations of fate.

At just 21, Sadie never expected to be recruited into the **Lux Bellator**, an elite band of paranormal warriors sworn to defend the veil between worlds. With her rare blend of witchcraft and angel blood, she's a prodigy of power—telekinesis, clairvoyance, and more at her fingertips. But it's her sharp tongue and fearless spirit that really turn heads.

Thrust into a team of supernatural misfits—snarky shifters, brooding vampires, and icy fae—Sadie doesn't just survive; she thrives. Especially when it comes to Nathan, the devastatingly handsome team leader with a glare that could cut glass and eyes that see too much. Their chemistry is combustible. Their arguments? Legendary.

Magic. Mayhem. Slow-burn romance. If you love witty heroines, brooding heroes, found family vibes, and enemies-to-lovers heat with a supernatural twist—*this* is your next obsession.

The Burning Vow Book 2 in the Lux Bellator Series

Heart-pounding, magical, and laced with a slow-burn romance that scorches, The Burning Vow is a fierce continuation of the Lux Bellator series—where loyalty is tested, love is forged in fire, and the only way out… is through the flames.